The Banished Medieval Queen

First Wife of Charlemagne

ACACIA OAK

At Last Communications

Published by At Last Communications

Printed in the United States of America

ISBN-10: 0-9842768-6-6
ISBN-13: 978-0-9842768-6-8

Library of Congress Control Number: 2011939525

Acknowledgments

My thanks and appreciation to the authors who devoted their professional lives to the study of the Carolingian empire and to Charlemagne the Great, in particular. Alessandro Barbero's *Charlemagne, Father of a Continent* (University of California Press, 2004), and Pierre Riche's *Daily Life in the World of Charlemagne* (University of Pennsylvania Press, 1978) were especially helpful to me. Volumes in Thomas Hodgkin's *The Barbarian Invasion's of the Roman Empire: The Frankish Invasion* and *The Frankish Empire* (The Folio Society, 2003 from a 1899 Clarendon Press edition) — contributed much to my understanding of the political developments of the time and the influence of Christianity on emerging rulers. The maps in these volumes were especially valuable.

Dedication

Dedicated to my beloved family for their unwavering belief in my stories, as well as in my writing skills. Also to those women whose lives have been challenged, disrupted, or re-directed by changes in life circumstance. May they draw inspiration, hope, and strength from the hypothetical struggles of a woman who, also, lost everything but recovered much more than she ever lost.

Chapter One
BANISHMENT

"You must calm yourself, Himli!" Queen Bertrada shouted, trying to break through the young woman's storm of tears. "You're frightening your son. Be strong! I expect more understanding from you!" She paced the room, clamping down on her temper and resisting the need to slap the silly girl's face.

"You must leave the court." The Queen Mother repeated. "Your presence here, yours and Pippin's both," she added, glancing at her grandson, "weaken Charlemagne. You are banished." She stated, her mouth firm, her eyes blank. "I can be no clearer." Her dark eyes bored into Himiltrude's face. In her anger, Bertrada's headdress sat askew, her thick brown hair escaping from the coil atop her head. Her cheeks, though the rest of her face was white with suppressed anger.

"I would hear this from Charlemagne's own mouth." Himlitrude struggled to respond. "How dare you! How is it possible…to stand there, to force your grandson out into the wilderness?" Her eyes widened in shock as she absorbed the Queen's words and, then, flashed in anger.

"What kind of a woman are you? I never thought you a **true** mother." She glared at the woman who so demeaned her place in the court. "Now, I am positive of it." She brushed her tears away angrily. Broken in both heart and spirit, Himiltrude bent over in pain. "Sending me away, are you? ...so your darling son can clamor into another bed, no doubt. Anything you want, anything the concerned mother decides—anything for breeding your precious heir!"

Tears splashed down her cheeks; a deep frown etched her forehead. Himli pushed her thick, dark hair off her neck. She felt ready to explode. The total lack of concern in Queen Bertrada's pronouncements increased Himiltrude's anger. She must get away!

"Go to hell, Queen Mother!" Himiltrude sneered into her mother-in-law's face. "Go straight to hell; you have earned a speedy trip there!" She flung a water-filled flagon. It just missed the Queen Mother's leg but liquid spread all over the bottom half of her gown. Lifting her skirt from the floor, Queen Bertrada slipped her left hand into her right sleeve. Shaking her head at Himiltrude, Bertrada struggled to remain calm.

"You make it difficult for me to be kind to you, my dear."The Queen Mother complained. "I have a gift from Charlemagne. He wishes you to know how much he values you." She withdrew her hand. Her fingers slowly opened, revealing an object with a chain dangling from it. A beautiful piece of jade, bound in a gold oval, lay in Bertrada's hand. The jade radiated calming warmth. Despite herself, Himli caught her breath, transfixed by the depth of color in the gem.

"This is the traditional stone for fidelity."Bertrada murmured. "My son knows he can depend on your obedience, on your understanding of his situation." She smiled brightly at Himiltrude, truly believing her bribe would dull the young woman's protests.

"Get out! Get out!"Himiltrude shouted. "Leave me alone in my misery!" She felt a momentary satisfaction. The Queen's gown was dark from the water flagon she threw. But Himli's delight dissolved, negated by the queen's crude effort to buy her acceptance. "I hope never, ever to see you again! Get out!" Queen Bertrada pocketed the necklace and marched toward the door of the bedchamber.

Himli wept bitterly as she walked quickly across the room to pick up her son. He whimpered, confused by the shouting in the chamber. Himli shushed and rocked little Pippin in her arms. Her tears dropped onto the little boy's face. He stopped moaning as a tear splashed into his mouth. At the salty drop, he squinched his eyes shut, reaching toward his mother. From the corner of her eye, Hilmi saw Queen Bertrada leave the room, a hand in her pocket around the jade amulet.

Himli sat on a near-by bench and buried her face in her son's stomach. His eyes stared into hers. His forehead creased in confusion. But he did not cry again. His slow, steady breathing calmed his distraught mother. Slowly she raised her eyes and looked into those of her son, the son who looked so much like his father, Charlemagne, king of the Frankish realm. Himli stroked little Pippin's cheeks. His smile began at his mouth and moved slowly up to his eyes.

She nuzzled his neck and he laughed. Suddenly, she clutched the small boy fiercely to her chest.

"My precious son," she murmured, "this doesn't matter. You're my life. Your grandmother may send us both away, away from your father and his court. But no one can ever deny you are the King's son! You are his first-born. The entire realm rejoiced at your birth, your first cry heralded throughout the realm. Charlemagne's need for an heir will sustain us, will guarantee a decent life for you. Don't despair, my darling." She continued to reassure herself.

"I will never leave you. Never!" So saying, she began changing the child's absorbent mosses, murmuring to him and kissing his little fingers. There's some plot here, Himiltrude thought. *The Queen is up to some thing…her banishing me. She must have another wife in mind for Charlemagne. Of a certainty, I am indispensable. But, Pippin, is he of no value either?* She swallowed the lump in her throat, more woundedfor her son's sake than for her own. *Charlemagne's hand is in this.* Her agonized thoughts would not cease. Queen *Bertrada would never act independently of him.*

Charlemagne wants a perfect son for his heir, one with no flaws. The tears threatened to overwhelm her again. She concentrated on Pippin, unconsciously rubbing and stroking his misshapen back.

"You have a quick mind.You understand my words. You're even-tempered and quiet." She kissed him gently as his eyes stared into hers. "You could surely be a king. Any man can fight but not any man is able to think. Your father takes another wife. He tires of this one, tires of me. I did love him dearly." Tears leaked from her eyes. "Clearly, my feelings and your future are of no consequence to him or to his scheming mother." She sat her son upright and pulled a tunic over his head.

"Well, there's no help for it, my sweet baby." Her mind moved forward, practical and realistic as she was. "We must pack our things and make ready for our journey. Here, let me bundle you up. We'll be leaving before the sun is straight in the sky this day. I'll put a larger tunic over this one. It will be cold in the cart as we travel." The little fellow gave a huge yawn. "You sleep, Pippin. We go for a ride when you wake." Himiltrude tried to inject enthusiasm in her voice. But it broke as she wept.

Through the long night, she ranted: against Charlemagne, against the Queen Mother, against their plots. Finally, the anger and, then, the fear helped her summon her strength. She must surmount her grief. She must be aware and focused to care for her son. *Who knows what the sun will bring?*

Her ladies watched her, their eyes downcast, their faces grim. They busied themselves removing linens and clothing from the large chests along the chamber wall. Himiltrude would travel with her own chests, provided by her father when she married. Her dowry and Charlemagne's bride gift were hers to take with her. *But this will be a somber journey.* She gazed with blank eyes at her clothing: the softness of the silk tunics, the rainbow of soft colors, the beauty of the embroidery, the encrusted gems along the neck and sleeves. What use will they be now? She wondered. Her embroidered headdresses, matched perfectly to her tunics, twinkled with rubies, jade, and sapphires which also marched around the sleeves and hems of her tunics. Pippin's breeches, a miniature version of Charlemagne's, were serviceable, made of linen or wool, though often embroidered. His blankets filled one whole chest. His hand-woven caps matched each of his little tunics. Seeing these clothes, Himiltrude thought, everyone will assume we are of the nobility. *How will we fit in…wherever we are being sent? How can we remain anonymous with the richness of our belongings?* She turned to her ladies, ready to ask for their guidance. But she caught herself.

She saw the shock in their eyes when the Queen Mother reminded them to pack Pippin's embroidered linens. They assumed the King would keep his son with him, never imagining the child banished with his mother.

Although Germanic custom allowed either wife or husband to ask for a divorce, most men demanded and got their children, especially the boys. It wounded Himiltrude that Charlemagne did not wish to keep Pippin. Impossible to believe, Himli thought, but perfect for me!

"Time is short. I must choose the furniture, clothing, weavings I wish to take." Himli spelled out her duties. "I feel so befuddled." She murmured, rubbin her eyes slowly. "If I could just think clearly..." She paused in her frantic movement. "I'll just take it all. It's mine. Who knows where we may be settled? I will take everything I can...for my little Pippin's sake. He will never forget. He is the son of a king! No matter what Charlemagne does next, our son will *always* be his firstborn."

Rinaldo, King Charlemagne's youngest Peer, hurried down the corridor, away from Himiltrude's chambers. He shook his head, trying to swallow the lump in his throat. How long he stood there, he had no idea. Hearing shouts from the Queen's chamber, he stopped outside, ready to provide assistance. The anger of the Queen mother, Himltrude's wail of horror, Pippin's frightened whimpering all echoed in his ears. But, mostly, he understood the anger betweeen the two women. Knowing the importane of their words, he had no idea what to do.

"How can the King do this - banish Queen Himli, a wife who has done no harm, and send his only son from court?" He rubbed his forehead. "Thank the Father, I am not a king." Rinaldo murmured, thinking of the departure of little Pippin. "I could not send my child from me, no matter what his affliction might be!" He hurried from the castle, wanting to remove himself as quickly as possible from the hateful scene he just overheard.

Hurrying to the stable, the young Peer saddled his own horse, a he dismissed the stable boy. *Praise God, we expect King Charlemagne to return soon.Mayhap, he will change his mind or....*" Rinaldo's thoughts stopped abruptly. "I wonder if he knows what Queen Bertrada is doing. If not, surely he will correct this injustice. True, he can never cancel out the Queen Mother's harsh words, but he must reassure Queen Himiltrude of his love for little Pippin. At the least, he must do that!" Rinaldo stepped back several steps, quickened his steps and sprang upon his horse. He turned his mount toward the river, thankful to leave the machinations of royalty behind.

Next morning, as the sun's rays broke the darkness, Himli's escort mounted their steeds and carefully surrounded her carriage, guarding her as always. I wonder, Himli thought, do they know Charlemagne sends me away? She looked around. *Don't they wonder that no one is here?* At this early hour, the courtyard was deserted. No one appeared to bid the banished Queen or her son goodbye. Himli felt thankfulness and regret. At least, no one would see her departure; there would be no first-hand report to the gossiping ladies of the court. Frowning with uncertainty, Himiltrude looked closely at her guards. It was then she realized not a single one of Charlemagne's personal guards was in the party. *I wonder who arranged this escort,* she thought vaguely.

Some three miles beyond the court, Abbot Fulrad, the court's priest and the King's beloved teacher, edged his horse beside Himiltrude's cart. He made the sign of the cross, an effort to bless Himli's journey. The Abbot smiled tentatively as Himli's red-rimmed eyes looked into his and nodded to him.

"Hello, my Queen," Fulrad greeted the weary woman. Her usually glossy, black hair was dull; her face splotchy. Her vivid, brown eyes, streaked like the red skies of autumn mornings, were dull. *Thrown out of her home, banished by her husband. Damn,*

Charlemagne! He persists in his own ignorance. The Abbot cursed in his thoughts. Then, he shook his head. *Nay,* he corrected himself, *it is the King's lack of faith, his lack of grace, his disobedience to the Church leads him to this choice.* The Abbot looked back at Himli and realized she stared at him. She waited for him to explain his appearance.

"I trust my presence here does not dismay you, my Lady," the Abbot began. "I want only to wish you well. And, for what good it may do, to reassure you. You have no blame in this sad journey, my dear, no blame at all. The King makes an incredibly poor judgment." His eyes filled with unshed tears as he looked at the young woman. Her tunic pulled askew around her body, her head-covering looked almost weary in its slanted position over her dark curls. Her pale face, usually so alive with vigor and good humor, signaled her distress.

"That changes nothing, Abbot." Himlitrude replied, hastily tucking an unruly curl away from her face. "I am banished from court, bundled off like some common thief!" She pulled her shawl close around her shoulders. "Queen Betrada ruins my life and condemns my son – her own grandchild! I must believe her words. Charlemagne concurs with her judgment. He does not appear but sends his mother to throw me out." She smoothed out her skirt. "I know you flinch, Abbot, at my next words, but I do hate them! I hate them both, for all they do to me, but, even more, for what is being done to my poor Pippin!" Himli dabbed at her eyes with her shawl. But she had no tears left.

"I understand," the Abbot acknowledged. "No one can blame you for your feelings. I hope the hate dissolves quickly. I would not have you separated from the Christ. HE would not wish this hate to consume you." The Abbot paused. "And you must grieve; give yourself up to it. In the weeks ahead, the grief will give you strength, strength to continue to live." The Abbot shifted on his mount. *Should I comfort her?* He asked himself. He heard Pippin cry out. Himli looked back into the cart. The nurse smiled reassuringly and mouthed 'only a dream,' to her mistress. Himli returned her eyes to the Abbot's face.

"How dare he banish me, Abbot?" She asked, her eyes wounded and dull, tears welling in the corners. "The whole realm knows I gave him a son. There's nothing wrong with Pippin, nothing which merits such treatment as this."

"True, my lady, true." Abbot Fulrad agreed. "Recent changes in Church law would require you and his Majesty to repeat your vows, repeat them within the Church ritual. A priest would, then, bless yours as a Christian marriage. But no one doubts your commitment and love for the King…or the sanctity of your past vows." Himli grimaced and turned her body away from the Abbot. "No one can deny you are husband and wife. Neither your son and his deformity or the King's need for an heir can undo such a sacred binding!" Himli turned a defiant face to the Abbot. Her shoulders stiffened. Her hands gripped the sides of the cart.

"Mine was a true and honorable marriage." She emphasized. "The Church is wrong, wrong to define a union by a new procedure, especially one it changes at will." Himli's shoulders crumpled, her eyes swept the ground. "But, now, it matters not, Sir. It matters not." Even though the wool of her shawl and the wool linens over her legs protected her from the winter cold, Himli seemed to shrivel into herself, shivering and trembling. The Abbot rubbed his forehead at her words.

"Still, you have no blame in this, my Lady," he re-iterated. "I wanted to offer you any assistance I can give." At the negative shake of her head, he spoke again. "If you ever have need, anything I might do for you, or for dear little Pippin, please contact me immediately."Himli nodded, trying to be gracious at the concern in the Abbot's words.

"You will ever be the Queen to me." Abbot Fulrad assured her. "There is no divorce in the Christian Church. You are the King's wife…for all time. Is there anything I can do for you?"

Himli found her voice, shocked at the Abbot's words. *Why would he take such a stand against Charlemagne, after all they are to each other? He's Charlemagne's teacher, almost a second father to him.* But the Abbot does as everyone else in the court, Himli thought. *Charlemagne decides and the Abbot obeys.These are but words he whispers to me.*

"Thank you, Abbot," she responded. "The need I have, you cannot fulfill. Your concern does comfort me on this difficult, sorrowful day." She offered her hand to the Abbot. He took it gently and continued.

"Of a certainty, my lady. I don't offer my help negligently. Should you have need, send a courier. I shall do whatever I can for you." He dropped his head. "I wish you Godspeed on your journey. I pray for you both, you and little Pippin. Surely, life must become kinder for you." He smiled into her eyes, squeezed her small hand, and turned his horse away. How strange, Himli thought. *Never before has the Abbot spoken three words to me. Now, when I am banished, he offers help. How odd for him - to oppose Charlemagne's decision and tell me of it.*

The little party trudged on, one day followed another. On the third day, snow began before noon. The wagons, heavily loaded with household items and furniture, seemed to make no progress along the ice-covered ruts. The horses struggled to stay upright. Frozen ice under the snow made footing treacherous. The little band camped for the night, unable to maintain more than a meager fire. Firewood brought with them began their little blaze. But wood on the ground, along the edge of the forest and encrusted with ice, would not burn. After only a few moments in the fire, water oozed from the soggy wood. As soon as it was light, the small group set out again. Captain Mortimer assured Himli this would be the last day of their journey.

"Even with this snow," he told her, "we will reach our destination well before sunset."

"And what is our destination, Captain?" Himli asked. "I daresay it does not matter, though I'll be relieved to end this journey. Those wolves in the night did nothing for my sleeping, I assure you." The captain laughed good-naturedly. Himli saw several soldiers nod to her fear of the wolves. Just as everyone hoped to stop for a cold, mid-day meal, Captain Mortimer rode up beside Himli's cart.

"The manor is but two leagues or so ahead, my lady." He pointed north. "I'll send three men forward. They can build a fire, warm the place up a bit. Or," he paused, "mayhap they
can offer some assistance to those workers who'll be waiting to ease your home-coming." The men came forward for instructions and, riding away from the little band, disappeared. No one saw any distinguishing landmark, so overcast, cloudy and dark was the air around them. Finally, as darkness descended, the captain rode up beside Himlitrude's cart.

"My Queen," he greeted her. "We shall soon arrive at your new home. Please follow me. You and Pippin enter as soon as we stop at the door." At the sound of hoofbeats, he stopped speaking and looked toward the south. Himli turned in the same direction. The Captain sat, waiting to determine who traveled in such weather.

"Well met, Sir." The rider greeted the Captain and nodded to Himiltrude. "Forgive me, Master. I took pains not to frighten you. Is there a manor close by? I am looking for a healer." The soldier quickly explained himself, wondering what this small band was doing out on such a day.

"What is the sickness," Captain Mortimer asked, "for which you seek a healer, if you forgive me?" The rider nodded and waved away the Captain's apology.

"Well might you ask," he responded. "My prince, injured a mere day after we started for home, worsens and is babbling. We took shelter in a cave, a short ride from here; but, today, his wound seems worse. Now, he is unaware of us. I'll lose my head if he does not recover. We all value the young man, Captain. I need someone with healing skill....and I need him quickly."

"We have no one to recommend." The Captain began, turning his eyes to the Queen as she stirred on the cart's bench. "We are passing through..." He startled as Himli spoke.

"Where is your prince, Sir? I shall take a look at him. I have skills with war wounds, accidental hurts. I daresay my limited skill is better than none." Himli glanced at the Captain's doubtful face. "It's necessary, Captain, for us to help. Who are we to deny care to a prince?" She hesitated as she reviewed the healing ointments and herbs in her cart. "It may benefit us...someday." Her voice dropped so only Captain Mortimer heard her last statement.

"Where are you camped, Sir? And, what is your name...and who is this prince? I must know these answers lest I take my group into danger." The Captain frowned, fingering his knife.

"Fear not, Captain," the rider replied. "I know you. You are one of the King's men, are you not? I am Kastron. We, my companions and I, serve the Prince of Lombard, Adelchis. These past many months we have been in King Charlemagne's court. We came for the fall hunt but lingered at the Queen Mother's insistence. Mayhap she intends the Prince for her daughter." The man shrugged. "But, now, we return home to Lombardy. It's been two days, Sir, since this accident felled the Prince. He worsens, even as we speak."He turned to look at Himiltude. "You are Queen Himiltrude are you not?" The rider bowed toward Himli and smiled. Captain Mortimer confirmed nothing.

"How many of you ride with the Prince?" He demanded. "Some of my men ride ahead, searching for a manor."

"I hope you know the way to one," the rider replied. "I searched far and wide west of here with no luck." He answered the Captain's question. "There are four of us and Prince Adelchis." Himli sat very still. She knew of Adelchis. He was one in a band of young nobles who came to hunt with Charlemagne and his Peers. Charlemagne liked him very much and praised his skill with the falcon. The Captain hesitated. He had no wish to remind the Queen of the court; but how to refuse to help a fellow soldier?

"We shall come."Himli decided. "Is there space for us to bed down? The night draws close." The Captain may not want to speak of the manor, Himli thought. "It's necessary, Captain Mortimer; send one of these riders to call our escort back. The soldiers took no provisions with them." Captain Mortimer nodded and waved his remaining soldier in the direction of the much-anticipated manor.

"It'll be tomorrow, then…before we have true shelter." He mumbled to Himli.

"We're in a cave, your majesty," the rider added. "It's warm and dry. And we will be happy to share our rabbit stew with you!" He smiled broadly at Himli, clearly relieved she agreed to provide some sort of help for the Prince. He hurried to lead them toward the cave, but the journey proved a slow one. Finally, he turned his horse to the right off the snow-covered path and ushered them into the cave's entrance, hidden between two massive rocks. Inside, the soldiers' fire made a welcome light in the dark air.

Himli handed her bridle to the Captain and hurried to look into Prince Adelchis' face. Her breath caught. My God, she thought, he's dying. *There may be nothing any human hand can do for this man.* But she did not voice the thought.

"Where is his wound? And how did this happen? Was he unconscious this morning or longer than that?" She felt his head, almost stepping back from the heat of a fever. His parched lips wrinkled as he labored to breathe.

"Help me, Captain Mortimer. Hurry; his clothes must come off. Off, now! Franco," she addressed the rider, "get me cold water, from the stream we passed. Hurry, man, hurry! We must cool his body." The Captain already had the Prince's tunic off and untied his breeches.

"I will lay this linen over him, my lady," he said to Himli, "to shield him from the draft. "He bent quickly to his task.

"Thank you, Captain." Himli smiled to herself. Does he think I never saw a naked body? She asked herself. *...well might he cover the Prince.* She chuckled as she soaked her hand linen in the cold water. *His body is well-muscled and very pleasing.* She dropped her head, struggling not to laugh aloud. The Captain will be scandalized if I laugh, she reminded herself. *It would be unseemly.* Himli smothered her chuckle, trying to still her amusement. She began wiping the Prince's body, hoping the cold water would alleviate some of the fever burning within. She sat through the night, wiping the cool linen over his chest and back. As the moon sank from view, she stepped to the cave entrance, stretching her legs and hands. When she returned, the Captain was in her place. As he wiped the Prince's chest, he looked into her face.

"He does seem less hot, your majesty," Captain Mortimer observed. "Do you think he's out of danger? His skin was like a coal...before you began with the wiping." He smoothed the man's hair from his forehead, imagining the weakness resulting from such heat.

"I know not, Captain," Himli admitted. "But he came through the night. He lives and seems cooler. I also think he doesn't struggle for breath as wretchedly as before. We have succeeded in keeping him alive...for now." The captain watched with her all night. He shook his head wearily and rose to waken his men. Quietly, he told two of them to break their fast quickly and to prepare to return to the manor they found yesterday.

"Prepare for the arrival of the Queen. Gather wood and light fires," he said to them. "We shall follow you closely, although more slowly, I am sure." He turned to Himli, knowing she could hear his words. She nodded in agreement.

"The herbs I have...they will not help this sickness. There is nothing more I can do here. If he weakens or makes another bad turn, Franco must come for me. It will be days before the Prince can ride. We must be on our way." Franco, hearing Himli's words, thanked her profusely for her help.

"I knew not what to do, my Lady," he admitted. "I am a fair setter of bones and have some skill with battle wounds. But this sickness, I had no skill to use."

"Be ever alert." Himli warned him. "Such fevers often ease and, then, return. If his body warmth rises again, you must seek us out." She nodded at Captain Mortimer. "The Captain will give you our general direction. Just ride until you find us." She asked Captain Mortimer to re-dress the Prince and told Franco to keep him warm. "But not overly so," she cautioned. "Let the sweat come. It is good healing for his body."

Himli sat near the firepit to break her fast, placing food aside for her little boy. Pippin was always hungry in the morning. As she ate, Pippin watched his mother from his bed on the floor. He didn't wish to move; he was so tired. All the riding, exciting at first, made his back hurt. He closed his eyes again but sleep did not return. His eyes traveled to the back of the cave; he frowned as the mystery of that darkness beckoned to him.

"Us 'top?" he asked his mother hopefully. Himli went to him, kissed his face, and smoothed down his tousled hair.

"Nay, sweetheart," she replied; "we don't stop right now, but soon." She laid him over her knees and began rubbing his back, moving first down one leg and, then, the other. "Soon. The Captain thinks this is our last day of riding. Won't it be good…to walk and use our feet, instead of those tired horses?" She hugged Pippin to her, whispering in his ear and squeezing him.

"Aye," the little boy replied. "Stop." He wiggled from her arms and went to stand beside the Captain. "Go?" He asked.

"… as soon as you break your fast, lad," the Captain agreed. He sat Pippin back on his sleeping linens and gave him the food Himiltrude set aside. Pippin ate as the soldiers secured their traveling bags on the horses and placed the linens in the cart. All mounted and re-traced the journey of the night before. In a short time, they were moving, again, toward the manor in the distance. Another furlong later, Captain Mortimer rode back to Himli's cart.

"We're almost at the manor, your Majesty," he said. "All should be in readiness for your arrival."

"Captain," Himli responded. "I appreciate your politeness and your concern for my feelings, but I am no longer a 'majesty.' You must not use the word with me again. Please. The King will be enraged…if he hears even a rumor of it. To break you of this habit, before you return to his court, call me something else." The Captain looked at a loss. He made no suggestion, just stared into her face.

"Let's try 'Mistress,' shall we?" Himli suggested. "I think 'Mistress' will be fine."

"Aye, Mistress." The Captain tried the word. "Shall we investigate your new manor, then?"

"Let me get Pippin." Himli answered. She turned to the back of the cart and mumbled to the nurse there. The captain wanted to ask her to leave the little boy in the cart but thought better of it,remembering the Queen's circumstances.

"Mayhap the child can comfort her," he muttered to himself. "God knows, I would need comfort to start a new life, forced to leave the people and life I have known." The Captain, holding Pippin, gave Himiltrude his hand as she climbed from the cart. The snow swirled about them. A white world stretched as far as the eye could see. Himli reached for Pippin and, then, followed the captain into the manor house. She looked around curiously, hearing one of the forward-riding guards speaking in an adjacent room. As she flicked the snow off Pippin's hat, a guard entered the room and began lighting fat-soaked torches.

"Captain, the place is deserted." The tallest soldier spoke.

"And, it's unsuitable. Wasn't there to be someone here....to clean, at least, before the Lady arrived?"His creased face frowned in the dim light. "I do apologize, Captain. We didn't have time to investigate yesterday...before we turned back to the cave. More's the pity you're already here. We had hoped to clean things up a bit before the Lady arrived."

"You found no one about?" The Captain questioned, looking around. He realized the chamber was cold and dark. "No one has appeared since you arrived?" He looked at Himli who stared first at him and, then, at the three soldiers. "We'll do what we can then." He turned his attention to the weary woman.

"Would you like to investigate the manor, my Lady?" the Captain asked. "There are several chambers. What say you to the cooking room?" He turned back to the three soldiers. This won't do, he thought as he stepped into the chamber. *The Queen must have suitable living arrangements. I cannot leave her poorly housed and unprotected, not her or the lad.*

"Pretty bare, Sir," one of them responded. A companion nudged him in the ribs.

"Well, then, let me see it," Himli replied. She handed Pippin back to the Captain who took the boy carefully. "He seems to like you." She smiled into the Captain's astonished face.

Himli went into the room which the soldiers had left. A cry tore from her throat. The chamber was horrible. And it's not just the mess, Himli thought, this room is unlivable. Deep gouges marked the old, wooden floor planks, almost as if someone attacked the wood with an ax. Around the rough window, a stain showed where water still trickled in a steady drip. The open pit, normally stocked with wood for cooking, held burnt leather, remnants of mantles, and broken trenchers. Even cleaned, it would still be unusable. The sides of the pit were caved in; the floor around the pit held puddles of water. Noticing an additional cold draught, Himli lifted her eyes to the ceiling. There were several holes in the roof. Much of the ceiling was open to the sky. Snow drifted inside, settling on the rotting table and benches. Huge holes decorated the walls, letting in rodents, birds, and blowing rain. Chunks of mud lay on the filthy furniture; old, moldy thatch poked through the cracks. The walls, the furniture, even the fire pit, looked ancient, worn, and ruined.

"I refuse to put my furniture in here." Himli said to the soldiers who hovered behind her. "This is not a manor. This is worse than the meanest stable. It cannot be used." She rushed back into the entrance, calling for the captain. Appalled at her description, he hurried to the cooking room. He re-appeared in a few seconds.

"I'm sorry, my Lady," he apologized. "I don't know what to think. Nay, there is no way I will leave you here. But I don't have another place to take you. This is our destination. The Queen Mother herself told me this was your home. She was very clear…"

"I care not what she said to you."Himli declared. She looked at the sleeping boy in her arms. "You can see. I will not accept this as a home. I will not stay here, Captain. Some other manor must be provided." The Captain looked at her in dismay. Clearly, he had no solution, not even a suggestion, to offer.

"Bring the others into this front entrance." Himli directed. "We need to sleep. At least, you and I must get some sleep. We will make a decision in the morning. Come, Come! Bring everyone in here. We have a roof." She looked around in the gloom. "…and there's a small fire-pit. Bring one-half of our starter wood; we must save some for the morrow. Build a fire. Burn anything which can be burned in these two rooms." The Captain began to protest.

"Never mind, Sir," Himli silenced him. "No sane person would ever use this furniture. No clean person would even allow it in a room, not for a minute!" She turned, closing the discussion. "We need warmth and rest. Please follow my wishes." Her voice firmed as she remembered to order the Captain.

There was little to be done. One of the guards parceled food out among the soldiers, Himli, and her nurse. Himli deliberately did not bring ladies from the court with her, even though the Queen Mother offered them. She knew none of them would serve her willingly, not banished from the intrigues of the court and their friends. Thank God no one else has seen this horrible place, Himiltrude thought. *I must be firm. Charlemagne must provide better than this. I will be happy with local people to work at my manor; they will be much more comfortable for me… and Pippin. But we must have a decent manor in which to live. Fishermen's huts are cleaner than this hovel.*

Luckily, the fire burned well. Each of the travelers slept warmly. It was early afternoon before anyone stirred. Himli woke lying on her back, her eyes searching the ceiling for any thing familiar. Then, she realized where she was. What will we do? She asked herself. *These few soldiers cannot repair this place. We would be better off to raze it all to the ground and begin again.She rolled onto her stomach, the better to think.*

"There is no one to help me," she moaned. Just after she married Charlemagne, her father and brothers left home, becoming fishermen many miles to the south. Although she knew Roland or Oliver, Charlemagne's trusted friends, would aid her, she did not want to compromise their loyalty to the King. *Charlemagne would not forbid them to help. He would insist on it.* But I prefer not to appeal to them, Himli thought. *What can I do?*

Pippin sighed and turned toward his mother. His small fists rested under his cheek. Himli thought. *I must do the best I can, for his sake.* Her thoughts lurched. *Fulrad! Abbot Fulrad! That's it; he promised me help.* She laughed bitterly. *He'll be surprised my need comes so soon.*

Himli rose and opened her pack. She had brought one precious piece of parchment, just as she left her old home, thinking to write to her sister-in-law, Gisela. *Gisela's letter must wait. I must use this parchment to write Abbot Fulrad. I'll have Captain Mortimer send one of our guards back to the court right away, this morning.* She penned her letter.

Dear Abbot Fulrad,

Forgive me for availing myself of your offer so soon.. But I appeal to you—for the sake of my son. We arrived at our destination late yesterday night, footsore and exhausted. My weariness and, then, despair deepened upon coming inside the structure.

Abbot, we cannot live here! The cooking room roof is open to the heavens; snow would be our most plentiful condiment! he structure is beyond repair.Even the fire pits have been mostly destroyed...completely unusable. I have not the strength to examine the other rooms in this manor but suppose them to be equally poor.

Captain Mortimer has brought us here, as directed. He has delivered us safely, but we cannot stay in this place. Please, please, Abbot, can you do anything to help me? I must have a home in good repair. Don't you see? The son of the King of Frankland cannot be housed in such a place! It is a denial of his heritage.

I am awaiting your response with great hope. Please hurry. I am afraid the Captain will wish to return to Court immediately.

With all thankfulness,
Himiltrude

And, then, Himiltrude woke Captain Mortimer.

"Captain," she began, "please have one of your soldiers deliver this missive to Abbot Fulrad quickly. The Abbot will find us an appropriate home. I am sure of it. He urged me to contact him if I had any need. This surely qualifies. Send a soldier as soon as he has eaten."

"Of a certainty, my Queen," the Captain replied as he rubbed his eyes. "I have no further directions, other than comfortably settling you here. I would welcome a response from the Abbot or the King," he added.

"As you can surely understand," Himli responded, "I'm not eager to communicate with your King. The Abbot will answer, I'm certain."

The soldiers spent the following days investigating the small manor and searching for additional food. They found a small stable and within it, near its rafters, discovered a large storage area. It contained dried fruits and nuts, salted meat, and old — but still usable — oats. Himli instructed the soldiers in grinding oats, promising them hot bread for their effort. She provided nourishing meals, having supervised her uncle's kitchen when she was fifteen. He had re-married within a year but, luckily, Himli retained her knowledge of cooking.

Himli visited each room in the manor and found the entrance area was the only livable space. In two of the other chambers, roofs were long gone. Walls and floors suffered much damage from rain and wind and, now, from the snow. All the furnishings were long-since ruined; those not rent and torn boasted nibble marks from mice or smelled of rodents. The more Himli discovered, the greater grew her anger.

"How could Charlemagne imagine we could live here?" she asked over and over again. "How can he be so careless? How dare he send Pippin and me to this — this decrepit, broken manor?" She ranted and raved, crying in frustration and disappointment.

On the fifth day after the soldier's leave-taking for the court, Himli took Pippin for a walk through the manor house. The little boy was restless, anxious to be outside their one, warm room. And, since the air was heavy with snow, Himli took him through the house, hoping the movement would entertain him.

"Can you find any treasures in here, Pippin?" She asked. "We could do with another blanket or, mayhap, a larger sleeping bench." She and her little son walked from room to room. She found that Pippin's presence soothed her hurt feelings. Pippin pointed at items. Himli named them and described their uses.

"Oh, that's a pretty ewer, son," she acknowledged as he pointed at a roughly-shaped vessel. "Someone here was able to mold leather. The water can be poured easily from it." Pippin lay down on a small bench, just the size for a child, and laughed. He walked into the fire pit. It was filled with rotten limbs, the stringy remains of an old tapestry, a carved chair with three legs missing, a pot and stand for hanging above the cook-pit coals, and tattered pieces of parchment. Pippin laughed each time they entered a new room, infecting Himli with his enthusiasm. As they returned to the entrance room, the Captain shouted for Himli.

"Rider coming, my Lady, rider coming from the southeast!" Himli and Pippin were at the door as the Captain ushered a soldier into the room. "He's come from the Abbot, my lady," the Captain announced, recognizing his courier.

"My Lady, a missive from Abbot Fulrad," the soldier began. "He told me to get here as quickly as possible. The snow is deep but I have come in less than four days." He handed a sealed parchment to Himli.

"Thank you, Sir," she responded. "We eagerly awaited your return. Please rest. Sit. Captain, bring food for this good man; and put more wood on the fire so he may warm his toes."

She smiled at the soldier as she sat Pippin on his linens, spread on the floor. The Captain leaned down to talk to the boy. Himli opened the Abbot's letter.

My Queen,

Please accept my apologies for the manor to which you were directed. I am appalled you have spent even one night in such unsuitable conditions.

I spoke to the King. He sends additional instructions to Captain Mortimer. You should leave for the new manor as soon as is convenient. I assure you this one will be suitable. I was a guest at this same manor in the late summer--just as the last battles were ending--and know of its sound construction, amenable furnishings, and pleasant environment. Its agricultural products are often sought by the residents in the near-by valley so you should be able to offer fruit and grain in trade.

Should you find anything not to your lik-
ing, inform me immediately. I will journey to
you myself to verify your comfort.

The court is not the same without you, my
dear.

With sincere good wishes,
Abbot Fulrad

"Is it too late to begin our journey, Captain?" Himli looked to the Captain who was reading his own missive. "I wish to depart from here, as soon as it is feasible."

"Aye, my Lady," the Captain responded. "The newly identified manor is about a day's march from here. It's being mid-morning now, we shall spend one night under the stars. Aye, it can be done." He tried to be positive. But, truth be told, he feared the cold.

Himli looked steadily into his eyes. Seeing his reluctance, she noticed, again, the wind howling around the manor. Nay, she thought, I should not press leaving today. *Pippin may be harmed by the cold, if we cannot maintain a fire at night. And we are warm here because we have old, broken furniture to burn.* She nodded at the Captain.

"You must trust your instincts, Captain," she admonished him. "We shall rest early, arise at daybreak and set out. With a long day, we should arrive before dark. Is that possible?" Clearly relieved, Captain Mortimer nodded his approval.

"Aye, my Lady. It's a far better choice to begin on the morrow." He immediately began planning for the next day's journey. "Identify your warmest clothing, my Lady. We will take it from the packs tonight and make all ready. You might consider two hats — one close-fitting on the head and another atop it. Mayhap, the top one will cut the wind a bit."

Himli nodded at his instructions and sat down to play with Pippin. They had one more day to pass in this pitiful manor. ...though I do give thanks we have only one day's march left to us, she thought, and that we have another destination. Each one in the group ate as much as possible the following morning before daylight. They knew their next meal would most likely be well after dusk, if all went well. Each traveler stuffed 'traveling sticks' in their pockets for munching. These were popular traveling food. The sticks contained mixtures of dried meat (mostly rabbit and squirrel), ground nuts, hog lard, and dried grapes. They were easily portable, provided much energy, and had a lingering, sweet taste — just the thing during a winter journey.

Every one of the travelers had on three layers of clothing and the two hats which the Captain suggested. The Captain, his face red with embarrassment, offered leg bands to Himli and her nurse, assuring her their legs would be much warmer if they wound the bands around them. Each in the party dressed warmly since their only activity would be sitting upon their mounts. As the day warmed, they would remove their layers of clothing and replace them in the late afternoon as the air chilled. The soldiers repacked the limited supplies left and departed the manor. It was just as deserted as when they entered, except now there was little furniture left. Each looked toward the northeast with a hopeful heart.

Chapter Two

In the early dusk, faint lights to their northeast beckoned to the soldiers of the weary, little group. Captain Mortimer rode quicky back to Himli's cart where the Queen was resting on a blanket.

"The manor is just ahead, my Lady," he announced, beaming at her. His eyes sparkled, thankful this unexpected leg of the journey would soon be over. He shrugged his shoulders, hoping to work out the tension. Nothing could ease the ache in his head. The responsibility of this escort was far more than he had imagined when he had volunteered to lead the small group.

"You will soon be safe in your new home," he added to reassure her. The Captain saw Himlitrude frown, saw the sadness mirrored in her eyes.

"Yes, thank you, Captain Mortimer." Himli replied, grateful for his continuing concern. "You will soon be free of your burden." Seeing his start of surprise and the hurt look on his face, she hurried to make amends. "Oh, forgive me, Captain. I did not mean to suggest your escort deficient in any way! On the contrary, you have cared well for us. It's just that, well, I would have….." Himli's voice stopped. She changed her thought.

"Captain, we shall all be more than ready to alight from these carts! Thank you for your dedicated protection. May there be a good meal for you and your men, as soon as we enter the manor."

The Captain, still watching her strained face, nodded quickly and rode back to the front of the small procession. In another few minutes, he dismounted and walked to the manor door, ready to announce their presence. Just as Captain Mortimer raised his hand to knock; the door opened. Light fell outside the door as it outlined a tall, imposing figure holding a spoon.

"Aye, young man," the woman spoke. "Who are you and why are you knocking on this door so late in the day?" Captain Mortimer handed her a missive and stood rigidly, waiting for her to read the Abbot's message. The woman sighed softly, looking into the Captain's face.

"I feared we would not be long without a master, but a mistress suits me even more pleasantly." She tugged at her headdress and smoothed her over-tunic. "Please, Captain, make your men comfortable in the stables." She pointed a bit to her left. "After they have settled, bring them through the side door of the manor. The evening meal is being prepared. We must just 'stretch the pot' with a little more preparation. How many are there in your party?" She asked, looking around the captain's body. She noticed his hesitation. "The manor is always in order, Sir. Now, let me see to the Lady and the child. Your meal will be served in the cook room." The woman handed her spoon to a young girl standing behind her and hurried to the carts now stopping behind the soldiers.

"Welcome, my Lady," she said as a soldier helped Himli from the cart. Himli staggered a little, holding the man's hand tightly. She had not stood for more than five hours and found her legs stiff and cramped. "I am Frau Woodslie. You must be exhausted." She took Himli's hands in her large, work-worn ones. "Come, come inside to the fire. Food will soon be ready for you all--hearty soup, barley bread, and tarts for your meal." She looked around keenly.

"But where is your dear little one?" she asked. Pippin's nurse, trying to work her legs as well, softly called Pippin's name. She gently rubbed his forehead, trying to wake him up. Silently, she handed her bundle to the woman. Frau Woodslie took him quickly, moving the blanket to look into his face. Pippin blinked his eyes slowly, moving them across the face of this stranger. Frau Woodslie kissed him on the forehead, softly tracing his jawline with her finger. Then, she tapped his little nose and smiled at him.

"What a big, brave boy," she praised as his little hand moved out of his linens. "You already look like a king, lad."

Pippin didn't take his eyes from her face. He wrapped his fingers around her thumb and smiled. And for Frau Woodslie, the heavens opened.

"Such an angel you are." She announced as she held him to her chest, "such a precious angel." Himli watched this little vignette with all the wariness of a new mother. She slowly released her breath and smiled at Frau Woodslie.

"He is very weary," she admitted. "We had a difficult journey, not made easier by the cold. But we are here now; thank the holies!" Himli turned to enter the manor, relieved with the concern and care she saw in Frau Woodslie's reaction to Pippin.

Frau Woodslie earned each traveler's thanks that night. They feasted on hot barley soup, turkey moist with cranberry juice and sprinkled with toasted walnuts, buttered turnips and parsnips, and hot loaves of rye bread, smothered in butter. The filling meal and mulled wine so lulled the diners that only little

Pippin could enjoy the apple-cinnamon tarts presented after the meal. Soon thereafter, all stumbled directly to their linens, apologizing to Frau Woodslie for their early slumber. Everyone lay abed the next morning until they heard a ringing from the cook room. Frau Woodslie announced breakfast.

"Cheese, bread, eggs and porridge are waiting to break your fasts." Hearing them stir, she then went to the stable to rouse the soldiers bedded down there. Within a very short time, all gathered in the kitchen, pouring milk over steaming bowls of porridge and murmuring thanks to Frau Woodslie. Each one paused, however, seeing the strange mix she sprinkled over the porridge.

"Ah..." she exclaimed, looking from one unsure face to the next. "If you weren't so hungry, you'd recognize the mixture. We grind pecans and walnuts, mix in dried grapes and roll it in a bit of honey. It does do well with the milk, though; does it not?" She smiled deliberately at each one in the room, delighted to have people smile in appreciation as they sampled their porridge. Offering bread, cheese, and eggs, Frau Woodslie looked to Captain Mortimer.

"And what is today's plan, Sir?" she asked.

The Captain looked a little uncomfortable as he glanced around at his men. "I have to inspect.... Well, look things over to.... You see, I must be positive..."

"Of a certainty, Captain," Frau Woodslie replied. "You need to inspect the manor and its properties — much more carefully now, in the light of day. I would expect nothing less of you!" She laughed heartily. "You will find everything in good repair. Of that I am certain. I do understand your worry...with what these soldiers told me about the previous manor! Have no more concern, Sir. Inspect your heart away and report to me if you find anything amiss... anything, Captain. Do you understand me?" She stared into the Captain's face.

"Aye, I do. You shall hear the right of it," Captain Mortimer replied. "As soon as all break their fasts, we shall inspect everything, starting with the barn. We will be out and about, in and around the manor, Frau Woodslie." She nodded seriously as the men grinned happily, downing their eggs and cheese. With one last gulp of milk, the Captain rose. "If you will excuse us..." He nodded to his men who immediately followed him out of the cook room.

Frau Woodslie turned to Himli, smiling in contentment. "I did not mean to make him uncomfortable, my Lady. He does show appropriate concern for you and the lad. But this *is* a flourishing manor, kept in fine condition by its previous owner." She looked at Himiltrude. "You do know the previous owner of your home, Madam?" she asked. Without waiting for an answer, she continued. "They were a family of good repute, stalwart and true."

By Frau Woodslie's manner Himiltrude could sense she was quite proud of the manor. Himli wondered at such a proprietary feeling. In her experience, court workers were more often envious of those above them, not necessarily proud of their positions. Yesterday night, Himli noted the beautiful furniture, the wall tapestries, and heavy floor coverings before she tumbled into her soft, clean sleeping covers. She delighted in Pippin's little sleeping corner. One wall was adjacent to the cooking room, so she need not worry about his warmth.

"Nay, Frau Woodslie," Himli responded. "I had nothing to say about my home, my journey, or my destination---as you undoubtedly have heard," she replied sternly. *How dare this woman believe anyone sought my opinion? Does she think I had a single word to say about my present circumstance? My God! If anyone sought my opinion, I would not be here. Nay, I would have re-*

turned to my father's house, to be with people who value me. She gazed at the floor, realizing anew the depth of her parents' worry when they heard she was no longer queen. *I must write and reassure them,* she promised herself. *I must lie.*

"Excuse me, my Lady," Frau Woodslie apologized. "I did not mean to make little of your trouble. I only wish to reassure you. This is a fine manor, one quite self-sufficient and prosperous. Its workers were all born here and elected to remain. They care for the house and stables, for the woods and fields, with pride and love. You have not only a home but a small community." She declared with satisfaction. Then, she had a different thought. "I do hope this is positive for you...and for the boy," she added.

"It may surely become so, Frau Woodslie," Himli replied. "Pippin and I need a community, to be sure, and a family — if we all here might grow into that," Himli declared. Yesterday night Himiltrude noticed the tunics and breeches of the manor workers. The linen was of good quality, the colors well-dyed. The cleanliness brightened her heart, suggesting both good fortune and good management. Frau Woodslie looked intently at Himli, inclined her head slightly and walked toward the cook-room door.

"Shall we inspect the manor, you and I?" She offered. "You may prefer to choose different chambers for yourself and Pippin. I showed you to the warmest in the manor yesterday night." She waited for Himli in the corridor. "Will any of the soldiers remain here, my Lady?" She did not wait for Himli's reply. "I ask because there are three barrack rooms in the stable, quite satisfactory for house soldiers, I should think." Himli paused, thinking. Frau Woodslie continued down the corridor. Himli followed her.

I've given no thought to protection of Pippin or of myself. We are in no danger, she thought. *All will understand the King no longer cares for me and that he repudiates Pippin. No one will give us the barest glance now,* she decided.

"I daresay that we need no protection, Frau Woodslie," Himli replied. My importance decreased appreciably, overnight, as soon as we left the court. Pippin came here with me at his grandmother's direction. I don't know if he will ever find a place at court. I assume we're safe. But I will give it additional thought." She inspected the manor, asking questions of Frau Woodslie as they moved from room to room.

This structure was as pleasing in its appointments and layout as the previous manor was appalling. The bed chambers each had a roaring fire-pit and deep, deep linens on the sleeping benches. Each room contained a wardrobe to hold clothing and a small writing desk. Thick tapestries hung from ceiling to floor, holding back sudden drafts from the corridor. Embroidered cushions lay on benches, along with wool lap covers for additional warmth. The more Himli saw of the manor, the more relieved she felt.

"This manor will be so much more comfortable than the traveling tents of the King's mobile court," Himiltrude observed. "When the court moves through the realm, the tent becomes home. But I did miss walls and separate chambers." Frau Woodslie shook her head.

"I cannot fathom living in a tent," she replied. "My goodness, did you never have a roof over your heads?"

"Aye … but never for very long. We stayed several weeks in one manor at Christmastide and in another at Easter. It was seldom the same places two years in a row. Nay, King Charlemagne moved all around the realm. Even when battle season finished, we visited counts and lords during the spring and much in the autumn. During the summer battle months, the court still moved. We weren't in danger…from the fighting, I mean," she clarified. "But we were near…to feed the soldiers, care for the wounded. It was a difficult life in many ways."

"I hope you're ready for the dullness of a permanent home," Frau Woodslie answered. "Come; let's go next to the stables." As the two women came to the stable door, Captain Mortimer entered across from them, on the far side of the stable.

"Good morrow to you, my Lady," he greeted Himiltrude again. "I trust you are more pleased with this manor than the snow-filled one. I did, though, enjoy the snow. It's drifting through the roof…very calming." He smiled.

"Good Captain," Himli answered. "Although I do, indeed, value the snow's calmness, I prefer to watch it fall from afar, not live with it decorating my headdress." She laughed and looked around the stable, spying the three 'barracks rooms' in the southeast corner. "And did you find your quarters adequate, Captain?"

"Far beyond adequate, my Lady," the Captain affirmed. "The rooms are much better than the usual soldiers' fare." Himli smiled at his words, but more so at his pleased expression.

"When do you return to court, Captain Mortimer?" she asked. "I can think of no reason to keep you here further. Your escort made this journey bearable for my son and me. You cared well for us, Captain. I thank you and your men."

"I need to discuss this with you, my Lady," the Captain

moved quickly to her side. He shifted his feet back and forth. "Might we talk about it? Now is as good an opportunity as we are likely to have."

"Of a certainty," Himli responded. What can he mean? She wondered. *I know of nothing to discuss.* Himli preceded Captain Mortimer out of the stable, walking toward the small pond in the distance. Frau Woodslie waved over her back and headed toward the manor. Moving toward the pond, Himli saw the distinct sheen of frozen ice on its surface. One of the stable workers broke ice along the pond edges, so passing birds and animals might drink.

"Not to usurp your wishes, my Lady, but I've given our return to court some thought...even so far as to write the King about it. I begged him to ask Abbot Fulrad's opinion." He stopped and looked at Himli. "I know it's not my place," he admitted, his hand rubbing the back of his head. "But the Abbot helped you before...in such a time that the King might have neglected his duty." The Captain's eyes quickly looked away, acknowledging he took a big risk when contacting the Abbot.

"I did want wise heads to consider my proposal, my Lady. Humm.... Mistress."

"And what is your proposal, Captain?" Himli asked, bewildered. "I believe your escort's purpose was to deliver me to my new home." She smiled. "You have done so. In fact, you brought me to two manors — the second one much more suitable than the first. Pray we do not have to make another journey."

"Nay, nay, you must worry no longer, Mistress," the Captain waylaid her fear. "Nay, you are to settle here. The King

and Abbot Fulrad were very firm about this manor." He nodded and, then, spoke again. "But, I am concerned about your
safety. You should not fear harm from anyone." His voice faded, as he noted Himli's stiff posture. I am certain you are safe,
safe here, and safe in general, I mean. But it is not natural for a
manor to have no guard, to have no protection about. Later, of
course, Pippin will be in charge. But for now, you two are
without any protection here." His voice trailed off. He tried
again.

"I know there are stable workers—farmers; but there's little
safety in their abilitries, my Lady, no matter how courageous
are their hearts."

Himli was astonished. *She gave her safety, hers and Pippin's,
absolutely no thought. How could they be in danger? But, of
course...my awareness of danger was not necessary. Once, we were
safely within the confines of the King's court.* But now, could there
be danger? Himli wondered. *...mayhap, for Pippin there might be.*

"Frankly, Captain; I did not consider our safety," Himli admitted. "I have no value. But, my son--now, that is something
else." She looked at the Captain steadily. "What did you propose to the King?"

"I requested to stay here, my Lady, me and the escort. Actually, two of us would be enough...to guarantee your and
Pippin's safety. We might each work extra at guard duty....for
that manor in the distance, the one we glimpsed from the
hilltop? Among us all, we can feed ourselves. I don't want to
burden you...with our upkeep, I mean." The Captain blushed,
unsure about protocol in hiring himself out. *I'm part of the
King's contingent, after all. I don't even know if I can do so.*

"I'm waiting for a reply now, Mistress. I sent Jasic two days
ago...to carry the missive." He squared his shoulders, took a
deep breath. "Forgive me, if I overstepped my duty," he

begged. "It seems someone needs to think about daily activities, your daily needs, I mean." He turned away from Himiltrude, seemingly engrossed in the distant mountain peaks.

Himli felt the tears well up inside her. *Here was a soldier in the King's army, a soldier-- worrying about her welfare.* The tears moved into her eyes; a lump rose in her throat. Sadness swept over her. *Her true husband could send her away, without a backward glance. But one of his soldiers now offered to protect her.* Himli thought of the Captain's gentle handling of Pippin. Her sense of fate and blessings reasserted itself as she walked over to him.

"Captain Mortimer, your concern does lighten my heart," she admitted. "Thank you for your worry. It does speak well of you and your spirit. I am very lucky to have you as my guide on this journey." She turned to the mountain peaks as well. "I know nothing of this safety issue. As I admitted, I do not even know if I should be concerned. Let's wait for the King's answer. I am certain he will consult with Abbot Fulrad. But, thank you again for your care, your concern for Pippin and me." She smiled into his face, then turned back to the manor.

Days later, the weather finally cleared, allowing Himli and Pippin to spend some time outside. Himli spotted the returning soldier as she and Pippin came down the hill behind the manor house. They were out visiting the sheep. Pippin eagerly became friends with every animal he could reach. A daily walk about the stables and fields to see his new friends assured them both a good night's rest. Yesterday, snow kept them inside; but today the sun, albeit weak and pale, beckoned to them. She strained her eyes to identify the rider.

Himli felt her heart lurch as she recognized the soldier. It was Jasic, returning from Charlemagne's court. Before the Captain spoke of his concern for their safety, she thought little about her small escort. But she realized, in the past three days, how much the men's presence comforted her. *If I must lose them,* she vowed, *I will be brave. After all, I never expected them to stay with us. But it will be with a heavy heart and an uneasy mind I see them return to court.*

Captain Mortimer held the soldier's reins as the man dismounted and handed him a rolled parchment. At the Captain's thanks, the soldier nodded and turned, heading to the back entrance of the cook room. The Captain walked the soldier's horse to the stable, surrendering it to the stable boy. He sat upon Himli's mounting block (used to get atop her horse) as he unrolled the parchment. Watching him as she walked, Himli could read nothing from his reaction as he looked down at the parchment.

Himli jumped as a rabbit ran across the path. Pippin let out an excited whoop. At his cry, Captain Mortimer looked up, saw them coming over the hill, and walked toward them. In his rush to catch the rabbit, Pippin fell over his own feet and began rolling down the path. Captain Mortimer rushed toward him and scooped Pippin up as he almost rolled by him. He stood Pippin on his feet, holding him steady with a hand on his shoulder.

"Thanks for righting my roll-away son!" Himli laughed, as the Captain slowly released his hold on Pippin. "He loves to be on the go," Himli added, "be that upright or rolling along." She thanked God every day for her son. His excited view of the world and his pleasure in small things helped her through the worse of her sorrow.

The Captain held out the missive. "I have a reply from King Charlemagne, my Lady," he confirmed. "He gave his blessing to my suggestion. Three of us may stay and be your small manor guard." Captain Mortmort nodded, almost to himself. "His response is far more than I hoped."

"Just tell me his reaction, Captain." Himli said, refusing to take the parchment. "I don't wish to read his words." His words, though penned in the Abbot's hand, will remind me of too much, Himli thought. *I don't want to see the parchment.*

The Captain hastily rolled the parchment, sticking it in his tunic sleeve. He could slap himself; he did not mean to cause the Queen additional distress. Her pale face and slow pace were already a concern. Even Frau Woodslie commented on the Lady's physical weakness this morning as they broke their fasts.

"He directed that three of us five should remain, as a small 'manor guard,' my Lady. I did not expect the second part of his response. The three of us who remain will no longer be his soldiers but will become guards, paid by the Crown. Abbot Fulrad will send wages every fortnight for us." The Captain's forehead wrinkled. His hands rubbed the top of the parchment.

"I hope I did not earn the King's wrath." Captain Mortimer worried. "I would not want him to feel I judge his decisions, though someone needs to remind him of his duty."

"Fear not, Captain Mortimer." Himli spoke hurriedly to lessen his concern. "I can assure you. No one intimidates King Charlemagne. He always thinks for himself and does exactly as he chooses." She smiled. "He admires you for clearly stating a situation. You may be certain. He does always want the facts."

"I hope so, my Lady," the Captain responded, smiling broadly. "This is good for us. The three of us who choose to stay here can, then, have some extra life." Himli looked at him, puzzled.

"…extra life, Captain?" She asked.

"We will be guards, soldiers no longer. And so, we will not be owned by the King. We can make some choices." The Captain laughed aloud and startled, hearing an answering laugh from Pippin. "He does like laughing, Mistress." Captain Mortimer reminded Himli as she smiled in the direction of her son.

"Aye," Himli agreed. "He has a happy soul."

"That 'extra life'…" the Captain continued. "To a soldier, that means a family, a little plot of land, maybe even a hut of his own." He turned his face, looking over Pippin's head, all at once shy about saying such things to the Queen. Himli smiled.

"None of those things should be 'extra,' Captain," she responded. "It's only what most people want for themselves. I'm relieved you don't mind giving up your soldiering."She looked at him seriously, asking a question. "What about the other men? Do any of them see becoming a 'manor guard' as positive? You'll be giving up booty, the excitement of battle, the comradeship of your fellows. What say the other soldiers, Captain?"

"Oh, we four talk of little else…since Jasic began his journey," the Captain admitted. "Tardt and I are eager to stay. Afore he left, Jasic said that he'd leave soldiering in a minute, if he could find any other kind of work. We're the three who will stay, my Lady. And it works out because Todd and Robs want to return to the court. They like the battles. They're still young, Mistress." The Captain nodded his head, shading his eyes as he watched Pippin fall again. He hurried ahead to set Pippin upright and brush the snow off his clothes. Pippin chortled with glee and rushed back to his mother.

"Then, I must thank you for your generosity," Himli bowed her head to the captain. "The 'manor guard' will make us all feel more secure. We will have a small celebration tonight as we take our evening meal." Himli took Pippin's hand, smiled at the Captain, and hurried to tell Frau Woodslie of their manor's good fortune.

The newly constituted 'family' settled down in the manor, eager for the first signs of spring. They were, each of them, beginning a new phase of their lives so the hope and promise of spring was on everyone's mind. Himli learned the history of her manor from Frau Woodslie who was second only to the previous mistress of the house. When the master, Duke Humbolt, died in battle—from an illness in his head, not from a wound—the mistress left the manor to join her niece's family. She herself had no children. The mistress hoped her gifting the manor to the King would aid in the crown's kindness to her niece's son. The young man wished to join the King's court, to earn his place as a peer.

Frau Woodslie pointed with obvious pride to the care given to the manor house and to the surrounding fields and orchard.

"This is a self-sufficient manor," she assured Himli. "Jakob is a good tiller of the soil, though the Duke did encourage him to expand the planting. He followed the Duke's directions to the letter. There's no faulting a man for that!" Himli nodded at Frau Woodslie's words. Her own parents inherited a small, but prosperous manor. She remembered listening to her mother's recountings of plantings, harvestings, and such.

Her new home supported the manor's needs and contributed to the tables of those in the near-by valley town. She was content. The farmers and shepherds welcomed Himli to the neighborhood, once they got used to having a 'former' queen in their midst.

"These are very welcoming people, Frau Woodslie," Himli commented.

"Aye, they are kind and hard-working, ever on the look-out to help someone. They hold you in much sympathy," she added, looking steadily at Himli.

"...in sympathy?" Himli questioned, not at all sure the meaning of this.

"Years ago, in the early autumn, King Charlemagne came here to hunt," Frau Woodslie explained. "Some small things went wrong—a falcon was lost in the field, one of the hounds broke its leg, a horse stamped its foot and spooked the retrievers. I don't remember the exact mishap. The King's anger flared. He blistered the hunt master and, then, the dog trainer with his hoarse shouting. He frightened all of us. Even the dogs sneaked away from his ire! Once the men saw that quick anger, they all prayed there'd not be another king's hunt here!" The woman laughed but, obviously, waited for Himli's reaction. Himli, for her part, said not a word. In this close-knit community, lessons learned passed from one generation to the next; an outsider must not question the wisdom of the manor's people.

It was obvious to everyone in the environs: working in the manor was a desirable vocation. Its straightforward farming values; its cozy quarters; its good, benevolent owners-- not to mention the plentiful meals--beckoned to young people looking for work. On this particular afternoon, Himli made ready to interview young women for house servants. At first, Frau Woodslie objected, reassuring Himli she could manage the running and upkeep of the house with the two workers she now supervised.

"Oh, nay, madam," Himli replied. "You have much responsibility here. We must have someone to undertake chores which require less thought or skill. We shall not continue to use your talents in this way. I need you for far more demanding duties!" Frau Woodslie could not easily argue with this outlook so she sent word to the village: the mistress of the manor would be interviewing workers.

Now, outside the door, there were about fifteen men and women milling about. Himli actually was not certain how many new workers she needed. The applicants' immediate skills would determine her choices. She wanted only to get her manor more adequately staffed, people to work in the manor as well as in the fields when necessary. Her first criterion for a new worker was an interest in learning. Such workers would be the most versatile, and, thereby, the most valuable.

"Frau Woodslie, please send the men to the cook room for buns and ale," Himiltrude directed. "I will speak with the women first. And you and I shall confer after I am done. We will announce no decisions today. I shall 'sleep' on the decision." She smiled widely at her next-in-command. Himli knew she must give Frau Woodslie the opportunity to form an opinion about these applicants. And, then, she must listen carefully to her opinion. I dare not alienate Frau Woodslie, Himli told herself again. *She's my right-hand man, much more so than the Captain.*

Himli sat in the garden beside the cooking room. The day was mild with sun shining boldly through gathering clouds. She did not want the applicants distracted by cooking activities nor by the equipment in the cooking rooms. So, she spoke with the women in the garden. Himli watched them as they followed Frau Woodslie. Three of the young women were caught up in each other, chatting continuously. They followed Frau Woodslie without once looking around, so interested in each other's tales. A fourth young woman turned to greet a young girl behind her, pointing to the small pond in the distance. The younger one turned, smiled and replied, though Himli couldn't hear her words. Himli motioned for the young women to sit on the benches and spoke to them..

"Thank you for coming up from the village," she began. "I am anxious to retain some workers, mostly for work within the manor. Except for a groomsman, we need no others for outside work. The farmers and gardener have agreed to remain. I am very fortunate with them, I know." Himli looked into the eyes of each young woman, gauging their attention. "But, before I explain the duties here, I want you all to meet my son, Pippin." Exactly on cue, Frau Woodslie patted Pippin's bottom and whispered.

"Go to your mother, Pippin. Do you see her sitting in the garden?" Frau Woodslie pointed her hand.

"M-o-m-a!" Pippin called as he darted away from Frau Woodslie, heading directly for his mother. Himli's eyes never left the group of five sitting before her. When arranging the benches, she angled them to her advantage. The young women would see Pippin as he rounded the curve. Just as she expected, each young woman's movements defined her individual reaction to the boy.

Pippin ran quite well. As he learned to walk, he also learned to compensate for his hunchback. And, though, his little body was not upright-- he leaned a bit to his right — he was steady on his feet, coming to his mother at a respectable pace. When he spied her, his face broke into a smile and he waved his hand. He decreased his speed just a little and skidded to a stop in front of his mother. Then, he crawled into her lap and softly kissed her cheek. Looking around, he saw the five faces watching him closely. He blushed and buried his face in Himli's neck.

"This is my son," Himli smiled as she stroked his head. "He is sometimes a little shy in front of beautiful young women." She smiled at the girls and whispered to Pippin to say 'hello.' He moved his head a little, looked up at his mother and, then, giggling, hid his head again, this time almost under her arm.

"Come, come," Himli urged him softly. "You must always greet visitors when you meet them. Let's hear a pleasant greeting from the 'man of the house.'" Pippin snuggled closer to Himli's body. He was very still. All of a sudden he shifted his feet to the ground, pushed himself upright, and turned to face the girls.

"Hullo," he said very quietly, "happy to see you." And he looked into his mother's face and beamed.

"Exactly right," Himli complimented him. "Now, please give our visitors one of your bows. I know you are practicing with the Captain." Pippin shifted his feet, fiddled with his shirt, and, then, walked slowly before the young women.

"Do one!" he announced as he bowed, his head touching the ground. Then, he ran toward Frau Woodslie, laughingly calling 'Bye' to his mother.

Himli had watched the young women carefully. Two of the group of three pulled back as Pippin approached, even though the boy was a good four feet from them. The third one in the group watched him, smiling at his serious efforts in making his bow. The youngest girl moved to the edge of her seat, smoothing and re-smoothing her dress. One minute her mouth would smile; the next minute, it trembled a bit. She smiled at his bow and mouthed 'Pleased to meet you," as Pippin stood upright before running off. Her hand reached out toward him as he rushed by.

"As you can see," Himli picked up the thread of the meeting, "Pippin has a problem which will affect his entire life. He does not look like other boys his age. But, I do assure you he has the same feelings, the same needs, as the rest of us. He is a little boy: happy, sad, enthusiastic, afraid, full of energy, sometimes slow. I would like to guarantee he will never be hurt." Here, Himli rose from her seat. "But I cannot make it so. And, as a result, I seek a friend for him. He needs someone who will keep him safe, who will play games with him, who will consider him no different from any other lad his age. He is smart, energetic, and quick. He will know if you don't like him, if you pity him, if you try to make things easy for him. Neither he nor I want this." Himli motioned to Frau Woodslie.

"Now, I offer you refreshments." Himli felt the ten eyes of the girls upon her. "Frau Woodslie prepared her ginger cake with lemon sauce and some nut-filled, sweet tarts. Please enjoy them and use the time to decide if you really do want to be a friend to my son. We shall speak again before you leave." Frau Woodslie began serving the sweets as, in front of her, Pippin handed each girl a small, wooden trencher.

"Please have more than one serving, if you like," Himli encouraged. "Frau Woodslie made them especially for us." Himli left the five young women to talk together. She nodded to Frau Woodslie, having told her to evaluate the young women as she served and talked with them. When they finished their treats, Himli returned to the girls. Frau Woodslie followed her and began to collect the trenchers. Himli looked into five sets of eyes.

"I would know your reason for seeking a position in this household," she said. "I want only one reason, so think deeply before you speak. Over the next day or two, I shall consider your words and your demeanors. When I arrive at a decision, I shall send one of the manor guards to inform you and tell you when you are expected to begin work." She turned and saw Frau Woodslie's lips, mouthing 'living arrangement.'

"Oh, I almost forgot!" Himli exclaimed. "There is a nice chamber for you to share, here in the manor. I would have you live with us, not come back and forth each day. Is that a problem for any of you?" Himli watched the girls absorb this last fact as she returned to her seat. "When you identify your most important reason for wanting to work at this manor, come and tell me."

The girls formed a line, each one seeming to know just where she wanted to be in reference to the other applicants. One-by-one they walked to stand in front of Himli. Frau Goodslie, at Himli's previous direction, stood within earshot, trying not to seem curious. The two young women who appeared uncomfortable when Pippin ran to his mother were the first in line. One of them spoke.

"I wish to work here because it is a beautiful manor, one filled with cushions and handicrafts, with huge hangings on the walls, and... she dropped her eyes, "you seem so nice!" Himli nodded at her, trying not to smile. The second of the pair seemed irritated at her partner's words.

"She said just what I planned." She explained. Himli raised an eyebrow but said nothing. "But," the second girl continued, "I want to work for you because everyone else in the village would envy me—the easy duties, these tasty treats, a warm place by the fire at night." She curtseyed to Himli. The youngest girl, Gerta by name, came next. She looked into Himli's face, turned to look at her companions, and, then, fixed her eyes on the far-away mountains.

"I know this is not the best reason," she prefaced her words, "but I like your little boy! My worry about going to work is my brother. I will miss him *so* much...but I think Pep...Peppi... Pippin would help me get over that. He seems so loving, just like our Harry." She smiled at Himli. Then, she walked over to Frau Woodslie who continued to gather trenchers, spoons, and flagons.

"Excuse me," the young girl said. "I wish to thank you for those cakes. I never had anything so good, not in my whole life!" She flashed Frau Woodslie a smile and ran away down the path.

The fourth girl, the one who was a companion to those in the group of three, curtsied before Himli. "I would like this position, Lady, because it would show me all the duties, all the work in running a manor....and all," she offered.

"Do you hope to manage a manor at some point?" Himli politely inquired.

"Oh, yes, Mum!" The girl answered. "It's exactly what I hope, someday down the road." She stepped aside, looking for her friends as the last girl came to stand in front of Himli.

"I hope 'the last one isn't the lost one', Mum," she said, her eyes twinkling. "My Paw, he always says to try to be first...so as not to be forgot!" She smiled at Himli. "My name is Marsta, my Lady. And I'd like this position," she began, "because I like your son, Pippin. I think he's happy. And I'd like to understand the reason for that." Himli almost stood, so taken aback was she by the comment. "Oh, do excuse me, Mum. I didn't mean to speak out of turn!" The girl's cheeks were red.

"I'd like to learn why he's happy. I mean, he has every reason NOT to be!" She struggled to explain, rubbing her hands together. Then, she was still. "Please forgive me, Lady," she begged. "I didn't mean to give offense or speak ill of your little boy." She did not take her eyes from Himli's as tears formed and threatened to spill out. "Please forgive me." Himli took her hand.

"It's all right," she said. "You didn't offend me. In fact, your words are well-spoken. It is true; Pippin is happy. May God bless him so it will always be so. I think we all wish to be around happiness." Himli reached out to stroke the girl's cheek. "Thank you for that reason," she responded. "It has made me happy....to hear you say it!" The girls' eyes widened even more. She turned to leave.

"Thank you for the tasty cakes," she added over her shoulder. "Frau Woodslie does have magic. I am certain of it." She waved goodbye.

Frau Woodslie silently sat down beside Himli. She balanced the dirty trenchers and flagons on her knee. "She is an interesting girl, the last one, don't you think?" she asked Himli.

"Interesting," Himli stated, "very interesting, indeed, Frau Woodslie. Shall we talk about the girls now or in the morning; do you want to sleep on this overnight?" She looked into the woman's face.

"No need of that, not for me," Frau Woodslie said. I know the one I would choose, my Lady; but, mayhap, I should let you have the night to clarify your own thoughts. I already know mine!"

Himli laughed with relief. "Frau Woodslie!" she shouted. "You are a wonder! Thank God, you will tell me your mind! Nay, nay; tell me now the girl or girls you prefer. While I do value your opinion, my own is just as important, of course. Name your choice."

"Oh, this last one," Frau Woodslie said with no hesitation. "Marsta, wasn't it? Let's have people who want to learn around us! It makes for a more interesting home. Don't you think so,

Lady?" Her lips twitched as she pressed them together. But Himli could see the laughter in her eyes.

"Aye, Frau Woodslie, it makes for a much more interesting place. But, you do realize, don't you? Learning makes for much change in the learner's mind, too? My grandmother always said that one must beware of change." She raised an eyebrow at the older woman. "Are you ready for the changes learning will bring?" she asked curiously.

"Of a certainty, my Lady," Frau Woodslie replied. "I'm ready, if you are."

Chapter Three

Himli nodded when Frau Woodslie named her choice of girls. *Aye, I liked that one very much, too.* Himli admitted to herself. *Her personality seems so positive and she gets to the heart of an issue. It is true that Pippin is pleasant, friendly, and outgoing. He is, also, shy and unsure of strangers. But the girl's choice of words goes beyond those characteristics about him. Pippin is happy-- that is the defining element of his personality.* Himli smiled to herself. She believed Marsta would be a fine addition to the manor but she really like the youngest girl, Gerta, as well. *The girl's reluctance to leave her brother touched my heart.*

"We shall have them both," Himli decided, sure of her choices. "Neither of them blinked at seeing Pippin's hunchback nor reacted when he ran...in his scuttling way. They will both care for him but help build his strength and confidence as well." *Aye,* she affirmed to herself. *This manor is productive enough to maintain two additional workers. And who knows? My house may be beneficial to them as well.* Frau Woodslie, taken aback by the addition of two girls to the house staff, was, never-the-less, clearly pleased with Himli's choices.

"I daresay," she confided to the cook, "there's enough work

here to keep us all busy, no matter the number." Himli sent for both girls and helped them settle in. On the evening after their arrival, Himli called all her workers together to discuss a 'production plan' and, then, to provide a manor party for everyone.

Although the manor's overseer conducted the discussion and, finally, made most of the agricultural decisions, Himli and he had spent hours discussing the manor's future. They agreed to continue planting oats, barley and rye. They would expand their breeding animals by acquiring another boar, two milk cows, and three ewes. And the size of the orchard would be increased with new trees in the spring.

"The household numbers expand." Himli stated, her eyes twinkling. "We have need of more wool for warm tunics."

"Aye, my Lady." The overseer, Jakob, was thankful for the Lady's grasp of agricultural concerns. "Tell me, my Lady, was your father a turner of the sod? You are more knowledgeable about planting than I would have imagined."

Himli inclined her head at the compliment and smiled. "Jakob, my habit is to listen to the talk around me," she admitted. "I do so love the green, the flowering in the spring and am always fascinated by growing things! My father was a fisherman, supplied the King's table and, eventually, bustled in and out of court, straightening out deliveries of foodstuffs. It 'twas my mother who grew things. She tended a large garden, providing all kinds of delight…throughout the year."

Himli smiled, remembering her mother's constant activity as she hoed and sowed, picked and dried, baked and roasted.

"I'm just too used to good food, I guess. I always like to know how a soup or a stew is made, how to put things together."

"A wonderful interest, my Lady," Jakob responded, "to know the work required to get food to your hearth!" He sobered. "I thought your idea to link people's interests with their manor duties a little odd. I mean, who among us ever asked a worker what he wanted to do?" He shook his head at such a notion. "But, seeing the interest each person shows in his job....well, I can scarcely believe the difference in their work. And if the men are content, it is to our good. So many manors lose the young ones to the army. The young men think the booty will make them rich."

"I know, Jacob. I remember my father's efforts to keep my two brothers at home. Soldiering seems so exciting and provides freedom that young men value." She shook her head. "But as to encouraging people to do what they like... I learned that from the King." Himli paused, thinking back. "His most successful plans were always those undertaken by the people who believed in them." It surprised Himli that she knew this; but it was a sure fact.

"King Charlemagne would solicit battle plans, tactics and such, and, then, have the Peer who suggested the plan carry it out. Ha!" she exclaimed. "It always produced good results."

"Well, it's remarkable to me," Jakob answered. "We'll talk at the end of harvest, to see how well 'our' peers fulfill their plans, shall we?" He smiled good-naturedly, relieved the manor had such an able and spirited lady to direct it.

"Aye, we shall, Jakob," Himli agreed. "May all our expectations be met."

Pippin grew quickly, completely unfettered by the usual restrictions placed on court children. His handicap was not one to him, for he had never been without his mis-shapen back. He compensated for it in his activities and, having no one who drew attention to it, he ignored it, most of the time. Only if he forgot and rolled on his back or played beyond his strength did he have pain. When the pain came, he did his best to ignore it. But, somehow, his mother always saw it in his face. She would rub his back and put warm cloths behind his neck. In no time he would drift off to sleep and, as soon as morning came, be on the go again!

"He is an active child," Captain Mortimer said to the other guards. "Keep him in your sight at all times. I would no harm come to him." The guards, delighted to be employed but out of the army, spread the directive to the manor's workers. So, unknown to Pippin or to Himli, someone always had an eye on him. Even though each of the manor's residents interacted with Pippin for specific reasons, all were equally aware of his whereabouts. Their devotion to the little boy and to the manor linked the workers even more. With his gentle ways and ready smile, Pippin earned the friendship of every one.

He spent hours in the stable with the animals, helped and encouraged by Nordt who was more a farmer than a soldier. Jakob encouraged Pippin to investigate all the corners and recesses of the barn, to watch the birds as they nested during the coldest days, to trace the routes of the rats which moved from building to building, to learn the beauty of silence and stillness.

In his wanderings all over the manor, Pippin became friends with everyone. Though shy at first, he was respectful and quiet. His manner, alone, earned him friends. Those who needed to talk, talked readily to him. He was the keeper of many secrets. With some of them, he didn't even know he had a secret.

"Mollie help?" Pippin said to Captain Mortimer, "... likes brushing horses?" Pippin laughed. When Mollie came to milk the cows at night, the Captain was there, currying his horse. They often lingered to help each other. They were good friends.

Pippin was sure.

Jasic, the youngest of the guards, braided cow hairs. Pippin asked him what he would do with them all. Jasic planned to sell them to the watchmaker. But Pippin noticed Sarta wore lots of braided bracelets on her arms. And Marsta, the new girl who helped Mama, Frau Woodslie and Cook Eagan, spent lots of time in the kennels, helping Tardt with the pups. Everyone seemed content to Pippin. He was equally happy with every-one himself.

His life was perfect for a small, energetic boy. He wandered over the hills, watched over by the shepherds. He climbed the fruit trees in the orchard looking, as Jakob told him, for a hint a green in those sleeping boughs. Every animal he met was a friend, even the gray squirrel who stole walnuts, right from his hand!

This morning, Pippin turned toward the manor's kitchen. He raced to find Frau Woodslie. He needed more walnuts. But, hearing the Captain's voice, he looked toward the stable and spotted Captain Mortimer waving, holding a fishing pole aloft.

"Wheee...." Pippin shouted as he sped up, bearing down on the captain from thirty feet away.

"It's time, Lad!" Captain Mortimer welcomed him, reaching out to stop him as Pippin ran up. "Let's go see if those fish are biting!" He led Pippin to the manor's small pond, picked the boy up and waded into the water. Carefully, he set Pippin atop a skift. The Captain realized Pippin would be unable to hold his fishing pole out, over the bank. *The lad will be in immediate pain from the strain on his back,* the Captain mused. So, he moored the skift a few feet from shore.

"Here, Pippin," Captain Mortimer offered. "Prop your pole on that bushel basket. I think it'll be just the right height for you," he explained. Pippin carefully set the pole on the basket and sat down. It was just right. He beamed at the Captain who turned to bait Pippin's hook.

Holding onto the pole was none too exciting for Pippin. But the pond's resident creatures, their comings and goings, immediately caught his attention. The dragonflies' wings dazzled his eyes, the colors breaking like a rainbow as the insects darted back and forth. Frogs - large ones with warts on their backs and small, green ones with slick skin - hopped all around his boat, dodging this way and that. Birds called incessantly from nests in the tall trees just beyond the pond. And the fishing herons stood in complete stillness before darting their pointed beaks into the water. The turtles sunning on the logs brought a smile to Pippin's face.

"Look, look, Cap'tin!" He sang. "...log has turt-els!"

"I see a snake, a heron, a fat bullfrog, and a duck, Pippin," Captain Mortimer laughed. "But you shout about the turtles. Why is that? Do you just like the turtle best, my boy?"

"Yes, Cap'tin," Pippin answered. "Like them the best- est, my fav-rite." He smiled at the captain, as if the turtle were the most wonderful animal in the world.

Noting Pippin's big smile and the warmth in his voice, Captain Mortimer answered. "That turtle, there, the green one? He'll always be here, I suspect. You know, turtles aren't much for moving. They love the pond, and that keeps them close. I'll bet you won't see them....down the road in front of the manor, for example. Maybe they're like you. They love their home." Pippin nodded and smiled.

"Luv them," he answered.

"We'll see if we can catch enough fish for everyone's evening meal, Pippin," Captain Mortimer suggested.

"...take many fishes," the lad replied. "...'dere's eleven people."

"Good for you, lad," Mortimer answered. "You're right; there are eleven of us, but if our fish are big, we won't need too many. You want to try it?"

"Aye," Pippin agreed, clapping his hands. The two fishermen were more than able to feed the manor that night. There were three large fish left over which Cook did not even need to prepare. Marsta dried them over the fire-pit, preserving them for later use.

Although the work pace was not as frantic as the spring planting, everyone worked steadily to prepare for the coming cold. At times, the workers at the manor were so weary at nightfall they ate only milk, cheese, and bread before tumbling into their beds.

On the following mornings, however, everyone broke his fast with huge, filling breakfasts: plump, sweet blackberries floating in fresh milk; warm rye bread as it came from the oven, covered with melting butter; boiled eggs and slices of ham; strips of meat roasted in the hearth. Although sluggish after such a meal, each worker warmed quickly to the duties of the day. Work began again in earnest. On the seventh day, mornings saw everyone at prayers. Pippin, Marsta, and even Jasic spent the afternoon gathering nuts and any fruits still on the trees. Then, there was time left to sit around the fire, to tell stories, and to enjoy each other's company, to share hopes and dreams. The days passed slowly, in stately procession, each one much like the last but with a little more work completed before the harsh, cruel days of winter.

Pippin, outside in all hours of the day, became brown and robust. His favorite pastime was begging everyone to 'race him to the manor.'

"Come, come, Moma," he said to Himli, "time for run!"

For Himli, this was a time of rejuvenation. Her pale face began to glow; her body, which was sharply angled, became more rounded. She lost much of her worn, haggard demeanor. Every single day she celebrated her ownership of the manor — and her freedom.

When Queen Bertrada banished her, her first thought was to return to her parent's deserted hut. She knew the small community there; the residents would welcome her and Pippin. Her breath stopped as she remembered her stupidity. Her shock at the banishment was so unexpected, she did not think immediately of the worst possibility. .

Charlemagne could have kept Pippin with him, at court. Her ladies fully expected it. She still remembered their faces - bright with relief, as they eagerly brought his linens, caps, and heavy, traveling cloak to her. *How lucky for me*, Hilde often reminded herself. *Without Pippin, I would not want to live. He is my baby, all the more dear because he's the only one I will ever have.* When Himli thought of this, she felt Charlemagne surely encouraged her in those dreams.

'We must have at least four children, Himli,' he often said to her as the court moved through the realm. 'Two boys and two girls but I welcome any more God gives us in HIS blessing.' *But, now,* she thought, *that dream, those old dreams, can ever come true.* At the thought and her regret, she slapped herself.

"Stop it! Stop it!" She chastised herself. "Don't think like this. Don't dwell on the past. Some choices are gone," she said. "We are healthy, happy, and away from the court. You have no one you must obey. Remember what it was like around Queen Bertrada...what a mean, controlling creature she was?" Himli's eyes widened as she thought of the Queen. "Thank

God for my blessings. I must remember to pray, to thank Him each day."

Her thoughts turned back to the court and, from there, to the battles which so occupied Charlemagne. Once or twice in the last light of darkening summer evenings, Himli saw the dust from a large contingent of soldiers' feet. They marched no more than two furlongs from her manor. In her mind's eye, she saw the carts bearing the wounded at the front of the column. The bowmen followed next, alert to any threat which they might thwart. Behind the bowmen were the mounted soldiers, their huge Destriers moving with unexpected grace. The thousands of infantry took up the rear. Moving in and out, but concentrated among the wounded, the priests forgave sins, offered encouragement, and tried to radiate calm and peace. The army moved slowly, as large battalions do.

Himiltrude knew the battle season stretched out this year, far longer than usual. Soldiers did not come home to help with the harvest. Jakob returned from the village, shaking his head at the lack of help. Often, she found herself thinking of those men who would never come home again. Imagining the grief of their deaths against the joy of the battles' successes, she felt doubly thankful to be away from the King's court, away from the killing, the wounded and the grief-stricken.

"How different can a life be," Himli murmured. "Duties and expectations change and determine our outlooks." She turned to her sleeping linens, thankful her life was no longer bound by the King's needs. Her life was good. Almost a year before, she arrived to begin her new life. Winter was half-finished then but, now, here it was on them once again.

In these quiet days of winter, Himli devoted herself to getting to know the people who worked at her manor. She evaluated them, improved their living arrangements, and committed the relationships and names of relatives in each household to memory. She knew people value those who value them. Her manor and Pippin's future depended on her ability to maintain this place. In this, she would *not* fail. As she told Jakob, she was a listener. She was also interested in agriculture, in growing of all sorts.

Now, as the warm days became memories, the manor's people began gathering and storing their crops. The daylight hours seemed to end more quickly. People woke early, breaking their fasts quickly with heavy breakfasts of oatmeal and cream, eggs and ham, thick slabs of buttered bread and honey. Every horse in the stable took its place in front of a cart, pressed into carrying people to and from the fields or in returning the harvest to the barns. The head cook, the baker, Marsta, and Gerta packed picnic lunches, complete with plum and nut tarts. Nothing took the manor's people from the fields. If bad weather arrived early, much of the harvest would be lost and the entire manor and its residents would go hungry during the last, cold days as winter lingered.

Butchering the cattle and hogs began, only a day after the crops were in. The fire for smoking meat and boiling pots in the slaughter hut helped keep all the workers warm as they skinned, cut, dried and cooked the meat.

Pippin ran so many errands during the harvest that he slept wherever he sat, often not finishing his evening meal. The manor's workers and a couple of wanderers hired for the harvest slept together, either in the cook room of the manor, in the entrance room with the firepit at the manor's south end, or in the stables. Those waking in the barn and stables could see their breaths in the cold, dawn air though the animals' nearness provided some warmth during the night.

Opening the small door of the chicken coop for Pippin to feed the hens, Jakob noticed the thin layer of ice formed on the water trough. Winter's near enough for us to finish this harvest, he thought, as he rang the bell to awaken the manor. *I'll hurry everyone along. We must try to finish in the fields by tomorrow.* He broke the ice in the trough just as an unexpected burst of cold air hit his legs. Jakob looked up into the sky.

"Snow clouds forming," he spoke aloud. "Damn, we could have snow by morning." Captain Mortimer came out of the stables as Jakob cursed.

"Aye, the cold is coming, Jakob," he agreed. "We must speed up our work today and finish the harvest. Rest for us all is only a day or so away." The Captain grimaced as he dipped water from the trough to wash his face. Jakob laughed as the captain carefully used his finger to splash water over his eyes.

"Hope you weren't thinking of bathing in the river, Mortimer," he laughed. "The water's likely to freeze your blood...or worse this morning!"

"Right you are, Jakob," the Captain agreed. "Never fear, bathing is for another day." The men pulled their mantles close, pinning them high to protect their necks. "Let's break our fast; we've much work to finish this day." The two friends walked toward the cook room.

Once inside, Jakob waited for Himli in the small room adjacent to the cook room. Inside, Jakob maintained the manor's accounts; Himli composed her few missives; and visitors were welcomed and given refreshments. Today, Himli and Jakob met to evaluate the year's harvest. As Himli entered the room, Jakob rose, holding his account parchment.

"We have just one more day of harvest, Mistress," Jakob confirmed. "The clouds threaten snow by mid-day. Mayhap, we will be lucky and not see it before dusk. But it's sure to come."

"Aye," Himiltrude agreed."Winter is almost upon us, Jakob." She poured him some herb tea, provided by herbalist Jaston and sat down for Jakob's report. He quickly summarized the manor's yield of barley, rye, and wheat.

"We have a wonderful harvest of beans, Mistress, and already dried bushels of apples and grapes—fifteen each at last count. The younger ones gathered chestnuts and walnuts already but have another day—possibly two—to finish under all the trees. There seem to be more than enough nuts for the next year." With a wide smile, he beamed in reporting each female animal produced an offspring.

"Our smallest ewe had twins, as you remember," he added, his eyes twinkling. "Getting two more of them in the spring was an inspired decision. And the ducks, chickens, guineas, geese—all successfully raised their clutches. During our last hunt, the day before Jaston came with the oil paste for our cracked hands, we killed four of last year's turkeys. Old Jackson smoked them, my Lady." Himiltrude nodded.

"Aye, we were very lucky with the fowl. It makes me think the foxes and weasels ate well in their hunts, too. They did not enter the barn a single time...so far," she noted.

"As for that," Jakob shook his head, "it's because of Pippin's dog, I do believe." Seeing Himli's startled look, Jakob explained. "That pup he claimed in the spring, the one with the black spot around his eye?" Jakob clarified the dog he meant.

"He doesn't sleep. Nay, he does not!" He re-iterated at Himli's laugh and amused smile. "I almost think he lies in wait at night for a marauder!" Jacob explained, knowing Himiltrude would question his certainty. "I hear him all hours, barking and growling. You would think he's a sentry in the barn."

"We are fortunate, then, are we not, to have such a protector, Jakob?" Himli questioned. "Pippin must be told. He'll be delighted to know we value his animal." She smiled to hear that Pippin's faith in his pet proved true, then turned her attention back to the news of the harvest and to her overseer.

"I salute you," Himli praised Jakob. "Thank you for the work, the manor supervision — all you did to guarantee us plenty for this year." Jakob grinned; he could not prevent it. He never heard a word of praise from the manor's former owner, just complaints if things were not as he wished. .

"Thank you, my Lady," he replied, letting his smile break through. "Thank you." He searched for something else to say. "We are having a bountiful harvest. It promises to ease the winter's harshness for all our manor people." Himli nodded, a smile forming around her eyes. She seemed to remember a thought and stood up.

"Jakob," she began, "please ask Jaston to bring us more of that oil paste of his. I would like for each woman at the manor to have a flagon of it."

"...a flagon, my lady?" Jakob asked. "I daresay a flagon is too little; it will not be enough for winter cooking. We store the lard in barrels which..." Himiltrude interrupted him.

"Nay, Jakob, this is not for cooking," she clarified. "Nay. Jaston suggested I rub the oil paste into my hands. They are so dry from water and cold." Himli's smile broadened. "You cannot believe how much it helps the skin! I would not have imagined it, if he didn't explain it to me." She held up her hands. "My hands are soft and smooth, Jakob; they no longer scratch Pippin as I rub his back. The oil paste is splendid! Everyone should use it on exposed skin." She looked solemnly at Jakob. "Mayhap, we should put it on our noses as well...since they are not as well-covered as our heads and ears." Seeing Jakob's surprise, Himli laughed aloud.

"Jakob, urge Jaston to produce more of this paste. Get him the lard ...or whatever...he needs. I want everyone to try it. I know the shepherds and the blacksmith in the village would benefit from using it. And," she added quickly, "I have yet another request of you." She tapped his parchment of harvest yield and continued.

"I wish you to prepare a Christmas bushel for every family," she announced. "We will share share our abundance with those who work so hard for us. Please tell me if the following items are appropriate. For every family, please set aside the following:

　　1 sizable ham
　　1 turkey (not any of this year's hatchlings;
　　　　find year-old birds.)
　　2 hens
　　1 bag of walnuts
　　2 bags of oats
　　1 square of dried apples

"My Lady," Jakob choked; he was almost speechless. "You are too generous, surely. Even half this amount would delight every hut in the manor holdings. Do retain the nuts and fruit for this manor, I beg you!"

"Nay, nay, Jakob." Himli laughed. "The nuts and dried apples are for the children—so their mothers will be able to make them tarts!" She shook her finger at him. "I mean every house will be so supplied. I will send Marsta and Gerta to help you pack the baskets. Pippin would love to help but, instead--if you don't object--I wwill ask that Pippin help you with your deliveries." Jakob nodded his head in assent. He tried to absorb everything she said.

"What say you as to the best time of delivery?" Himli asked him.

"Usually, I would suggest the night before the Christ Child's birth, my lady," Jakob replied. "But since you want sweets," here he looked at her in some amusement and smiled, "let us deliver the second day yet before Christ's Day...to give the women time to make them!" And he laughed aloud.

"So shall it be," Himli agreed. "What time would you like Pippin to be ready, after we break our mid-day fast?"

"Aye," Jakob agreed. "The families will have the day, the eve of Christmastide and Christmastide itself with no duties to the manor. Everyone should be home. Let's say two hours after our meal."

With Christmastide almost upon them, the manor residents settled in to make their gifts, to bake tarts, sweet dough, and all manner of pies. Sometimes, after a day of cooking, day workers spent the night in the manor, so harsh was the outside weather. They were all busy during this season, busy with the work of preparing for spring planting and of keeping people warm and fed. Himli used the time to learn all she could from Jakob about the manor's productivity. She also expanded her knowledge of record-keeping and evaluation of the yields of her fields.

The winter storms kept people indoors. Captain Mortier, Nordt, and Jasic helped the stable hands pull dead trees and heavy limbs home, to add to the wood for the fire-pits. Women, girls, and some of the men mended bridles, saddles, horse linens, foot coverings and clothing.. Cook's helpers mixed fresh mud, bound together with chaff from the wheat, to spread, poke, and smooth over the stable walls. It was left to harden, to keep out unwanted winter chill. The manor women worked long hours carding wool and, then, working on the looms. But there was little done outside, other than feeding the animals and bringing food from storage in the stable. The world was sleeping, surviving heavy ice storms and absorbing moisture from the deep snows.

Finally, the day to deliver the Christmas bushels arrived. Jakob was truly thankful. In the past two weeks, Pippin asked him twenty times a day if 'treat day', the day of delivery, had come. And for days, he told him 'nay.' Where did the boy get that name? Jakob wondered. "Treat day? Treat day?" He shook his head in amusement and exasperation. "It really is difficult to say 'nay' to him. There's been many a day I was ready to make my own 'treat' to give to each family, anything to fulfill the boy's wish!" Himli smiled and settled into the depths of the delivery cart. She was to accompany Jakob and Pippin in their deliveries. She was adamant in her wish to remain unseen.

"Nay, my Lady, this will not do!" Jakob objected vehemently. "You must not hide in the cart. You must be up front, up front where the families will see you and thank you. Please, come up front and sit."

But she refused. "The people may thank you and Pippin." She shrugged her shoulders. "I don't want to be thanked, Jakob. But I do want to see my son's joy. I want to see him with these people. Surely you can grant me one Christmas wish. Aye?" Jakob was outmaneuvered and knew it.

"Of course, my Lady," he answered. "Here, get in the cart; try to stay warm." He held up the cover as she slipped back down into the linens. He placed the cover over the bushels.

"P-i-p-p-i-n." Jakob called. "It's time, son. Let's go!" Pippin ran to the cart, stretching his arms to the Captain to help him up. Captain Mortimer handed Pippin to Jakob on the cart seat.

"'Tank you, Cap'tin," Pippin spoke solemnly. "Jaycub and me take food to fam'lies," the child explained. The boy wrapped his hand around the rope beside the seat, all the better to sit safely in the cart. "Back later," he said to Captain Mortimer. Earlier in the day, his mother promised a 'special trip' in Jakob's cart. So, he knew that 'treat day' was finally here. With the help of a tart and milk, Pippin slept before the midday meal. He ate little so great was his excitement. To the small boy, waiting for Jakob to finish his meal was a misery. Now, he was doubly anxious to be on his way.

"Have a great time, both of you," the captain called as Jakob clicked his mouth to the horse. Moving slowly, he circled behind the manor and turned toward the first hut. Hearing the cart crunch along the frozen ruts, several faces peered out of the hut's flap, ready to greet whoever visited. Seeing Jakob atop the cart, the family startled and hung back, waiting for him to climb down. By pre-arrangement, Jakob told Pippin that he must offer the bushel basket.

"Just say you're Father Christmas!" he suggested to the delighted boy. Pippin's eyes danced with anticipation, so happy was he to be 'helping' Jakob. As Jakob stopped the cart, Pippin stood.

"Hello frum Fath'r Crist-mas!" Pippin shouted. He waved to the families as faces peeked out of the door of their hut. "Come! See!" He motioned the families forward. They inched out of their hut, pulling on woolen mantles and caps as they came. Seeing Pippin beckon to them, the older children moved slowly toward the cart to say 'hello.' The brave ones greeted him as their parents came up. The parents solemnly wished Pippin and Jakob a Happy Christ's Day. Pippin waved the children closer, encouraging them to stand beside Jakob. Jakob, hoping to reassure the children, told them he had a surprise for each of them.

"Wait here until I find your surprise," he said to them as he flipped the cover linen back from the baskets. There, atop the first basket, Jakob spied a round mass, bundled in red cloth. He remembered that Frau Woodslie told him she slipped something into a bushel basket. But he thought she meant only one of them. She bustled out of the cooking room so fast he didn't asky her to whom her item should go. Now, he realized she put a red-cloth bundle in each basket. Jakob saw a stick figure drawn on the red cloth. The figures are small, he noted. He immediately knew they were for the children of the families. At this first house, he picked up a red bundle and handed it to the oldest child.

"This is especially for the young ones," he said, nodding to the group of children waiting. There were five of them. The oldest boy carefully unknotted the top of the red cloth. Jakob heard the intake of the youngster's breath. Turning from the cart, Jakob looked over at the boy.

"Let everyone see," Jakob suggested.

The boy nodded and slowly stooped over, putting his hat on

the snow-covered ground. He laid the red bundle atop his hat and pulled back the edges. The children gasped and laughed in surprise. Pippin craned his neck to see. The oldest boy stepped to the cart, offering his arms to Pippin. Pippin looked into his face and held out his own arms, snuggling immediately against the boy's shoulder. Then, they both looked down at the red bundle.

There, speckled with bits of dried purple grape skin; pieces of dark, red plums; and chunks of nuts lay small, star-shaped tarts. There were even tarts in the shape of crescent moons! The children's mouths were wide open, as they nudged one another and called to their parents to look. Pippin patted the head of the boy holding him.

"Ohhh…" he breathed, "pre-ti, pre-ti!"

Jacob, looking from one amazed child's face to another, felt his own eyes fill with tears. He spread his hands wide and said to them all. "Taste one, taste one. They're meant to be eaten, you know."

The eyes of the children widened in amazement. They had never seen such colorful food. The idea they should eat these bright, cheery tarts was beyond their comprehension. But Pippin was not so hesitant.

"Eat! Eat!" he urged them, as he bounced up and down in the boy's arms. "Tast' yummy!" He chortled, delighting in the children's surprise. The children's mother picked up the bundle, hat and all, and offered one to Pippin.

"Nay, 'tank you," Pippin answered. "You eat." Each member of the family enjoyed a tart. Then, the mother wrapped the bundle carefully, handing his hat back to her son. At that, Jakob left the horse and handed a basket to the father of the house. The father's eyes bulged, as he hefted the weight of the food inside. The father and, then, the mother turned to Pippin and, then, to Jakob.

"Many, many thanks, kind sir," the Father began. He could say no more. Soon, everyone surrounded Pippin. The girls kissed his cheeks; the boys clapped him on the shoulder. And everyone laughed! Only Jakob heard the rustle of the cover as Himli peeked out. Tears filled her eyes as she saw the delight in the family's faces — not to mention the joy and excitement in her dear Pippin's face. *How kind and loving he is*, she thought as she watched him with the family. *He would have been a much-loved king.* She pulled the cover back, obscuring herself and the other baskets.

Pippin talked of 'Christ's cart' for months. After their adventure together, he considered Jakob his dearest friend. They spent many an afternoon working side by side: storing baskets of pecans, walnuts, and hazelnuts and relocating containers of dried fruit in the barn, searching for the driest places. They counted the sides of salted pork in the curing room, checked the oats and barley for rodents, and plugged leaks in the stable roof. The coldest nights of the year came regularly now, almost denying their memories of the warm, sunny days of summer.

Chapter Four

Some fifteen days after the manor's celebration of the New Year, Jakob donned his warmest furs and went out on his horse, seeking downed trees to replenish their store of wood for burning. The substantial stack of wood from the autumn had become alarmingly small. On this clear day he decided to haul any limbs or logs lying along the edge of the forest back to the stable. Captain Mortimer and Nordt had agreed to chop the wood of a size to fit the fire-pits. Jakob's mount, a massive plow horse, was up to the task. They began by pulling the top quarter of a large beech tree toward home. As Jakob turned his horse, he heard the faint clop of another horse's hooves, doubly muffled by the fallen snow. The sound drew closer to him, coming from the southwest. It was then he spotted the rider.

Jakob watched the rider, hunched over his horse's neck, draw near. Although the tree top tethered to Jakob's mount was heavy and the deep snow made his progress slow, he walked his horse steadily toward the approaching horse. Just as Jakob opened his mouth to hail the rider, the other man reined in his horse and waited. As Jakob came to within three feet, the rider held out his empty hands to show non-threatening intent and walked his horse slowly toward Jakob.

"Good morrow to you, Sir," he greeted Jakob. "Your job, there, is slow going. Does winter always bless you with so much snow?" And he chuckled.

"Aye," Jakob nodded. "It's been just this way, every since I can remember. But not many are moving about in it. Have you been riding a long time, Sir? Your horse seems weary, nor to mention yourself. Have you need of directions? Mayhap, you are lost... wandered off the trail in this fog?" The rider shook his fur, sending clumps of snow toward the ground. He nodded to Jakob.

"Not lost, exactly," he responded, "though I do admit I don't know these parts. My traveling party is a small one. They are about three miles back. We journey toward Lombardy. But our master, the Prince of Lombardy, has fallen ill. I seek help for him. Please, Sir, do you know a healer or anyone knowledgeable in healing? ...someone who is close?"

Jakob's forehead wrinkled. *A healer...?* He asked himself.

"Nay," he responded, "not around here. We have no healer as such," he said. "Our herbalist is making a trip south but he'll be gone for another two moon turns. No healer close by...at least, not one you can get to through this snow. Down south, there was a healer last spring. But the village had a bad outbreak of lung fullness. It spread quickly. I advise you to avoid that place." He saw the rider shake his head in weariness.

"What kind of sickness did you say your prince has?" Jakob asked, thinking of Himli's healing skills. He said nothing more; he did not want to put her or others in the manor at risk. I wonder who this fellow is, he thought to himself. *...the Prince of Lombardy? Isn't that the man who was hurt, back last winter before Christmastide?* As if reading his thoughts, the rider unfurled a standard which was bundled behind him.

"As you can see," the man said, "I have the Prince's banner here. How I would love to see him carry this himself." He shook his head. "He is the only one sick, Sir. None of us has any idea of the illness—he's very hot to the touch and doesn't seem to know any of us…or where we are."

Sure enough, that's Lombardy's banner, Jakob told himself. "Tell you what," Jakob said, thinking rapidly. "Will your horse seat another rider, other than you, I mean?"

"Aye," the man replied. "He's a good horse, pretty gentle to everyone."

"Let me ride him," Jakob suggested. "I'll bring a woman from home; she knows a lot about healing." He saw the man frown in surprise. A man would not lightly give his mount to another, not one he's meeting for the first time, Jacob thought. "I need to ride quickly," Jacob explained. "My horse is shackled with this wood. You ride my horse to your camp. I'll get my mistress and follow the tree's print in the snow." Jacob saw the man hesitate. "If time be important for your prince, this is the best way."

"Here, take Jetty," the rider said, dismounting and handing the reins to Jakob. "He's tuckered out; but he'll move toward a warm fire at a good clip."

Jacob dismounted, took Jetty's reins and mounted the man's horse. The man mounted Jacob's horse and turned back the way he came. Jacob watched as the rider turned his horse and headed south, the trail of the tree top engraved in the snow. Then, Jakob turned Jetty toward Himiltrude's manor. *He won't get far with my horse in this snow,* Jakob reassured himself, *and he won't be back with his friends long enough to plan any surprises.* Jakob walked the horse quickly and carefully, knowing cantering would only exhaust them both over the snow-covered track.

In another few minutes, Jacob could see the manor house, directly in front of him. Just as he was sighing in relief, the door opened and out raced Pippin, followed closely by his mother. She waved the boy's cloak, begging him to put it around his shoulders. Pippin's smile warmed Jakob's heart as he called.

"Where you been? We's worried!" He trudged through the snow to pat the horse's nose. "Who's this?" he asked, as he examined Jakob's mount.

"A friend," Jakob replied. "I've found someone lost in the snow, Pippin, someone who's hurt. We need your mother to come...with her medicines. Can you fine her herb bag for her?" Pippin's eyes tightened, his forehead wrinkled; his hand stopped midway in rubbing the horses' ears.

"Hurt?" he asked.

"Aye," Jakob confirmed, "...someone who needs your mother's medicine." With that, Pippin turned back to the manor, calling to his mother.

"Someone hurt, Moma, hurry!" The lad struggled through the snow, pulling Himli's hand as he led her toward Jakob. Jakob told Himli all he knew, it being very little, and admitted he offered her help.

"Do you know this Prince, Mistress? Adelchis, that's the name his man called." Himiltrude startled and looked into Jakob's face.

"Aye." She replied. "I saw him ill once before. Let's see if we can help him again, then, Jakob." She said immediately. "Why don't you get another horse from the stable, tell the Captain what we're doing, and come back here? I need warmer clothing myself and should get some blankets, some broth or porridge, to take. Oh, here's Pippin with the herb bag. Please put it across your saddle. I'll be back directly." With that, she turned to re-enter the manor. Jakob went to the stable for a different horse, saddling him. Just as he mounted, Captain Mortimer came in from the woodpile.

"Not going out in this cold again, Jakob, are you?" the Captain asked. "There's a bad-looking storm cloud over in the northeast; we'll have snow before sunset."

"Seems the Prince of Lombardy is ill along the road, Captain. Our Lady is going to see if she can help. We don't even know what made him ill but it sounds serious. We should be back well before dusk, even with the bad state of the road." Jakob nodded his head at some blankets nearby which the Captain passed to him.

"I best come with you," Captain Mortimer decided. "If our Mistress is out in this, I must see to her safety." He began saddling his own mount. "The Prince of Lombardy, did you say?" The Captain frowned. "He does seem to get hurt a lot." He laughed, seeing Jakob's puzzled face. "The Mistress treated him once before, just before we came to your manor. But, no matter, I'll accompany you."

"I'd be relieved, Captain," Jakob admitted. "It's hard for me to trust men's explanations, life being so uncertain these days."

"Right you are, Jakob," the Captain nodded. "Come; let's see if our mistress is ready." Himli waited for them at the front of the manor, wrapped in long blankets, wool linens tucked under her arm. She nodded and smiled when she saw the Captain.

"I knew he wouldn't stay behind, Jakob," she acknowledged as she thanked the Captain for his help in mounting. Her horse raised its head, looked forward, and began walking. The three rescuers bent their heads to the wind which steadily rose, whipping snow all around them. Himli knew Jakob must lead so she concentrated on breathing down the front of her tunic. Her warmed breath would keep her torso from getting chilled. Captain Mortimer rode on her left side, doing his best to shield her body from the gusts of wind which raced across the fields. Back nearer the house, the thick woods diminished the wind's speed; but, here in the open, it was harsh. They did not ride before Jakob turned to take Himli's reins in his hands.

"Don't want to lose you in this stuff!" he shouted. It was almost impossible for Himli to see him, though he rode just beside her. Captain Mortimer, still on her left side, reached out to hold to her horse's mane. The three rode side-by-side as Jakob searched the ground for tracks. He shook his head in dismay when he saw a figure run from a small clump of trees. Jakob knew there was a cave inside the nearby rocks. *With this storm, it's no surprise someone shelters there.* .

At least they knew to take shelter, he thought as he raised his hand to the man. The man struggled to Jakob's horse, clutched the bridle and led the little group into the trees. He walked them right to the cave entrance and helped each dismount.

"We're inside here," he volunteered, his mouth muffled by his blanket. "Go inside; you'll see the fire's light. I'll unsaddle the horses and bring them. There's plenty room for them near the back." Himli, Jakob, and Captain Mortimer clung to each other for support until they passed into the cave, away from the clawing wind. Each shook snow off cloaks and headgear.

"Not a bad ride," Himli laughed, "the kind I like in this weather—short." She laughed with her two companions, then turned to follow the flickering light inside the cave. Jakob and Captain Mortimer continued to guard each side of her, pacing their steps to hers. All three rounded a corner and stopped. There in a large recess was another man, adding wood to a fire in the ground. He turned as they came up.

"Thank the Christ someone has come!" he exclaimed. "I fear my Prince is dying! He stopped speaking two days ago and refuses even to drink now." He put the last limb on the fire and walked to a prone body, one covered with blankets, lying not on the cold floor of the cave but on the men's saddles which had been softened with dead leaves and grasses. Himli knelt next to the sleeping form and placed her hand on his forehead.

"Aye, he burns with fever," she acknowledged. "I do always see this Prince on his back. He is very prone to fever, is he not?" She looked up at the soldier. He shrugged.

"I do not know, my lady. This is my first journey with the Prince. After the king's hunt, Charlemagne's I mean, he returned home. But, in less than a moon's turn, he journeyed again to the Frankish court. I was in his escort. When we arrived at the Frankish court, the workers gossiped that the King's marriage failed. And it's a fact: our escort was to take Achelis and his sister to Lombardy." The soldier explained. "But she, Queen Desiderata, I mean, she wished a rapid return home. Prince Adelchis bade her go on, ahead of him." He shook his head. "And here we still are."

"Captain Mortimer," Himli called. "You're needed once again. Please help me undress the Prince. We need to get his fever down, just as we did before." She beckoned to Jakob. "Get some snow for me," she said. "I want it to melt but I do not want the water hot. We will wipe his body, try to decrease the fever's heat." Captain Mortimer was already removing the heavy blankets from the sleeping man.

"My Lady," he cried, "the blankets are soaking wet! Will taking them off so quickly chill him even more?" Himli stared at the Captain. Oh, she thought. *The Captain has a gift for healing, if he even thinks to ask that question.*

"Yes, Captain, you are right," she affirmed. "His body is hot to the touch, his blankets are absorbing his sweat. But the wetness on his body will harm him, especially if there is closeness in the lungs." The soldier who had been tending the fire came to Himli.

"Forgive us, Lady," he begged. "We did all we knew to do. Is there anything I can do to help you? Don't say we have harmed the Prince. That cannot be the truth of it."

"You did the best you could, soldier," Himli replied. "Now, don't dawdle. Build that fire up, please." She softened her voice, seeing the look of regret in the soldier's face. Looking around for firewood, she asked: "Have you more wood? Can you get the fire roaring…and keep it that way?"

At her question, he smiled. "'A course I can, Lady--been cutting firewood, dragging limbs and such for days. I know the weather, you see. I knew this storm was a-coming three days ago. I told them all when Prince Adelchis became ill. But, not 'til later did they stop." He shook his head, as if to control his mouth. "We do have wood, my Lady, and good food as well." He hurried to the back of the cave, pulling dry limbs and stumps to the edge of the blaze. Soon, everyone in the traveling party removed layers of clothing, so warm was the cave.

As soon as they removed the Prince's over-tunic, Himli began wiping his chest with the snow-water Jakob brought her. The patient flinched at the cold water but did not waken. Then, she saw the scar along his left hip. She consciously kept her eyes on the man's upper body. She remembered its beauty from the last time. *Oh, but he is well put together*, Himli thought, admiring the smooth stretch of his skin over hard muscle. *His shoulders don't bulge like Charlemagne's did and his chest is not so prominent. Still, I find him very pleasing.* Himli turned her face away, looking for the Captain. *He mustn't think I am lusting after this stranger.*

"What is this scar?" Himli asked aloud. "When was the Prince wounded?"

She need not have concerned herself about the Captain. He was industriously removing the Prince's boots. His attention was focused there. What excellent tanning... and look at that scrollwork on the side, Captain Mortimer thought, examining Prince Adelchis' boots. Then, he laughed silently to himself. This is a prince, after all, he thought, the prince of Lombardy. *I suspect he can get any boot or scrollwork he imagines.* Hearing Himli's question, he moved to the Prince's side. The scar was just above the hip bone, angry and red.

"It does puff up mightily, my Lady," the Captain observed. "...a strange place to be struck. He felt around the wound and down the prince's legs. "The wound is very hot while his legs are cold." He pulled extra linens around the man's legs. "The skin around his wound is very tight; what can that mean?"

"The skin stretches...to accommodate hurt flesh, I guess." Himli replied. "We must keep his body warm, Captain. I'm going to dry his hair and wind this linen around his head. That will warm his skull, though we must continue to bathe his face." She looked into the pale, weary face. The man's skin was ashen, his fair hair wet and limp. His eyes moved rapidly under the lids, though he gave no sign of consciousness.

"We need dry clothes for this man," she announced to the cave. Immediately, the man who brought them to the cave disappeared in the back and returned with an armful of clothes.

"My Lady, what would you want first?" he asked, clearly worried about the sick man. He has two clean under-tunics left. ...and this overtunic is fresh. I washed it myself yesterday night." He offered them to Himli. "As for the wound, he fell when his horse reared. He hit the sharp edge of a boulder. The wound's covered itself up; but it seems full somehow. I can't explain it. Prince Adelchis did tell me it felt sore there and was hot to the touch. That was three days ago."

"Put all the clothes on him," Himli decided, "the two under-tunics and, then, that over-tunic. That should make him warm but not enough to sweat them through. We must keep his body dry, as much as possible.." She declared. "Remove his breeches, though. I have to drain this wound." The soldier, Franco by name, stepped back, immediately wary. "It must be done," Himli added, seeing the soldier's hesitancy. "The taut skin suggests the wound is not draining."

The soldier held the Prince's back from the linens as Himli removed the sweat-dampened tunic and pulled the fresh ones over his head. Then, she motioned for the soldier to lay the Prince down gently.

"Mayhap we should change his sleeping place," the soldier suggested. "Would closer to the fire be good?" He looked at Himli as if she were a priest, waiting on her every word.

"Yes," she smiled at him. "That would be a good idea. Smooth away as many stones as you can and, if there are any dry leaves to cushion his body, place them under a blanket. We'll put double blankets over him him and lay him there, near the top of the firepit." When the soldier completed the bed, he and his companion lifted the prince to the new position. Jakob brought Himli the herbal bag which she promptly emptied in the firelight.

"Hot water to seep this packet, Jakob," she explained. Captain Mortimer came over to smell the herb and guess the packet's contents. Much to his delight, he was able to name all the herbs but one. Himli was impressed and told the captain so. "Very good, Captain," she praised him. "Don't fret that you didn't name the chamomile. It's to relax the patient. I don't know that it has any qualities that would ease his breathing. His body will just relax a bit...if we can get some into him."

The Captain raised the Prince's head as Himli put a cup to his lips. Adelchis swallowed quickly but little of the liquid went into his mouth. Himli motioned for the Captain to hold the Prince's head as she spooned the liquid into his mouth. She moved slowly, each time waiting for him to swallow. Either the spicy taste of the concoction or the warmth of the liquid pleased the prince because after each swallow, he re-open his mouth.

"That's fine," Himli praised all their efforts. "That should dull some of the pain." She looked into Captain Mortimer's eyes. "Your knife, Captain," she said, "it *is* sharp, is it not?"

"Very, Mistress," the Captain answered, handing his boot knife to Himli. It was a small knife which, regardless, looked very dangerous. Himli eyed it with distaste.

"I wonder you do not cut your own leg, Captain," she commented. But she held the knife securely in her hand and pressed its tip into the edge of the Prince's wound. The skin seemed to rise around the tip and, then, burst open. White-yellow pus flowed from the wound, staining the linens under the Prince. Franco quickly placed dry leaves under the Prince's hip, using them to absorb the draining fluid. He shook his head. The smell was putrid. Captain Mortimer swallowed quickly, amazed at the amount of pus still leaking from the wound.

"My God, Mistress!" He exclaimed. "No wonder the man is sick. This is a serious wound." He gazed at the Prince's face which was sallow and still. "Can he survive this, do you think?" The Captain whispered.

Himli shook her head. She wiped the Prince's sweating face. As the liquid leaked out, he sighed deeply. Now, even his eyes stopped moving. She opened her herb bag and motioned to Franco. "Grind this up, please," she directed. "Then, bring it back to me. I will need warm water to mix it." Franco nodded silently, taking the leaves along with the mortar and pestle Himli handed him. He was back quickly, holding a flagon of water out to her. As Himli nodded, he stuck a heated sword into the flagon, warming the water for her. Himli stirred the mixture and then spread it over the puncture in the Prince's side.

"You may clothe him, Captain," she said. "And cover him warmly." The Prince's two soldiers came near to gauge his improvement. Seeing less puffiness around the wound, they thanked Himli for her efforts.

"We must wait," she responded. "Improvement will come slowly. We may have to drain the wound another time yet." The soldiers turned to thank Captain Mortimer as well.

"Not me!" the Captain exclaimed. "I am a soldier myself, just like you. The Lady is the one with herbal knowledge. Let us all hope for the Prince's rapid recovery." He hesitated. "But, none of us can be healthy without food. Shall we take a hunting party out?" He asked, knowing the ferocity of the still-howling winds.

"No need," the older soldier, Jarvis, responded. "We've been hunting for the past four days. We've plenty of meat. Let me prepare some for all of us." The two groups ate quickly, talked a bit around the firepit and retired to their blankets. All were exhausted, either by their worry or their travels. The Prince's companions felt more hopeful and said so to the Captain. But Himli frowned and shook her head, afraid to think her paltry effort could be successful. She spent a restless night, checking and rechecking on her patient.

Just after they awoke the next morning, Jakob realized the constant winds had died down. He left the fire and the cave to determine the difficulty of getting the Prince to the manor. It is cozy by the fire, he told himself. *We have plenty of supplies; but this is no place to get an ill man back on his feet. Best it is that we leave now ...while the winds are low.*

"We have to wait, Jakob," Himli replied to his suggestion. "The Prince cannot be moved now. Take the soldiers to the manor and bring back a cart. Mayhap, he can be moved tomorrow. Better to have the cart here, if that proves to be true." Jakob bustled about, bringing food and water close to Himli. "Captain Mortimer and the Prince's captain will remain here," Himli decided. "The rest of you need activity; be gone with you!"

The sun beamed brightly down on the little band as they emerged from the cave's warmth. Snow crystals glittered in the tree limbs; ice crunched underfoot.

"Let's be on our way," Jakob said to them. "We must turn around and come back, so time is an issue." He turned slowly. "...looks like no more snow for a while; but weather is changeable this time of year." The men mounted and turned in the direction the Captain indicated. They could see neither road nor path in any direction. It would take hours to get to Himli's manor. Snow was falling even more heavily than yesterday.

The day passed slowly for Himli and the two captains but they felt hopeful because the Prince appeared not to worsen. The next day passed as the one before, the Prince's face seemed a little less pale. He lay listless. Himiltrude spooned warm herbal water into his mouth and fed him potatoes beaten soft and flavored with bacon fat. As she rubbed his neck softly, he swallowed the food. Early the third day, the Prince's captain rushed back into the cave, happily announcing that the soldiers and Jakob were returning.

"Let's get the Prince on the cart," Captain Mortimer suggested as the men appeared at the cave's entrance. "We must move as quickly as possible toward the mistress' manor. The day is clear; pray that our journey will be quick." Himli judged the Prince could not be harmed any more by moving him.

"It won't be an easy journey," Himli warned them all. "We must not overtax his strength." She looked out onto the snow-covered terrain. "The snow drifts will slow us down, but that is all the better for Prince Adelchis. Thank God, he has no broken bones!" The Prince's soldiers carried him out of the cave and gingerly laid him in the deep straw of the cart. He moaned and frowned, but, otherwise, gave no sign of understanding.

Looking at the glistening ice frozen underfoot, Himli turned back to Captain Mortimer who was at the rear of the group.

"Captain," she called. "This ice looks treacherous. Should we all walk our horses, do you think? I wouldn't risk a single leg on this slick surface." The Captain looked up, gazed northward toward their destination, and replied.

"If we move along, my Lady," he said, "we will be better served by riding our mounts. It's going to be a lengthy journey because of our slow pace. Mayhap, if the weather warms, we will need to walk; melting snow will increase the hazard for the horses. But, just now, ride with a light heart." Himli nodded in acceptance and gently clicked her mouth; her horse responded, following the cart. The returning men entered the cave, first to break their fast and, then, to pack up their camp. They would follow the Prince and his escort shortly.

True words the Captain spoke, Himli thought. As the sun rose toward mid-day, she could not measure their progress at all. The snow-covered land blurred any distinctive landmarks. We seem to move through a white blanket, she noted as she turned in her saddle. Captain Mortimer, peering behind him, could read the frustration in Himli's movement. He smiled to himself.

"Don't worry, Mistress," he called back to her. "You sat hours by the Prince's sickbed, wiping his sweat away, keeping the blankets close, and, sometimes, fanning Adelchis' body. Take a deep breath. You must find patience. We ride slowly because we must. My Lady, we are making good progress," he reassured Himli and all the other ears listening. "See that great mound to your right?" Himiltrude nodded. "That's the hillock which the vines cover in the spring. You just aren't able to recognize the signs along the way!" Himli turned to her right and realized the mound looked about the same height, similar to the green-covered hill she remembered. She raised her arm in acknowledgement of the Captain's words and settled back into her saddle.

I can manage this, she told herself. *We can move no faster than is safe for the Prince, after all.* She relaxed into her saddle, finally giving way to her weariness. Himli woke from a fitful doze, feeling one of the Prince's soldiers ride up on her left.

"My Lady," he said, "the Captain has sent me with meat sticks for everyone. He says we should not stop for the mid-day meal. He's fearful the wind will rise again before we reach your manor. Do you have water?"

"Yes, Fritz, I do have water, thank you," Himli replied as she accepted three meat sticks from the soldier. She demurred when he offered her more. "This is enough." She bit off the tip of one of them. The group plodded through the snow. There was a faint depression where the trail had once led, a bare outline for them to follow through the white emptiness.

Captain Mortimer rode by every half- hour, checking on everyone's horse, making sure each rider was bundled up. He didn't want blankets or tunics carelessly open, allowing the tendrils of cold to sneak over the riders' bodies. The Captain and Jakob took turns relieving the soldiers leading the Prince's cart. Although the others fretted, the Captain judged their progress acceptable. Near mid-afternoon, he gave a shout to get their attention, pointing to their left, ahead of the band. Himli's intake of breath graduated to a wide smile. There was her manor, just a bit away, looking like a gift from God. She turned to look back at Captain Mortimer and raised her hand as the men broke into a cheer. In a little more than a quarter hour, stablehands from the manor ran to the group, taking reins from stiff hands and urging them all into the manor house. Two of them brought the Prince's cart close to the door and helped Jakob and the soldiers move Prince Adelchis inside.

"Put him on my sleeping bench," Himli directed. "He cannot be in the center hall. There's too much going and coming there for him to have adequate rest. I'll sleep alongside Pippin until the Prince recovers." At the mention of her son, Himli saw Pippin darting toward the front door of the manor. Keeping a lookout from the loft in the stable, the boy had straw sticking to his hair. Falling from his shoulders was the blanket he wrapped over his shoulders. He raced toward them. His hair was unbrushed, his face smudged with dirt. He looked wonderful to his mother.

"My dear, my dear," she covered his face with kisses. "Did take care of the manor while we were out? You are truly the 'man of the house.'"

"Aye, Moma," the boy answered with not a hint of a smile. "Is good…with me and everybody," he declared. "That man … he hurted?" The boy asked, his eyes widening as the Prince's blanket was lowered to the floor.

"Aye, my dear; he is very sick," Himli responded to Pippin's question. "We shall put him in our bed chamber. I can watch him there in the night. Go and tell Cook we all need food, something warm and hot—as quickly as he can make it ready." Pippin nodded, gave his mother a quick peck, and raced toward the cooking room. The Captain piled wood in the firepit as everyone came to stand in front of the fire. As their hands throbbed from the heat, Cook called for them to come and eat.

"Let's all eat lightly now," Himli suggested, "and, then, try to sleep. I'll tell Cook we'll want a large evening meal." She laughed. "But, right now, our bodies need rest more than food." She tried to reassure the Prince's men. "The Prince seems no worse for this day's exertion. We shall let him rest as we do. Then, if you will help me later, we will change his linen and get some hot broth into him." The men made quick work of the stew and bread. Then, they followed Captain Mortimer to the stable rooms. Jakob lingered to be certain Himli needed no help; then he, too, left to take his well-earned afternoon rest.

Chapter Five

Himli 'rested' lying next to Pippin but she could not sleep. Her mind repeatedly searched her memory for an herb which eased labored breathing. She knew Prince Adelchis' major sickness was in his chest, not in the hip wound. It was healing well. Although she used most of the herbs in her bag and the color of his face was better, the deep rumbling of his cough worried her. I will send for Jaston on the morrow, she consoled herself. *Mayhap, he returned from the south earlier than expected. He has herbs which I do not know. One of them may ease the Prince's burdened breathing.* Himli pulled the thick trapestries over the bedchamber windows, piled more wood in the fire-pit, and wrapped another blanket around the prince.

As she lay down beside Pippin, Himli realized that she, herself, breathed much easier here than in the cave. *What has happened to me?* She felt the moisture in her nose and rose to blow it from her nostrils. Then she stopped short. Mayhap it's the heat, she thought. *Can it be the warmth of the chamber eases breathing?* She did not lose a minute. She took the top blanket from off the Prince's body. She folded it once and stood in front of the firepit, holding the blanket as close to the coals as she dared. Then, folding the warm inside, she held the blanket once more in front of the coals. After this second warming, she hurried to the prince, removed the covers from his chest and pressed the hot blanket against him.

He flinched at the heat. Himli watched him closely. She didn't expect an immediate change in the sound of his breathing; but she looked for any physical change in his body. She re-heated the blanket twice but saw no reaction from the Prince. All at once, his eyelids twitched. He looked directly into her eyes and smiled. His right hand trembled and, then, settled into its former position. Himli stood transfixed, staring into the Prince's face. His eyes had been so kind...even in his weakened state. As she turned to the fire pit, Himli heard a sigh.

She turned as the Prince's shoulders relax. He seemed to sink into the linens. The frown between his eyes faded. He sighed again. That sigh sounds like relief, Himli thought. *Mayhap he's no longer in pain. His body does seem less stiff, his limbs less rigid.* She turned to warm the blanket once again.

Within three days of Himli's hot blanket press, Prince Adelchis began to recover. On the fourth morning, he woke and asked for milk. At the mid-day meal, Himli had to discourage him from over-eating on bread and cheese. He slept most of the day. Himli saw the lines of tension around his eyes lessen and, then, disappear. His mouth rested easily - his lips no longer pressed together, no longer clenched in pain. After an evening meal of barley soup and bits of pork sausage, he slept once again. Finally, his body relaxed; he was truly resting now. The next morning, Adelchis asked to see his soldiers.

"Might I talk with Franco?" The Prince asked as Himli spooned porridge into his mouth to break his fast. She smiled at him and replied.

"You may... but just for a short while. You're weak and need much rest." He nodded, slid into his linens and slept. He awoke to eat but could not keep his head steady. That evening, Adelchis ate little but asked repeatedly for cool water. The following morning, he asked to speak to Franco again. Himli sent for the soldier, cautioning him of the prince's weak condition. She watched anxiously as the men talked; and, seeing Adelchis' hand tremble, she asked Franco to return the next day. Prince Adelchis smiled.

"You understand I am weary even before I do," he acknowledged as his eyes drooped. He ate three small meals and, again, asked for water throughout the day.

On the sixth morning, the Prince insisted he must stand up; and so he did, for all of two minutes. As Adelchis grappled for his linens, his face white from exertion, Pippin rushed into the bedchamber. He came from the stables, eager to report on the puppies there.

"Pups listen good," he told everyone. "Jakob claps 'n the pups run to him." Pippin's eyes rested on the Prince. "Are you sicker?" The lad asked, moving to Adelchis' side. "You look bad- d-! Here," he said as he selected a tart from the table. "Eat, be strong. Me need tarts, like you... 'coz learning pups is work." He helped himself to two more tarts and returned to lean against Adelchis' knee.

The lad held a tart up to the Prince's mouth, urging him to eat. He took a bite of his tart and, then, held the other one to the Prince's lips.

"Eat more," Pippin directed, "you feel better." Throughout the day, Pippin came in to examine the foods sent to tempt the

Prince. Pippin would choose certain tidbits and spoon them into Adelchis' mouth. In the afternoon, he climbed into the Prince's lap. But as he climbed down, Pippin saw Adelchis wince. Thereafter, he stood quietly beside the sleeping bench. Just before their evening meal, he came from the stable and presented Prince Adelchis with a frozen pine bough which had one broken cone hanging from the limb. Himli looked into her son's pleased face.

"Prince Adelchis likes the flowers you brought, Pippin," she praised him. "Mayhap you should tell him your favorite bloom." Pippin climbed from his mother's lap and stood beside the Prince's sleeping bench. He frowned, looked at his mother, seemed to think and, then, raised his arms and let them fall to his side. Himli did not understand the boy's reticence. Then, she realized he didn't know the names of flowers yet. So, she said to Adelchis.

"Pippin likes the smell of roses, don't you?" She turned to the boy. "He was always sniffing the red roses in the garden at Rouen." She took several dried, rose petals from her traveling cabinet and held them out to Pippin. He opened his hands, and stuck his nose into the petals. A huge smile spread across his face as he thrust the petals for Prince Adelchis to sniff.

"Ahhh," the Prince inhaled deeply. "What a magnificent rose!" He smiled as Pippin nodded.

"Ro, ro...zzzz," the boy repeated.

"That's right, Pippin," Adelchis answered. "Rose. This red rose smells very sweet." And he sniffed the petals in Pippin's hands again.

"...sweet 'n good!" Pippin declared, his eyes crinkling, shining at both Adelchis and Himli. Pippin laughed, closed his fist and raced from the room. "Want Cook and Fra Wudsly to smell the ro-zzes," he called to them, running to the cooking room.

"He's a dear child, Himli," Prince Adelchis commented, "such a happy personality. I commend you with all my heart. You have created a wonderful home for him—safe, active, and full of love."

"He is a special boy, Prince Adelchis," Himli answered. "How could one not be hopeful and grateful around him?" She closed the small drawer in her traveling cabinet and glanced at the Prince.

"Your soldiers would like to speak with you," she said. "They are delighted you are recovering so well…after these worrisome days."

"Aye," Adelchis answered, "I should like to see them. They have been faithful in their concern for me. They are a new escort. I was so long at court my usual guards returned to Lombardy long before I. Please send them in." He settled back on his sleeping bench.

"Oh, before you fetch them, I would ask you a boon. What is the most direct route to my father's court? I propose to send a soldier to my father, to tell the Lombard Court I am recovering. May I prevail upon your hospitality yet a little while longer? I fear I am yet too weak to ride but I must speed my recovery. My mother and sister will have need of me."

"Of a certainty." Himli agreed. "Had a soldier been able to cross the mountain, we would have sent word earlier. The snow makes the mountain paths treacherous. You are welcome here, Prince Adelchis, for as long as your recovery requires. You are our guest."

"I understand my debt to you, my Lady," the Prince replied. "And I thank you." His eyes went to the firepit and returned to hers. "I shall repay you; I promise." Himli nodded but demurred.

"There is no debt, Sir," she replied. "And I do apologize for my son's easy familiarity. He considers you one of the family, as you surely see. We have few visitors here, so he has no understanding of strangers." She quietly left the chamber to summon the Prince's soldiers.

"What coin shall I use to repay her?" The Prince muttered to himself. "How does one pay for his life? I was all but lost in the cave. My soldiers did all they knew, but my life faded fast. Even in my delirious state, I could feel it seeping away." The Prince looked around the bedchamber, suddenly distressed.

"Damn," he muttered under his breath, not for the first time. "I am still in Himiltrude's bedchamber! She has not had a decent night's rest since I came here. How can I repay such a large debt?" As he repeated that question to himself, the Prince looked up, hearing a small scuffle in the corridor.

"Who's there?" he called. "Whoever it is, come in here and tell me how cold it is outside. I feel like going for a walk." Adelchis surprised even himself with this statement. Realizing that even a short walk would tax his strength, he, then, made himself content on his bench. As he sat, a head peeped around the door into the room.

"Gud morrow!" Pippin shouted to the Prince. The little boy scuttled over to the bench, reached up and hugged the Prince's neck.

"Good Morrow to you, Pippin," Adelchis responded, his eyes misting a little as the little arms squeezed his neck. "What a wonderful greeting, just the thing to get me up this morning." He hugged the boy back, being careful not to upset his balance. "Have you broken your fast?" Adelchis asked.

"Aye," Pippin replied. "Ate eggs and fuit," he added, patting his stomach and smiling at the prince.

"F-uit?" Adelchis asked to confirm that he had heard rightly. "Really? What kind of fruit was that? The winter snow has covered most of the trees and bushes, my good man," he answered. Pippin laughed aloud and scampered onto Adelchis' sleeping bench, falling back into the linens.

"Sweet, sticky f-uit!" he exclaimed. Then, seeing Adelchis interest in the 'fuit' question, the little boy stopped squirming to think.

"Brown, soft, good f-uit!" he screeched, burrowing under the sleeping linens.

Adelchis had no idea which fruit Pippin described. Maybe he means figs, the Prince thought. Unsure, still, about the fruit, he stripped off his sleeping tunic, replacing it with a freshly-laundered one from the chest.

"How can this shirt smell of lavender," he asked Pippin. "It's the middle of the winter. The tunic must have dried hanging in the cooking room."

Pippin giggled as he tunneled out from the bed linens. He scampered to a cabinet under the window, pulled open a drawer and stuck his thumb and forefinger inside. Taking his two fingers out, firmly pressed together, he came directly to Adelchis.

"Open," he commanded, tapping the Prince's hand. Adelchis spread his hand as Pippin opened his little fist and dropped bits of broken leaves into it. "Lav-dah?" he asked, his face wide with a huge smile. Then, the child sniffed Adelchis hand, turning back to Adelchis' face. Adelchis brought the leaf pieces to his nose and inhaled. The perfume of basil tickled his nose. As he pressed the leaves before another sniff, the clean, pungent smell wafted through the air.

"No, Pippin, not lavender," he laughed, "but just as good — basil. These are basil leaves." Pippin sniffed his hand, then Adlechis' hand again.

"Basil," he repeated. "No lav-dah. Ba-sil." He wiped his hand on his butt, laughed at Adelchis, and ran from the room. The Prince, intrigued by the availability of the basil, went to the cabinet. Each drawer, as he opened it, revealed mounds of dried herbs. And, yes, he found lavender. Surrounding it were small drawers which contained other herbs: peppermint, rosemary and thyme. The spices blended together to diffuse a light play of smells in the corner of the chamber. At just that moment, Marsta knocked on the door and came into the room.

"You are awake, Sire?" she inquired. "Good. All wait for you in the cook room. I will bring your meal here, if that be your preference. Are you too weak for walking?" She hesitated, her face full of concern. "I have come to change the bed linens."

"Aye, I am eager to join everyone in the cook room," Adelchis confirmed. "Pippin was just here, introducing me to spices and I forgot the time." Adelchis turned back to the cabinet. "What is this cabinet for, Marsta; can you tell me?"

Marsta smiled. "'A course," she nodded. "This is one of the King's spice cabinets, Sir. King Charlemagne designed it himself, to transport spices when the mobile court travels. It is a cunning little thing, don't you think?" She asked. "My Lady brought two from the court. She put one in the cooking room for all of us. That way, we can store our special treasures." She ducked her head in embarrassment.

"I mean, you know Sir, little 'membrances' or tools: a pretty pebble, thimbles for those who got them, a set of needles, pieces of left-over yarn. Why, Frau Woodslie even has her hair comb in her drawer. It's beautiful. All of us mean to have one...someday, Sir," she added.

"I see," Prince Adelchis replied. "Thanks for the information. Aye...very interesting, indeed." He smiled at Marsta as she stripped his sleeping bench. He left the chamber, heading for the cook room.

The household gathered around the cook room table, each with a bowl and flagon. Last week Himli declared the open hall, where they usually took their meals, was too cold. The firepit could not warm it enough for the diners to be comfortable. So, everyone now ate in the cook room. It was warm from the heat of the cooking pit and ovens. Himli invited all to eat here: the Prince, his soldiers, Pippin, the guards and Captain Mortimer. The kitchen and house workers, along with any stablehands, would eat after them. As a result, the cook room often seemd ready to burst with people. Somehow, it contributed to the *esprit de corps* of Himli's manor and added to the general camaraderie of the entire group. Pippin bolted down warm, baked bread spread with butter as the Prince took his place at the table.

"Pippin," Himli placed her hand on her son's shoulder. "You're eating much too fast. Slow down. I despair that you will ever learn any manners." The boy, with no hint of remorse, turned an oily mouth to his mother, promptly kissing on her the cheek.

"Hungry!" He laughed but he began chewing more slowly, fingering the last piece of bread and butter in his bowl. "Tastes good." He pointed to the cook and smiled broadly.

"Aye, he knows who to thank! Wouldn't you say?" Captain Mortimer asked as Cook's face flushed with pleasure.

"Yes," Himli admitted. "I daresay appreciation will endear him to the cooks but, mayhap, not to the hostess, as he matures and spends time in other manors." She smiled at her son, nodding in praise for his thanks to the cook. Pippin was already looking away, though, turning his young appetite to the promise of the ribs being placed in his bowl. Everyone at the table could hear his "Yum, yum, yum" as he picked up a small, well-braised piece of meat and popped it into his mouth.

"We are all happy to see you at table, Prince Adelchis." Captain Mortimer said as their attention shifted from the little boy. "Are you up to walking?" Not waiting for a reply, the Captain continued. "I know you are eager to be out of your chamber, Sir, but be cautious. You lay abed for several days. It will take time but your strength will return. Just don't try to hasten it...unnecessarily."

Prince Adelchis flushed. He felt winded, just from his walk down the stairs, and knew his breathing was faster than normal. I would not have the Captain think I am a fool, Adelchis thought. *He has done much to keep me alive.*

"You're right, Captain," the Prince answered. "I am feeling, mayhap, more frisky than my body can deliver!" And he laughed. "But, neither may I stay abed, basking in all this attention, not another day." He tried to look determined but succeeded only in getting a laugh from those around the table.

"I must re-build my strength, sooner rather that later," the Prince sobered as he spoke. "I must leave for home, as soon as I am able. My father will be angry beyond measure...at my sister's return to Lombardy. His temper will flash 'til spring. Already, I fear I stay away from home too long." Adelchis saw Himli's flush of anger, her eyes hard and bright. "But," Adelchis held up his hand, "I cannot go until I am well-healed. I know that. It is difficult for others to understand sickness they cannot see. The cough and fullness in my chest--they do not show the true severity of my illness....not to those who will question me." Adelchis turned his attention to his meal, assured all understood he would be leaving them soon. Much to his heart's delight, he saw Himli's face absorb his news. Her eyes softened, her cheeks flushed, her right hand rose quickly to her throat.

Aye, the prince thought. *Mayhap, she will miss me._* He was surprised to note how much pleasure the thought gave him as he looked again at Himli. Her presence alone would heal any hurt, he thought as he accepted another piece of buttered bread. His hand stopped half-way to his mouth as he considered this thought. Then, blushing at his understanding, he took a long drink from his flagon.

Much to Adelchis' surprise, his strength seemed to quadruple every day. Now, knowing his return home was imminent, he thought more often about Himli and her gentle care of him. She was away from his chamber most of the day now, supervising the carding and grading of the wool, overseeing the tanning hides, making suggestions to those sewing and weaving tunics for the coming winter. Although she confided that her knowledge of manor activities was superficial, she impressed him with her fervor to learn. She would, she said, understand every job in her manor and the resources she must provide to her workers so that the manor could prosper. .

"How could King Charlemagne give up such a woman?" Adelchis constantly asked himself. "Pippin is a fine boy. Aye, he has a serious problem. But, as far as I can see, it does not prevent his growing, laughing, learning—all the things a so-called 'normal' child would do! What a waste! What a waste….to banish such a woman and this dear, energetic boy." Adelchis' admiration for Himli and his genuine fondness for Pippin grew as he thought of their past struggles. "I shall lessen the burdens of their futures," he vowed to himself. "As God is my witness, I will care for and protect them."

Adelchis, though correct in some of his judgment, did not know the true facts of Himli's banishment. He, like Himli and the Frankish court, assumed King Charlemagne himself decided to banish his wife and child. After all, who could banish a wife but her husband? But such was not the case. It was Charlemagne's mother, Queen Bertrada, who banished Himli and little Pippin. She, intent on Charlemagne's marrying Adelchis' sister, sent Himli away, removing her overnight from the court, denying her the most basic courtesies due a queen.

On his return from Septimania, King Charlemagne found his wife and son gone. While he battled outlaw bands, and dealt with rebels-- attempting to provide some measure of safety for his people-- his mother secretly deprived his wife and son of their court lives and their futures. By the time Charlemagne returned to the court, his first family had disappeared and his betrothal to Desiderata, the Lombard princess, was complete. He easily determined Himli did not undertake a visit to her family. But, otherwise, no one could tell him where she was. When the Abbot approached the King about Himiltrrude's problems with the manor, Charlemagne was embarrassed to admit that Queen Bertrada had so fooled him. And so, he did nothing. Many blamed the King for an overt act which he did not commit; but neither did he refute the act or rectify the pain.

Adelchis, more than most, thought about the fate of Himli and Pippin often. One day, he stopped in his tracks.

"How ironical," Adelchis muttered. "Charlemagne rid himself of this wife and child and, then, banished my sister for lack of a child." He shook his head, trying to understand the mind of a king. "Dear God, spare me that job. Although I am my father's only son, I do not wish to be king of Lombardy or of anything else. Allow me to live my life, away from the court and all its insanity." He knew such a wish was a dream. But he fervently prayed that, somehow, his desire might come true. Adelchis threw his mantle over his shoulders and left the manor, looking for Pippin. He turned toward the stables, knowing the boy was likely there, among the animals he so loved. Seeing Adelchis leave the manor, Frau Woodslie turned to Himli.

"Shall I prepare 'traveling food' for Prince Adelchis?" Frau Woodslie inquired as Himli entered the entrance hall from the cook room.

"Do what?" Himli asked, turning to look into Frau Woodslie's face.

"Make traveling meals for the Prince," the Frau replied. "It is surely time for him to return to Lombard. You must agree with that, my Lady."

"He is mending, for certain," Himli concurred. "The herbalist is coming tomorrow to look once more and listen to his breathing. We will know then if it is safe for him to travel."

He should be on his way," Frau Woodslie insisted. "It is not seemly. He has been here too long…if you want my opinion." She stood very straight, her hands ramrod by her side.

"Nay, I did not ask your opinion," Himli answered. "Neither do I seek it now." Her neck tightened with the effort to say no more.

"Then, it is my duty to tell you," Frau Woodslie continued. "He must leave here. He must leave now, even before the herbalist comes, if is possible."

"What is the matter with you, Frau Woodslie?" Himli asked. "You do overstep your place, to decide who will leave this manor and when they should do so. Do you tire of the effort required for Prince Adelchis' recovery or..." Himli paused, thinking, "do you resent the extra work? ...the usual duties I am unable to continue which you perform?" Himli's forehead wrinkled, her lips pressed together. "You assured me you wanted to continue to supervise the manor house. Have you now altered your opinion?" Himli questioned.

"My wishing the Prince to leave has nothing to do with my duties," Frau Woodslie answered quickly, her words slicing the air. "I wish him gone, gone ...for the disgrace he brings on this house!"

"Disgrace?" Himli asked. "...disgrace? What disgrace can the Prince possibly bring to any house? He is polite, quiet, amenable and pleasant. I do believe, Frau Woodslie, you are quite overworked."

"Not I," Frau Woodslie replied. "You do not see the favor in his eyes, when he looks at you. He goes beyond seemly behavior. A Prince may not consort with a married woman. He must not damage his chance of an appropriate marriage." Her words battered Himli in the face. "Interest in you will only harm his reputation. You have been banished and are ... should be ... beneath his interest." Frau Woodslie stopped her ranting, as she realized all she had said.

Himli froze in place, unable to breathe. *Why, she believes me unworthy of Prince Adelchis. He is too far above me, in his princely station.* Himli's shocked mind could not accept Woodslie's implications. *He is not interested in me,* Himli thought, *not in that way.*

"Frau Woodslie, your worries are groundless. The Prince has no interest in me," she responded. "Yes, we are friends. We spend much time together and I have nursed him for these few days." Her mind moved back to the woman's view of her. "There is nothing more. It is not your place to voice such thoughts. Of a certainty, you speak untruths." She considers me unworthy, she thought again.

Himli was completely still as the pain of the Frau Wood-slie's words flowed through her mind. *I, unworthy! I...who show her nothing but kindness, who take her advice--unsolicited as it is--in good spirit? I...who defer so often to her way of doings things? I ...who was the King's wife? How dare she speak so to me!* Frau Woodslie shook her head, denying Himli's words, and began walking away. Hilde's answer stopped her.

"You do forget, do you not? I was King Charlemagne's wife? How dare you speak of anyone being above me? You make a serious misjudgment!" Himli stared at the woman, holding her immobile with her anger. "How dare you!" Him-li's voice broke, then firmed. "Wait." She stood staring into Frau Woodslie's face. Himli's mind raced madly. *What do I do? I cannot be around someone who values me so little. But can I manage the manor without her?* In an instant, Himli decided.

"Pack your belongings. At the first thaw, you leave this manor. I no longer have need of your services." Himli paused, seeing a shudder pass through the woman's frame. "You shall be Cook's assistant...from this minute, until you depart. I will be in charge of my own manor." She turned her back. "You are no longer needed here."

"But, but..." Frau Woodslie began to protest. Seeing Him-li's pale, closed face, she faltered. Nodding once, she opened the door into the corridor and left Himli alone.

"Dear God, help me," Himli prayed. "I'll get Pippin to bed and, then, think about what I've done." Himli found Pippin on his sleeping bench. Prince Adelchis recounted a story about a bear and a turtle. Pippin's sleepy eyes turned as his mother came into the room.

"Moma." He reached for her. "Hear story wid me?" His dear, loving face beamed at his mother and, then, turned to the Prince. "Moma wants hear," he said firmly. Himli sat beside him and smiled at the Prince.

"Please continue, tale-teller," she said. The Prince, spoke more and more slowly, as he saw Pippin's eyes droop and, finally, close. Himli moved Pippin from her lap to his bed and whispered a 'thank you' to the Prince. She covered her sleeping son and left the chamber. As she walked out, the Prince softly called her name. She ignored him, pretending she didn't hear.

She sat in the entrance room, developing a plan for supervising the manor house alone. Within two hours, she realized she would need more help. *I cannot possibly do all this.* Himli told herself. *I cannot see to the manor: to the cleaning; to the cooking; to planting the vegetable garden, not to mention the herb garden. Then, there are the stables, the farmers, the plans for spring planting, the new dove-cote to construct... How will I ever get it all done?* After a while the enormity of it overwhelmed her. She drifted off into a troubled sleep. Prince Adelchis, getting up for a drink of water, found her asleep on a manor bench.

"Himli, for heaven sakes," he breathed. "What are you doing out here? I thought you were in bed hours ago. Come, you exhaust yourself." He led her to her sleeping bench and covered her with linens. "Sleep as long as you can." He gently squeezed her shoulders. The next morning, Adelchis got up with Pippin, helped the boy dress, and accompanied him to the cook room.

"Himli slept very late yesterday night," he told the household. "She must be exhausted. Let's not disturb her; let her wake after she gets enough sleep." He noticed Frau Woodslie look at him strangely and mutter to herself. But he forgot her strained face as he and Pippin went to the stables to curry the horses, their morning ritual. Just before the mid-day meal, the herbalist came down from his hut on a near-by hill to examine the Prince. He found him almost recovered but warned him not to strain his breathing and not to get chilled.

"May I travel any time, then?" Prince Adelchis asked.

"Aye, but you must ride slowly at first: no longer than the time between breaking your fast and mid-day," Jaston answered. "And you must dress warmly—cloth wound around your neck, a wool hat atop your head." He smiled at the Prince. "Walking about the manor and currying the horses helped you regain your strength ... and the good care of this young man." Jaston added as Pippin came to give him a hug. Pippin's eyes lit up at the herbalist's words. He took Adelchis' hand as they all left the stables to take the good news to Himli and to have their mid-day meal. After eating, Pippin lay down for a nap as Himli and the Prince returned to the stable rooms. A cobbler was making new boots for Prince Adelchis and needed to mold the leather around his feet.

"These are the most handsome boots I've ever had," Adelchis thanked the cobbler. "You are a master with leather, Sir."

"I thank thee," the cobbler replied, "but it is not my skill, Sire; it is the Lady's leather. The quality of it makes my job easy. It is soft and easily fitted. See? It makes a glove around your foot." And he laughed as he turned back to his work. Adelchis acknowledged the cobbler's truth and tipped his head to Himli who was asking the cobbler about shoes for Pippin. She smiled at him over the cobbler's head, bent to answer a question, and turned back to the Prince.

"You are feeling much better. It is true, is it not, your highness?" she asked gaily. I feel the returning health flowing from him, Himli thought as she noticed the Prince's bright, alert eyes; the easy manner of his gait; and his regular breathing. "You are almost well, Sire, no matter what the herbalist says."

"I am recovered, Himli," Prince Adelchis replied, "thanks to you. Without your care, I would have joined the spirit world. What an angel you are." Himli put her hand to her lips, shushing his words. She preceded him out of the stables, going toward her mounting stump.

"Please, Aldelchis, no such talk. You will cause speculation all around the valley." She frowned at him. Then, accepting his hand, she mounted her horse.

Adelchis looked into her eyes, searching for disapproval but found none. Her eyes do belie her words, he thought as he swung onto his own mount. As soon as he sat, Himli raced away, toward the east. Adelchis clicked his mouth to encourage his horse, following her path. But he did not try to overtake her. I know she likes riding alone. I'll give her some space between us, just now. He thought back to the early morning cook room. Tension had been rife in every worker, though he could not discern the reason. Cook stirred the oatmeal until I wondered if the pot's contents were only water. The house girls, contrary to previous mornings, spoke not a single word, not to each other nor to Pippin as he smeared large amounts of blackberry sweet on his bread. Himli ate only a mouthful of bread and cheese and turned from the table. And Frau Woodslie was all over the kitchen: tending to bread for the mid-day meal, blowing on coals for roasting the haunch of meat, straining milk as it came in from the stable. No one had seemed able to look another in the face.

Finally, Adelchis saw Himli tire of her frantic ride, turn her horse and ride back toward him. The cool, morning air and her horse's energy served to lighten her mind. She knew lashing out at Adelchis was not the way to deal with Frau Woodslie's accusations. Himli, lost in her worries, did not imagine the picture she presented to Adelchis as she rode.

Her cherry-red cheeks were bright from the cold, her hair blew out from under her headdress. She looked full of life. But to Adelchis, she rode stiffly, erect--without the easy assurance she usually displayed. He dismounted as she rode up beside him.

"Just look at the pond, Himli!" he exclaimed. "It appears to be ice from one side to the other." Seeing three ducks try to drink at the edge of the pool, Adelchis hurried forward, picking up a broken tree limb. "I'm going to make a hole, here on this edge, for the animals to drink."

"Thank you, Adelchis," Himli answered, swallowing some of her frustration from his previous words. "The animals thank you as well."

"No need," he smiled. "Their thirsty gulps are thanks enough for me." He turned to face her.

"What is it?" he asked, his forehead wrinkled, his eyes staring intently at her. "Have I offended you?" He did not wait for a reply. "If so, I beg your pardon...though I cannot imagine what I have done, to irritate you so much." He spread both his hands, palms up, and stood waiting. Himli's stomach lurched. The apology, so unexpected and sincere, turned all her worry away. She gave no response.

"Please, Himli," Adelchis begged, "you must tell me what wrong I committed, so I do not repeat it." Here, he paused to smile. "I would bring no cloud to your face, ever. I would do nothing to cause you pain!" Himli answered not a word, just stood looking at him. The Prince walked toward her, looking around to verify no one else was about.

"My dear," he said as he caught Himli's hands, "please do not be angry with me. My heart cannot bear it." He held her hands tightly, caressing her wrist with his thumb. Himli jerked her hands out of his and dismounted.

"What *are* you talking about?" her voice demanded. "I have no reason to be angry at you. You are imagining things, stirring up trouble to make me uncomfortable, I daresay." She walked to her horse, got out an apple and fed it to him. Adelchis' horse ambled over to the two, nuzzling her hand for an apple of his own. Himli laughed at the horse and looked over at the Prince. He stood with his hands still outstretched, completely dumbfounded. His eyes dropped quickly to the ground as Himli turned, but not before she saw the hurt and pain caused by her outburst. She walked slowly over to him.

"Adelchis," she began, "please forgive me! I don't know what's wrong with me. I didn't mean to ... upset you." Warm tears dropped on his arm as he reached for her, pulling her to his chest. She sobbed quietly, murmuring words he could not understand.

"Himli, what's the matter?" Adelchis' voice trembled. "Do you wish to be rid of me? What did I do? I don't know your mind, can't fathom what is wrong," he finished softly, his hand following the spread of her hair over her shoulders. He felt her tremble and bent to kiss her cheek. Suddenly, her mouth was right beside his.

"Such a perfect, little mouth," he murmured as his lips met hers. And then, her arms stole around his neck. The day, the horses, the unhappiness were all forgotten. They spoke very little the rest of the afternoon. Their eyes drank in each other, their voices joined in little bursts of laughter, and their hearts flared in discovery and in disbelief. But the wonder of their feelings for each other grew and grew.

"Adelchis," Himli savored his name on her tongue. "Adelchis," she said again, as if the sound of his name were the most beautiful one in the world. "My darling, we must stop this. I cannot allow this to continue." And she pulled from his arms.

"What?" Adelchis had to force his mind back to reality. "What are you saying? You cannot continue...? Are you insane? You think you can control these feelings. Himli, wake up! We love each other! Is it not as clear to you as it is to me?" He pulled her again into the circle of his arms and nuzzled her neck.

"That's just it. I cannot love you." She felt Adelchis' body stiffen as he held her at arms' length. Himiltrude fought to be clear. "I mean ... I cannot let this go on." She shook her head and sat down on a near-by stump. "Adelchis," her voice begged, "please try to understand. We are caught in a quandary here. Give me a solution. Help me."

Adelchis stared at her. "What can be the quandary?" he asked. "I love you; you love me. That's a quandary?" He smiled. "The situation seems pretty clear to me."

"But, I am the King's wife," Himli stopped. "Well," she acknowledged, "I was the King's wife. And you were his brother-in-law during this last marriage. This is very awkward..." Her voice trailed off.

"Exactly," Adelchis laughed. "We have both, you and I,

been put away by the King. He regretted sending you away, at least so he said. He regretted sending me away, so he said. We are two banished souls...so what is our problem?" Adelchis laughed. "He no longer has use for us. Nothing could be clearer."

"Said in those words we seem two victims, don't we?" Himli smiled. "But, dear Adelchis, there are other realities beyond the one you describe. You are a Prince. One day, you may be Lombard's king. Who can say what Charlemagne may do next in the governing of your land? You must not love the wife the very same king rejected...or his concubine, as he probably now names me." She paused, thinking of the shame. "Nay, this will not do. No matter how Charlemagne feels about us, together or individually, we are still his subjects, bound by his law. He will never accept you and me together, Adelchis. He will never allow it. You know how he thinks!" She felt the tears course from her eyes, as she recognized the hopelessness of her tomorrows.

"In fact," she added, "he would never allow me another love at any time, not anyone. He would feel it detracted from his image, from his stature as King." She looked miserably into Adelchis' eyes.

"I cannot risk his taking Pippin, Adelchis. In a temper, he would take Pippin from me. A love affair, my love affair, would be a wonderful excuse to demand my son's return to court. The place would kill my son, Adelchis. Surely, you understand the problem." She walked back and forth between their two horses, her heart breaking. Adelchis walked over and took her into his arms. He said nothing, just kissed her head, smoothed her hair, and rocked her gently. Noticing the dying day for the first time, he raised her face.

"My dear, Himli, my dear; it's near to sundown; we must

go back…before we are caught in the dark. Here, here. Let's wash your face in the pond and think through a plan." At Himli's confused look, Adelchis continued. "We've been *'riding'* a long time, dear; we must have some explanation for our rather lengthy absence. What can we say?" Himli stared at him, hardly seeming to understand his concern. She gasped. The worry raced across her face.

"I've heard no rumors in your manor. We are good friends. But we must have some explanation for the time we have been away from the manor. Don't you understand, dear?" Adelchis asked again.

"Oh, Adelchis, I am so stupid! I opened us both to question. You felt the tension in the cook room?" At Adelchis' nod, Himli continued. "Last night Frau Woodslie was very unpleasant. She decided it is time for you to leave, to leave my manor. It is her opinion I am not good enough for you." Himli smiled. Having experienced Adelchis' kiss, she knew she was quite good for him, indeed. *But that was their secret — not anything the world could know.* "What are we going to do?" she asked, worriedly. "I dismissed her. I will not have someone so judgmental about reputations in my home." Adelchis nodded, surprised Frau Woodslie spoke so harshly to Himiltrude.

"Let's ride toward the manor," Adelchis suggested. "Tell me. Is there anything of importance around here? Any possible errand we might have undertaken for the better part of the day?" At Himli's negative nod, he re-emphasized their position. "Think, Himli, think! We must protect your reputation, at least! Mine, I fear, will not be harmed by a liaison with you. But it would not be wise for your sake, for the King's possible reaction." He helped Himli mount her horse, then mounted himself and rode beside her.

"Consider everything around here. Is there anything of interest, of importance, to anyone in your manor?" Himli pulled her horse to a stop and looked around, thinking of their location and casting a mental eye about. All of a sudden, she gave a squeal of delight.

"Aye, aye, I've thought of something! It might just cover us, Adelchis. Come with me. We must hurry through those trees." She reined her horse toward the huge forest on their right. Before Adelchis could ask, she rode quickly toward the tree line. In twenty minutes, Himli stopped at the edge of the forest, dismounted, and began walking north along the forest edge. Adelchis dismounted.

"What are you doing?" he asked. "Of what good is the forest to us, Himli?"

"Late in the autumn," Himli began, "Drak and I, searching for a wee lamb, came upon a chestnut tree. Its limbs were covered with chestnuts, so many they almost seemed painted on the tree. We found many nuts on the ground, much bigger than those from the trees around the manor. He and I picked those nuts up and stored them near the base of the tree." Adelchis was confused.

"What good is that?" he asked. "The nuts will be ready to sprout or they have rotted by now." His eyes scanned the trees. "We need something which will give us a cover, dear."

"Oh, but Adelchis, this does. It does. We found a cache near that tree, one some previous rider made. Lined with small pebbles, it was quite a large cache. Mayhap, a soldier passed this spot on his way to and from battle and wanted to leave something. I don't know, but it was a perfect storage space. Drak said our own chestnuts produced few nuts this year. He thought this cache with our nuts inside would keep the manor supplied with chestnuts throughout the winter." Himli closed her eyes, her smile slowly fading.

"Then, you remember," she added softly. "Drak was gored by that bull, just as the harvest began. I told you about it; he suffered so much!" She ducked her head. Adelchis could feel the wetness of tears drop on his cloak.

"Alright," Adelchis responded. "That might do. It's a weak tale but better than none at all. Can you find the chestnut tree again, find it quickly, I mean?" Himli nodded, her eyes shining brightly.

"This is the one. It's right there," she said as she pointed to a huge, majestic tree just inside the edge of the forest. "The storage hole is on the other side." Himli called as she hurried to the tree. And sure enough, when they scraped the dirt away from the base of the tree, they scratched river rock which lay atop the chestnuts stored inside.

"There were more chestnuts than this," Himli noted as they filled their leather bags. "Someone else must have discovered the place." She looked around.

"Relax, dear," the Prince said. "No one is around now but us. I guess these are your and Drak's chestnuts." Just as he spoke, his hand hit a hard object under the nuts. "Did you hide anything else in here, Himli?" Adelchis began digging.

"Nay. Why?" Himli responded. Her mouth formed a big "O" as Adelchis brought out a small chest and placed in on the ground. "I've never seen this before," she said to him.

"Well, let's see what it is," Adelchis said. He brushed the loose dirt off the chest and prized up the top. Inside was a soft leather piece, wrapped tightly around some dried herbs. "This looks like some kind of herb," he said. "Do you recognize it, Himli?" He asked.

"It isn't an herb," she answered as she pinched a little between her thumb and forefinger, bringing the dried leaves to her nose. Memories washed over Himli as she breathed in the fragrant odor. "Aye, I know this plant. At court, one of the caliphs offered it to the King. It is an esteemed gift. Aye!....if I could only remember the name." Himli sat back on her feet, sniffing and sighing as she held the small pinch under her nose.

"Aye, Adelchis! I have it. Its name is *chai*. It makes a wonderful drink when you steep it in hot water! It is a treasure, a treasure!" Adelchis looked at her excited face. "The caliphs of the east gave it to Charlemagne. He absolutely loves the taste."

"I have heard of such a drink," he acknowledged, "though I have never tasted it. Good! Then, we have a true gift to take back to the manor." He was all seriousness again. "Himli, we will tell this story when we return. The only change is we searched all morning before we found 'your' tree. Agreed? That will explain the length of our absence. And, everyone must have a taste of this liquid. If it is as wonderful as you say, no one will think to question us." He sighed with relief, looking into Himli's delighted face.

"Aye, it is delicious!" Himli cried. "This will work, Adelchis. I am sure of it." She smiled happily at him, then her eyes dropped to the floor. "But, one other thing, love, we must be very careful and look sternly at each other." At Adelchis' surprised expression, Himli chortled. "We can't let anyone see how we feel about each other....right?" she asked.

"Aye," Adelchis agreed, "you are exactly right."

Adelchis and Himli made much of their chestnut tree cache, promising everyone a taste of the liquid to be made from the 'treasure' they discovered. The chai-tea was delightful, both in its aroma and its taste. If anyone doubted their tale, no one questioned them, nor, as far as Himli could hear, were there any speculations or rumors around their lengthy ride.

The next day, Adelchis, playing in the newly-turned soil of the garden with Pippin, told Himli he must leave for home. At her stricken look, he explained.

"I cannot postpone it any longer, my dear. Your workers are breaking the sod, readying it for planting. If crops can be put in, the roads are surely passable. I must go. But, I will return." Himli's head popped up from the hole she dug for planting onions. Her eyes filled with tears. She reached out to touch Adelchis' hand.

"I know you must go, Adelchis. But how can I bear it? I don't want a day without you, here close beside me. How wretched a day becomes, in only a moment!" Pippin, hearing the distress in his mother's voice, ran over to kiss her cheek.

"Moma? Are you sick?" He asked as he looked to Adelchis for an answer.

"Nay, your mother is fine, Pippin." Adelchis responded. "This spring day makes her happy, even if the wind hurts her eyes." Pippin nodded his head as he shielded Himli's eyes with his dirt-stained hands.

"I'm fine, my boy," Himli echoed Adelchis' words. "Thank you for the wind shield. That's fine for now," she assured the lad. Pippin turned away, going back to his little plot of soil. He wanted to plant carrots.

"If you're willing, Himli, to have a relationship with me, it will be marked by separation." Adelchis said. He spent yesterday night pondering their options. They were few. "At least, that will be true for a while. I must return to my father's court...and I will be caught there for some time. I know the court is chaotic. My father will still be livid over Desiderata's return from Charlemagne's court. Charlemagne rejected her; father is humiliated. He will see this rejection as her biggest personal failure and he will punish her." At Himli's frightened look, Adelchis spoke quickly.

"Nay, Nay. He will not beat her, but he will criticize and reprimand her whenever he chances to see her. Desiderata's coming home will produce additional reasons for my father to rebuke, judge, and be unpleasant. Everyone in the Lombard court will pay for my sister's failure. Father nurses his grudges. He will strike out, particularly at the innocent - even after all these days!" Himli nodded her head in understanding and shuddered.

"I must see to my mother." Adelchis continued. "She will be wracked with worry for me and with concern for my sister. Undoubtedly, Mother can still find Desiderata a husband, but she will share in the blame for the annulment of the marriage." Adelchis shrugged.

"I am not much surprised that King Charlemagne did not like Desiderata. After you, how could he?" Adelchis asked as he touched Himli's hand. "My sister is selfish and self-centered, I admit. She has been much sheltered, not asked to adapt or to change. I know such characteristics are not a hindrance in previous royal marriages, but I doubt they helped her in Charlemagne's court." He smiled at Himli, trying to move her mind from their shared problem.

"Obviously, I know nothing, Adelchis," Himli answered. "Queen Bertrada sent me away in secret, in the dead of night. I have no close contacts in the court and, so, have no knowledge about the marriage or the state of the relationship. Of a certainty, I wish to know nothing."

"But I did learn that loving Charlemagne is not enough. Mayhap if she gave him a son, one perfect in every way, he would have kept her. I loved him and look what happened to me." Her forehead wrinkled. "He wanted a perfect male child;

that's the one thing I learned. The manor women here say Desiderata herself did not want to continue the marriage." She lifted her shoulders in confusion. "I know not where such a tale came from. Mayhap, it's only court rumor." She straightened and looked into Adelchis' face. "The King's affection for me was gone, Adelchis, before your sister arrived at court." She frowned, her smile trembling. "Somehow, with Pippin's birth, he saw me as an enemy," she whispered. Her smile was wistful.

"But I must be brave and help you on your way. Of a certainty, I know you must return to your court. I know you must, even though it is difficult to accept." Himli squeezed Adelchis' hand and returned to her work in the garden. They talked at length throughout the afternoon, as they worked side-by-side. The next morning, Adelchis bid the people of Himli's manor farewell.

"Although I am reluctant to leave this warm manor, I must return home." Adelchis said to them all. "There are not words enough to thank you...for all your care and goodness. I will return to visit, if you will have me again!" Adelchis mounted his horse, waved goodbye, and slowly rode his horse from the manor's courtyard. As the sun touched the morning sky, he and his small escort began their journey toward Pavia. He had left coin with Himli so she could thank everyone in the manor appropriately after he was on his way. Adelchis particularly asked her to choose hair combs for the manor's women and present them in his name. He was happy to avoid their thanks, thanks for mere tokens. They did, after all, return his life to him.

"Bid me goodbye, Pippin," Adelchis begged as he squeezed little Pippin that morning, knowing he would miss the boy. The lad's 'gud morrow to ya' each day encouraged Adelchis to move about, to walk, to regain the strength in his leg. Life won't be the same without Pippin, Adelchis admitted to himself. He said only a very brief farewell to Himli. It was the only way he could bear to leave her. Although she appeared cool and proper on the outside, he knew the effort it cost her. Seeing the distance grow between them, Adelchis stopped, waved once more, and turned his horse east toward Lombardy.

"Stay, Moma, stay," Pippin commanded. "You and me watch 'A-del-shus' til he go. Okay?" Pippin stood resolutely by Himli and held her hand.

"Aye, my dear," Himli responded. "We will stand right here. Let him see you wave as long as possible." At Himli's comment, Pippin raised his hand and began waving to the Prince. He waved until Himli could no longer see Adelchis. Still, she and Pippin stood watching.

"He does go in good health, my Lady," Captain Mortimer said as he headed for the stables. "I will be on the road by tomorrow's sunrise, taking Frau Woodslie to Mainz. That will be a thankless trip, I am sure." Himli nodded at his words but made no reply. The sooner Frau Woodslie departed the manor, the better she would feel. As they finished the early-morning meal, Himli spoke to Frau Woodslie.

"Tomorrow morning, Frau Woodslie, you and Captain Mortimer set out for Mainz," Himli said. "This is the optimum time to depart; make your preparations."

"Of course, my Lady," Frau Woodlie replied. "I have happily anticipated this journey for weeks, as you undoubtedly know." She paused. "But I wish to clear up a mis-impression. It is clear to me now. I can say with certainty. The Prince cares nothing for you. He is anxious to be off, to re-take his place in the Lombard court." Her mouth kept a firm line but Himli saw the pleasure in her eyes.

"As I told you, Frau Woodslie," Himli replied. "As I said... the Prince is a man with responsibilities and interests far beyond the scant resources of my manor. Most people understood his need for nursing from his first moment here. It was only you who jumped to outlandish, wild conclusions about his interest in this manor." So saying Himli left the cook room, secure that Frau Woodslie suspected nothing of her feelings for Prince Adelchis.

Adelchis rode his mount homeward with little attention to his surroundings. He pushed his escort and their horses, riding from early morning til dark. Of a certainty, he was not eager to return home but knew his presence would spare court members additional criticism and fright. Although his Father would not value his presence and his being there would likely feed King Desiderius' anger, Adelchis felt he must bear the brunt of his father's unhappiness. Desiderius would yell and rage at him, instead of at members of the court. They could go about their duties as usual, not continue to be caught up in Desiderius' disappointment.

"I'll make plans in his stead." Adelchis decided. "Desiderata must be married as soon as possible. The sooner there is a marriage, the sooner all this will be forgotten. I will encourage Father to prepare for battle: increase the number of his troops, expand the size of the cavalry, train more horses for battle. His attention must be moved from Desiderata, focused elsewhere. And, I will broaden my knowledge of diplomacy. The Lombard Court and its nobles must learn to think and negotiate, rather than be offended and draw swords. I may unwittingly save lives." Adelchis smiled to himself. "All will be as before."

he muttered to himself.

As the sun sank in the west, Adelchis and his soldiers stopped for the night. He found his legs stiff as he dismounted. His chest ached a bit, probably from the constant coldness of the air as he rode. But, all in all, he felt good, fully recovered from that debilitating closeness in his chest.

"I must stay strong," he reminded himself. "I must journey back to see Himli as soon as possible." He knew anticipating a return visit would help dispel some of the loneliness and hopelessness now gripping his heart. So, he dreamed as positively as possible.

Late on the fourth day of his journey, Adelchis arrived at the Lombard court. His Father's anger, his Mother's anguish, and his sister's lack of concern flood over him. Each of them evaluated the end of Desiderata's marriage to King Charlemagne in a different light. Of them all, Desiderata appeared the least troubled. And Adelchis, at least, thought that a very good thing. She so values herself, Adelchis thought. *She doesn't second-guess her behavior or her desirability. How excellent it must be to feel so confident, so certain your decision is the only possible one. I am just as sure of my love for Himli...and of my need to steal away from here, to steal any time with her I can.*

"God," he prayed, "may I be as steadfast in my devotion to Himli as Desiderata is to her own well-being." Adelchis practiced the art of keeping silent, perfecting the ability to shape and hold his face into an immobile visage. No matter what he heard, no thoughts or feelings surfaced on his face. This served him well. His Father continued to plot against the Frankish King.

"I promise you, Adelchis, We shall take Frankland from Charlemagne! I understand all his tactics. I do out-think him." He spoke with no hesitation. "Carloman and I did constantly revise battle plans. We would have overcome him, if Carl had lived." Desiderius was firm in his expectations. "Those plans will work now. Already, we train one hundred additional war mounts and expand our troop levels." Happily, he described changes in his army's strength.

"And we bait the great Charlemagne with 'strike and hide' tactics." Desiderius paced around his battle room, full of his own ambition and resentment. "We shall prevail and Frank-land will be mine." He smiled at Adelchis.

"Ride with me for the next few days. I travel to speak with the nobles throughout Lombardy. They will carry my message to others, to their friends and mine. The King holds no sway here. The nobles know he cares nothing for Lombard...only wants our allegiance and our men to fight his battles." Desid-erius never dwelt on the King's strengths. He persisted in be-lieving that King Charlemagne could be deposed. He thought only of victory, never of the cost of battle. "We shall overcome him, son; we shall. And, then, your kingdom will be secure." He tried to elicit Adelchis' interest.

"Father," Adelchis replied, "you cannot defeat King Char-lemagne. I don't care if you have the support of every noble in Lombardy...and you will not. The King cannot be so easily overcome." He paused, watching his father's anger build. "But you must do as you see fit. I will say nothing." Adelchis knew his father's behavior, his plotting, would eventually earn him banishment. But Adelchis had no more arguments to give.

"This is your land, won over and over through combat; I know you must ever try to rescue it from a ruler you despise." Adelchis would not undermine his Father's values, even though they did not reflect his own. Surely King Charlemagne knows I do not wish him ill, he prayed. *My service while at his court should guarantee my loyalty to him, despite my father's blind wish to return to the past.*

The truth is, Adelchis admitted to himself, I cannot rouse such anger and resentment. *My heart is brimming with love for Himli and her son; I cannot contaminate my feelings by hating the boy's father. I cannot.* Adelchis' mind jumped back to Himli's manor and the carefree days he enjoyed while recovering there. He sat immediately to write her. Many days later Himli unrolled the parchment the courier delivered

"It's from Adelchis." Her lips moved as her heart shouted. But she kept her face fixed, showing no emotion. *He will not be coming soon.* She interpreted Adelchis' words, coded to say he was not able to get away, not yet. She looked into the eyes of the courier.

"Thank you for the message," she said. "I will have a brief reply. I shall bring it to you. Go to the cook room, refresh yourself. You must eat and, then, bed down here in a barracks room. You need rest and sleep. Stay here with us, regain your strength for your homeward journey." The courier nodded, thanked her for her hospitality, and handed his reins to the stable boy nearby.

"Thank you, my Lady," he replied. "With your word, I go to find meat and bread." He took a leather bag from his horse and headed toward the cook room, eager to rest from his journey and to quieten his growling stomach.

Before Adelchis departed, he and Himli devised a code for their communications, one which rested on the position of the words. Himli remembered his dedication to that task.

"We must have some way to speak to one another," Adelchis worried. "How will I let you know when I can get away, when I plan to arrive? We must devise some method to send true messages, lost in the mundane correspondence the world will see." That day, he took Himli's hands in his.

"Just know," he added as he kissed her cheek, "just know-- every word is sending my love to you. All my love, dear Him- li." Himli remembered resting contentedly in his arms, filled with the wonder of his love. Since that precious day, she felt surrounded by a completely unexpected glow; it warmed all her days. Never did she think of finding another love or, even, that she wanted one.

"And I want no other," she admitted to herself. "No one but Adelchis could ever move my heart."

Chapter Six

On the seventh day of Adelchis' return to Lombardy, his hi father summoned him to the battle chamber. Inside, King Desiderius' most competent tactician unrolled maps of Lombardy and its outlying regions on the room's huge tables. Desiderius' captains had long ago devised various methods for crossing particular regions: mounted, on foot, hidden in carts, disguised as vagabonds or entertainers. Their knowledge of their own realm and of those lying nearby was unmatched by other commanders. The room itself radiated battle preparations. Adelchis was shocked. The upcoming spring assembly was yet more than a month away. His father had only yesterday received the location of this year's gathering.

The spring assembly gathered the King and all his supporters. Charlemagne and his commanders shared information, evaluated troop strength, and ranked threats to the realm, as well as to individual counts' manors. Then, always considering the King's interests, they decided the battles the army would undertake: the dates for marching; the duties of commanders; the numbers of soldiers, horses, and carts; the routes they would follow; the methods used to live off the land as much as possible. Preparations for the wars of summer consumed them all. Commanders and seneschals identified the plateaus and plains for the animals to graze. Commanders and their captains presented battle plans for specific geographical sites. Included with the battle tactics were bivouac requirements and food stores. Each commander answered these questions for himself, before he took part in battle plans with King Charlemagne. All looked to protect their men and gain as many concessions and as much booty as possible. In this, King Desiderius — regardless of his ambitions, was no different from the other nobles - Lombard or otherwise.

What is Father doing? Adelchis asked himself, as he sat near the back wall of his father's battle room. He had not seen this much preparation for battle in years. The seasoned commanders in the room smiled, fingered their swords, and bragged on the readiness of their individual cohorts. There was much battle enthusiasm in the air. Although the nobles shared tense glances, they eagerly identified their personal goals for the campaign, those goals apart from King Desiderius' wishes. Most of the nobles hoped to acquire more land. Desiderius, in addition to granting it to them, would be expected to help them protect it. They talked as if their goals were the same as Charlemagne's, their needs and battle successes duplicates of his.

But it was clear T Adelchis. None of them truly thought of the King. Their single concern was Desiderius' wishes. His wants outweighed anything else. Each commander worked to obtain additional lands for himself, to increase his manor's wealth and influence, to attract additional soldiers to his court. But all results centered around the wealth and glory King Desiderius would gain.

Something unusual is afoot. Adelchis realized as he watched the commanders interacting. *It will, for certain, be something I do not like.* He predicted with certainty. He shifted back into the shadows of the room, hoping the Lombard commanders would forget his presence. King Desiderius sauntered into the room, trying to look nonplussed, attempting to hide his excitement. Seeing the broad smiles on his captains' faces, he laughed aloud.

"You seem to have become bored during this dull winter!" he exclaimed, as the men nodded their heads vigorously. "Ready for battle, are we?" He asked, as his eyes scanned the faces of gathered there. He looked, as if searching for someone specifically. Then, he refocused his attention as three nobles knocked and came into the chamber. Duke Justin of Milan, Duke Aquillers of Genoa, and Duke Guerier, also of Genoa, hurried forward to clasp Desiderius' shoulders. These three were soldiers and friends, their loyalty to each other constant and unquestioned. Adelchis, hidden in his corner, shifted uncomfortably.

"Welcome!" Desiderius greeted the other men in the room, his eyes making contact with many of them. "All of you, welcome! Thank you for journeying here before the Spring Assembly. This is the year we need to plan together, both to respond to King Charlemagne's battle plans and to make our own, ones he surely does not expect." Desiderius beamed at those in the room, entirely comfortable with his perception of their loyalty and military support. "I appreciate your presence and your support. Thank you for this extra effort. Let me get right to the point." Desiderius turned slowly, deliberately nodding into each man's face.

"As you've heard, the Saxons, those unwelcome heathen, do threaten Frankland. And, although King Charlemagne controls them at the moment, I feel we could do him an extra service...by strengthening our control of the Susa Valley road. We will re-enforce the clusae,* so invaders may not easily move into the Italian plain." Desiderius watched the commanders, alert for any sign of resistance to his idea. "This will, of a certainty, also protect us from unwanted invasion—from anyone attempting to travel into Italy." There was a loud buzz around the battle room. Men were talking at once, some in astonishment, some with a heady optimism shining in their eyes.

"But, Desiderius," Guerier spoke first. "Clearly, this is a duty for the King! He will not take kindly to a Lombard force marching toward the Susa Valley." He looked keenly at Desiderius and, then, smiled. "What plan do you make for us, cloaked in service to the King? I ask you frankly." And he stepped back into the circle of his fellows.

"Well might you ask." Desiderius nodded his head. "Of a certainty, the King will, at first, be angered." His face was solemn and intent. "But, my dear Guerier, I do not suggest an army, not men marching for battle. Nay, I am asking for soldiers to strengthen the clusae. These fortifications have served Lombardy well since the Roman period. I suggest repairs only: the watchtowers' weak points patched, the walls strengthened, methods to dislodge grappling hooks—the better to prevent entrance to our own land." He looked steadily at Guerier, gauging the man's reaction. Then, smiling broadly, Desiderius continued.

"Charlemagne will be immediately angered by our suggestions. He will question our effrontery, but the clusae's value to our defense will be obvious. I will remind him of our loyalty, of our support of his conquests. He will, then, be less able to turn against us. Don't you think such an action could work in our favor?" The room was silent, every man considering Desiderius' words. Each of them, for his own individual reasons, would prefer their friend, Desiderius, command the realm, not Charlemagne. Looked at in a different way, these fortifications could just as easily keep King Charlemagne out of Lombardy as protect the Frankish king's army. Desiderius sought to convince Charlemagne the fortifications would hold the Saxons at bay.

"This is an idea with merit." Aquillers announced, nodding at Guerier. He looked around the room once and, then, turned to Desiderius. "But its presentation to the King must be neatly done. We must present such support for *his* ambitions that he does not think of ours. Is this not so?" Talk erupted throughout the room.

Adelchis immediately understood his father's intent. Display filled his mind. *He baits the King.* Adelchis realized in horror. *Father does not understand the King's tactical mind. King Charlemagne will see throught this immediately. He will be doubly alert to anything my father plans.* Adelchis stood, surprising many in the company as he walked from the shadows into the light. He passed Aquillers and Guerier, nodded casually and stood beside his father.

"Though I understand the necessity for increased fortifications, this explanation will not fool King Charlemagne." Adelchis stated boldy. "He will see immediately the implications of our restoring those fortifications, our marching into that region, repairs or not. Any explanation we give for strengthening these fortifications will seem seditious to him. His wrath will be inflamed." Waving his hand dismissively in his son's face, Desiderius replied, frowning.

"We will not be foolish, Adelchis, in the explanations we give the King." He hoped to placate his son. "We're able to make appropriate defense of our actions, to so couch our words in order to emphasize our eagerness to defend the Frankish realm. We will convince the King this is a prudent and peaceful undertaking. Besides," Desiderius smirked, "we need not explain the extent to which the fortifications will be strengthened. We shall lead him to believe we make miminal repairs.

He will never leave the battlefield to inspect our work." He raised his right hand in victory to the assembled men who smiled and nodded at his proposal.

As the gathered lords and dukes voiced their support of Desiderius' plan, Adelchis backed slowly to the edge of the chamber, returning to the shadows. He wished to absent himself from these traitors, but knew he should wait. He should hear all the plans, everything being said ... and not said ... among these men. His father, not seeing Adelchis at the front of the group, assumed he left the chamber and assured the gathering he could control his own son.

"Do not despair at my son's words," Desiderius said quietly to the men. "His regard for Charlemagne confuses his allegeance to his comrades here. He just lately returned from the King's court where Charlemagne's attention befuddled both his mind and his heart. He remembers Charlemagne's favor and welcome, the King's respect for him. They did hunt together for weeks. The boy will be with us. I do assure you. He will see the serious chance we have for ruling Frankland. What a day it will be!"

Despite Desiderius' desire for Adelchis to rule Lombard eventually—after he obtained it--he never allowed his son to discuss tactics, plan troop movements, or delineate battle strategy. Adelchis strengthened fortifications for his father. He was uncanny in his ability to find money, materials, and daily rations for the workers. As always, though, Desiderius did not invite Adelchis to confer or even to listen to military plans when he and his commanders talked long into the night. Little did Desiderius realize Adelchis knew King Charlemagne far better than he or his fair-weather friends—the Lombard nobility.

Adelchis understood clearly. The last man to rule Lombardy was his father. He would never follow his father as king. Charlemagne would not allow it. Desiderius' power would soon be decreased. King Charlemagne would have it so. Incrementally, as time went by, Desiderius' rule would weaken. The King would begin making major decisions.

King Charlemagne surely understood Desiderius' ambition. His ambition, his obsession with conquering, had dominated his life. Even if his father managed to conquer lands beyond Lombardy, Desiderius would rule them for a short space. They would soon be incorporated into Charlemagne's realm, along with Lombardy itself. Desiderius would never hold those lands. His continual plotting made it impossible for the King to trust him trust him.

Knowing his inability to re-route his life among his father's supporters and their lack of interest in his words, Adelchis left the chamber to spend some time with his mother. He proposed two appropriate suitors for his sister's hand and plotted with his mother to move his father toward a betrothal. Adelchis thought this his most important duty, one which would deflect Desiderius' anger from his family.

"Adelchis," Desiderius addressed him a fortnight before the spring Assembly. "I want you to take a small number of our best scouts and seek information about Charlemagne's military strength. I must be well-informed before we begin to plan summer battles. Select only the best scouts. Take the army's spies, if you prefer, to accompany you. You are to travel as Septimanian farmers, move with stealth through the land, as if you are renegades. Gather information about the King's expected movements, military strength, and the speed of marches. Talk to soldiers who are planning to travel to this year's spring assembly. They will know of last year's losses, weaknesses, wounded or dead commanders—that kind of information." Desiderius consulted his list of duties and looked back into Adelchis' face. "Do you understand what I expect?"

"Aye, Father," Adelchis responded. "But I would learn more, if you would assign me to Count Guerier. Let me soldier under his command."

"Nay," Desiderius refused. "Nay, you will serve in the position I choose. This way, I can assure your mother you will come to no harm. You won't be dodging arrows, should we meet unexpected resistance. Nay, this mission may well save your life."

Adelchis schooled his expression. Playing it safe, once again, he thought. *I can never make a name for myself—certainly not. Father would never want that!* His grim face reflected his inner frustration but he answered evenly.

"...as you wish, Father." He saluted and left, moving among the tents bivouacked in the field beside the stables. Adelchis had already identified the men who would accompany him on the spying expedition. They worked with him in the past on the very same kind of assignment. He greeted each one, relieved to have an occupation with his friends. They were well-trained, men he could admire and, more importantly, trust.

"Each of us will work alone," Adelchis began, "just as we have done in the past. I head west. Anyone who wishes to camp with me this night, meet me at the river." He gave each of the men provisions: a new, wool cloak; new foot coverings; and a leather bag of 'traveling sticks' and nuts. He continued speaking. "We will gather information, then meet to compare: to weed out the chaff and misleading reports; to sift through rumors; to distill the facts. Let's give it three weeks." Adelchis decided. "By that time, we must march to the spring assembly." The men picked up their weapons. Anticipating this journey, they had their woolen mantles, traveling bags, and food with them. All left to do was to mount their horses and ride.

"Each of you, Godspeed," Adelchis said. "Let's meet at the hill cave, in three weeks time. Be alert. I expect to see each of you at our rendezvous point. Do not linger, gathering information. It is best we arrive back here together...or as closely as is possible." The men all nodded in approval, took their leave of each other, and wished the prince a successful trip. Adelchis waved them off, mounted his horse and rode out of his father's court.

"I shall go to Himli," Adelchis decided. "I can pick up rumor and talk as I journey there. Nothing I can do will improve Father's chances of ruling the realm. That's what he wants. He wants Frankland...and all the peoples the King has added to it. But he cannot defeat the King, the Peers, the loyal commanders, or the King's army! No one has the strength!" Adelchis shook his head.

Over the years, he made repeated attempts to reason with his Father, attempted to direct Desiderius' ambitions toward a more fruitful harvest. Father will not be moved, Adelchis admitted to himself. *His hatred and jealously of King Charlemagne overwhelm his reason. He condemns himself and anyone who aligns with him.*

Adelchis finally accepted it: his father rejected his cautious words, put no value in his thoughtful suggestions. Desiderius would never cease his plotting or re-think his megalomanic ambitions. Despite Adelchis' efforts, King Desiderius would eventually confront Charlemagne and, finally, battle against him. Nothing could save Lombardy from his father. Through such behavior would his father seal Adelchis' fate. He was the final pawn in his father's ambitions, certain to be sacrificed for an impossible dream. So be it, Adelchis decided. *Now, I am free to do what I can, what I can for Himli and and for us before I am imprisoned or killed.*

"God, he whispered, please help... that I might keep Himli and Pippin safe."

As Adelchis began his journey, several of his spies joined him. They left the Lombard court together, just as the sun's rays began kissing the mountains in the east. They rode long in the night, finally building a fire as the stars' splintered light looked down on the world. While eating their evening meal, the men discussed the questions they needed to answer, made suggestions to each other, shared the routes they would follow, and described individual town and villages to ease their fellows' travel.

"I prefer to go westward," Adelchis told them, as their talk wound down. "...probably, a bit northwest. Does any one else prefer that route?" All the men shook their heads negatively.

"Truth be told, Prince Adelchis," one of them answered, "I'll go where you say. Between us, this does seem a fool's errand to me. Charlemagne is our King. Your father has sworn his allegiance. Support of one does show loyalty for the other. I do hope." He looked at his companions. "I don't mind working on the fortifications. They make us all feel safer, I'm thinking. But no matter what strength we give them, King Charlemagne will find a way through them, or over them, or around them. We know his skills, don't we?" He turned to the other men around the fire.

"Of a certainty," one of them replied. "Charlemagne's a great fighter...the best any of us is ever likely to see! But, if King Desiderius wants me to repeat rumors, to count soldiers, to report on past battles, let it be done. I share in the army's booty. I'll do my job. I'm here to soldier, just trying to feed my woman and my son. I leave battle plans to the king, whichever one of them wants to make them." Wishing each other 'God-speed,' the men banked their fire, turned to their blankets and were soon asleep.

The scouting party broke up the next morning, each man riding off in a different direction. They wouldn't see each other for more than three weeks. They planned their routes so their travels would not overlap. All would return to the rendezvous point, would ready the cave and hunt. When the men gathered three weeks hence, they would discuss the conservations over-heard, glean the truth from their many disparate reports, and distill their observations into information for King Desiderius. As in the past, Adelchis would deliver the report, verbally, to his father at the spring assembly. Their oldest scout would ac-company Adelchis. He was the one King Desiderius respected; he represented the credibility of the spies' findings. Each clapped the other on the back; shared any special 'traveling foods' they had; and, with a backward wave and a "Be Alert" wag of their fingers, rode away.

Adelchis knew he had a hard ride of five or six days to get to Himli's manor. It was cold. Patches of water still froze overnight, though they melted by mid-day. He didn't want to chance getting sick again. So, he decided to live up to his prince's role. He would stop in small inns along the way and glean any information that he could. He would carry some tid-bits back to his father, however discouraging they might be. He knew the other soldiers would, most likely, only report pos-itive rumors. He would balance their positive reports with real-istic evaluations.

Adelchis rode hard. The quicker he got to Himli, the more time he would have to stay with her. The slow encroachment of spring had turned the roads to slush. He stayed alert to boulders shifting in the mountain passes, to slick patches which might throw his horse, and to any riders who might lie in wait for those traveling alone. Despite the efforts of the King and his nobles to safeguard the roads, there were always small bands of men, escaped prisoners, soldiers of fortune who posed danger. Adelchis' training, however, came from the best spy and tracker in Desiderius' army. He remained alert but pushed his mount, riding until he and the horse were both close to ex-haustion. Having crossed these mountains and plains before, he remembered shallow caves where he and his horse could rest or hide if he spotted other travelers.

On the fifth morning of his journey, about mid-day, Adelchis spied Himli's manor in the distance. He saw the smoke from the manor's cook room. But he had to round the massive forest to see the house itself. All seemed calm. He spotted horses outside the stable and someone throwing straw from the stable's second story. Mayhap, all were spring clean-ing! Adelchis jumped from his horse as he came to the garden.

There, brittle twigs snapped as someone gathered up the dead debris of summer plants. A second look assured Adelchis; it was Gerta, not Himli. He shouted to her.

"Good morrow, Gerta! Adelchis here, come for a visit! I'll need no nursing this time. How are you this fine morning?" The girl's face broke into a broad grin.

"Welcome to you!" she shouted, as she stood up, wiping dirt-covered hands on her apron. "It's wonderful to see you again." She smiled. "We will have a party tonight, Sir, for certain!" She came to the Prince, curtseyed, and grabbed his hand.

"Let me run and tell....! Oh, my Lady and Pippin went to the herbalist's yesterday after the mid-day meal." Seeing Adelchis worried face, she put out her hand.

"Nay; they are not ill! Do not trouble yourself, Sire. Their health is fine. My lady went for the usual spring tonic; we expect Jaston here to douse us all in another day or two." She laughed merrily.

"My Lady wants Pippin to spend some time with Jaston so that, whenever Pippin gets sick, he'll be already familiar with the herbalist. The familiarity will make for a better recovery, I guess." She smiled at Adelchis. "But, come, I expect Mollie and the Captain are sharing a flagon...of milk!" She shrieked in delight at Adelchis' face. She could immediately see he thought she meant the two were drinking ale together.

"Nay, nay, the Captain has sworn off spirits, Sir!" she laughed. "Let us go so you can be welcomed."

Adelchis had no recourse. As much as he wished to see Himli, he must not show his impatience. He must meet the workers, expresss his joy in returning, greet each one of them to emphasize his delight at this visit. Truth be told, he was as delighted to see each of them as they were excited to see him. All spent a pleasant two hours as Adelchis spoke of his return to his father's court and of his return to good health. He showed his delight on hearing that the Captain and Mollie had recently married. To his surprise, Mollie now filled the position vacated by Frau Woodslie, and all at the manor were more relaxed for it. Nothing would do. Adelchis must go to the stables to greet everyone there and chat for a bit. As the day grew old, he turned to the stable hands and spoke.

"If I am to find Jaston's cave before dusk, I must start out before the air becomes any darker. Nay, there's no need for anyone to come with me. Just point me in the direction I should go. And how far up the hill should I walk?" His forehead furrowed. He had not investigated this particular place, though the herbalist treated the cough which accompanied his chest thickness last year. He repeated the directions to Jakob for confirmation, left his horse for the stable boy to curry, and set out for the herbalist's cave...and for Himli.

As he walked, Adelchis tried to plan his approach. He knew all he wanted to do was take Himli in his arms and lose himself there. But, that would not be wise. He must be discreet--to protect Himli's reputation. He would have no one talk unkindly of her or judge her actions.

"Pippin will be delighted to see me, as I will him." He muttered as he walked. "I will cherish holding the lad again, fishing with him and, generally, hearing about his days. I have missed them so much!" Adelchis hurried up the rambling path, slowing his steps as he came close to the crest of the hill. He wanted to surprise Himli and Pippin, if he could.

But his careful plans were all for nothing. Himli emerged from the shadow of the herbalist's cave, going toward the small stream which Adelchis passed. Humming a jaunty tune, she looked up as Adelchis rounded the curve. She gave a shout of joy, dropped her leather flagon, and sailed into his arms. Ever afterward, Adelchis could not remember putting his arms out to catch her, drawing her to his chest, or picking her off the ground. But he did all those things. Himli laughed and cried at the same time. She gently touched his cheek, as if afraid it would break. Adelchis' eyes softened, his cheeks flushed, and his hand cupped her face.

"My darling," he breathed softly, "my darling, finally, I have come home." He kissed her forehead, her cheeks, her nose and her forehead again. Then, her lips found his mouth and all time stopped. There was nothing else in the world, nothing between lips and hearts as they merged into each other. Adelchis breathed in slowly as Himli's lips pulled away. He felt, rather than saw, her snuggle under his chin and sigh.

"My precious Adelchis," she whispered. "You are here...at last." Both of them turned as they heard a loud "Huh...hummm." Jaston emerged from the cave. He stood smiling at them both, his eyes twinkling, his smile almost obscuring his face.

"Welcome back, Prince Adelchis," he chuckled. "You seem to have recovered your health. My welcome may not be quite as intense as Himli's; but it is sincere, all the same. It's good to see you here, my boy... very good, indeed."

Adelchis' heart jumped in shock. *Oh, God!* He thought. *What have I done! I, who was going to protect Himli's reputation, have ruined her! What IS the matter with me?* Reluctantly, he put Himli's feet back on the ground and looked up to smile at the herbalist. The man came forward, squeezed Adelchis' shoulder, and shook his head.

"Create no pain for yourself, son," Jaston chided. "I say

nothing of all I see and hear. I am a healer and any fool can see you are exactly the tonic this woman needs." He laughed heartily, patting Himli on the cheek as he beamed at both of them. "It does my heart good to see this feeling between you, and why not? You have your own destiny to follow. Far be it from me to interfere! Nay, you two take some time together, right now. Pippin will soon be coming back. I have no doubt he will demand his share, mayhap more than his share, of Prince Adelchis' attention. Be still, my children. Calm your hearts. I am the master of secrets!" He smiled at them once more, squeezed Himli's hand, and walked around the corner of the hill.

"I'll fetch Pippin," he said as he disappeared.

Himli's hands reached for Adelchis' face as she caressed his face. "Oh, my dear," she breathed. "I cannot speak of my happiness. It is so deep. Why didn't you tell me you were coming? How long can you stay? Have you eaten? Are you exhausted? How long have you been in getting here? Oh, Adelchis, this is a dream come true!" And she burrowed her face in his chest, her tears wetting his tunic.

"My darling, I know these tears are of happiness. But, please, don't cry. Here, let me see your face." Adelchis pulled away, just a fraction, and looked into Himli's eyes. "I love you so very dearly," he said to her. "You must never doubt that."

"And I love you, my dear," she answered. "That love has kept me afloat on my most trying, difficult days. It is a miracle you're here. Thank God for his blessings!" They sat outside the cave in the now-meager sunshine, marveling at their love for each other. It seemed to have only grown stronger since Adelchis' departure. Each spoke of the peace which suffused their minds, now they were together. They were holding each other, crying softly, when they heard Pippin's voice calling to the herbalist.

"Surprise?" he asked. "What surprise? Tell it!" They could hear him run to the herbalist, run back, and then return to Jaston as he called him. Himli and Adelchis hastily wiped away their tears and quickly exchanged kisses. They were all smiles as Pippin burst around the corner, clutching dogwood blossoms to his chest.

"A- d- e- l- c- h- i- s!" he sang out as he spotted the Prince. "You come, you here at last!" And he ran directly into Adelchis outstretched arms, patting his cheek and stroking his hair. "I miss you!" Pippin added as Adelchis threw him into the air, catching the chortling child as he shrieked in delight.

Herbalist Jaston beamed at them all. His smile, again, covered his face as he looked from one delighted face to another. Finally, he saw peace in Himli's face. The drawn, worried expression of this morning had given way to warmth and laughter. Watching her, Jaston thought: she is always positive, reacting to each challenge with a strong spirit. *But, I've not seen this certainty in her face before. And how this man loves her...Pippin, as well,* he noted, as he watched the home-coming play out. He disappeared into the cave, returning a bit later with chamomile tea and fruit tarts.

"I'm lucky," he said, offering Pippin a tart. "You and your mother stocked my food supplies when you came. I believe Marsta made these tarts! Hummm?" He inquired.

"Nay," Pippin answered. "Not Marsta! Gerta made. Tarts are Gerta's!"

"Amazing," Adelchis responded. "She is young to be cooking, is she not?" He turned to Himli.

"She delights in special treats for Pippin. And when she goes home for a visit, she takes a 'sample' to her young brother. She is a sweet, sweet child." Himli added, remembering Gerta's excited, if messy, cooking. They turned back to their tea, though Adelchis ate treat for treat with Pippin. They looked the same, one small boy and one man gobbling treats.

"I would have thought fruit tarts the most delicious in the world, Pippin." Adelchis admitted. "But these nut-filled ones are yummy! Don't you think so?" Pippin nodded his head vigorously. Little bits of pecans flew into the air. He had almost as much nuts and sugar on his face as in his stomach.

"Yum, yum, yummy!" He agreed, laughing with delight. Herbalist Jaston brushed the crumbs of tarts from his own mouth and held his hand out to Pippin.

"Are you ready?" he asked the boy. Pippin's face broke into an even larger smile.

"Me full!" he announced, patting his stomach. He ran to Himli, gave her cheek a peck, and turned toward the herbalist. Then, he changed his mind and ran back, clambering onto Adelchis' lap. Pippin kissed the Prince on the cheek and, then, scrambled to stand.

"Now ready," Pippin insisted, pulling at Jaston's hand.

Jaston turned to Himli, winking at Adelchis at the same moment. "I have promised Pippin to walk around my hill, here, to show him the small animals which hide as people come by." Jaston patted the excited little boy's back. "He's very anxious to spot a ferret, a weasel, and — we hope — a beaver!" At Himli's open mouth, Jaston continued.

"We will stay only as long as it is fun for him, my Lady," he assured her. "And he knows we must use the night...to spot the weasel and, probably, a ferret as well. I know where there is a small dam. Beaver will surely be busy there." Jaston looked at Himli and Adelchis, sitting side by side. Their bodies were not touching but he could see the closeness between them.

"You are not to worry if we are out late," he told them.

"Taking night journeys among our furry friends demands stealth and patience." Pippin tugged at his hand. "Pippin, what did you promise me?"

"Be quiet," Pippin replied, "me be quiet!" And he danced wildy at Jaston's feet.

"And you will be very tired. Let's get a tart to take with us, a flagon of water and some nuts. How about it?" Jaston continued.

"Aye." Pippin agreed, "...but hurry!" Jaston turned to Adelchis.

"We'll be gone until late," he said again. "I leave you in charge here. Keep the fire roaring. Spring is peeking at us, but it will be cold for many days yet." Adelchis nodded, unable to believe he and Himli would be alone, only the two of them, for hours." Jaston's eyes twinkled as he nodded at the young man.

"The manor expects to see us all tomorrow. Himli and Pippin often stay with me. It will seem natural for you to do the same. Be easy with this night." He turned before Adelchis could reply and, smiling to himself, held Pippin's willing hand in his own. "Let's go, my boy." He turned his attention to Pippin. We must hurry but move quietly. The animals are waiting!"

The herbalist and the excited child turned the corner from the cave, speaking quietly to each other. Himli and Adelchis could hear Pippin's voice: "Why? ...b'coz what?" As the voices faded away, they heard the boy's excited shriek: "A turtle, Sir, a turtle!"

Adelchis turned to Himli, pulling her close to his chest. He smoothed her hair from her forehead, following it with his hand to the middle of her back.

"My darling," he whispered, "what a gift has Jaston provided. What shall we do...with no one else about? I hardly know how to start our 'stolen hours.'" Himli laughed. Her laugh was so merry, along with her flushed face. Adelchis delighted in just looking at her.

"My dear," she cried; "how can it be?" She asked him and waited for a response. Adelchis did not understand the question. He was watching her eyes dance, the beat of her heart at her throat, her quick glances at him and her equally quick looks away.

"God, my love, you are so beautiful!" Adelchis breathed.

"My love, my love," Himli snuggled her head under his neck, "if you do not know how to use these hours, I have no doubts! Mayhap, I should take the first step!" And, saying that, she took his face between her two hands, guided his face to hers, and kissed him gently. She dropped her hands, moved them under his tunic, and pulled him to her. "I know just how to start." She breathed in his ear. Then, her teeth nibbled his ear, moved to the nape of his neck while her hands caressed his torso.

How can her hands move so quickly? Adelchis asked himself, just before realizing he must feel, not think. He clasped his arms around Himli's body, pouring all his yearning and love into his kiss. He felt her legs falter and realized she clung to his shoulders. Their breath mingled, as first one and, then, the other remembered to breathe. *I must get these clothes off!* Adelchis almost cried out. *I'm too hot, for all the cold of this morning.* He looked into Himli's face, realizing that her breaths came in little gasps. She moaned and thrust her hands back under his tunic.

"Darling, darling," he mumbled. "We should go into the cave. Come, come with me." He picked her up, pressing her chest to him, feeling her tremble as his hand touched her neck. He stepped forward but felt too weak to move.

"Put me down, Adelchis," Himli whispered. "I can walk...but not too far!" She laughed aloud and reached with her legs for the ground. "Come, come, love," she added, "do hurry. I have real need of you!" She giggled at those words and reached up to lock her lips against his again.

"At this rate, we might get to the cave for breakfast," Adelchis laughed. He picked Himli back up and walked quickly to the cave, passing the firepit which was burning brightly." There was a trail of straw leading to a small indentation at the left side of the cave. Following that, Adelchis instinctively understood Jaston prepared a bed for them. There, in a little alcove, was a huge spread of hay, covered by several animal skins and three linens. He carefully placed Himli in the middle of the linens, removing his tunic before he lay down. Her hands came to his chest immediately, as she kissed his nipples, rubbing her body against him.

"Ohhhhhhh, Himli!" He breathed. "Don't ever stop doing that!" He heard her happy laugh. Adelchis was totally aroused but knew Himli needed his intense attention. She moaned as his tongue licked her ear and his hand began its descent toward her navel.

"I don't want to move away from your body, Adelchis," she whispered; "but I have to get out of these clothes. You're still not touching me everywhere I want you." Adelchis helped her with her clothing, untying her tunic as she untied his leggings. They had legs and arms and bodies everywhere, it seemed. But none of it hindered anything important. "Ohhh, touch me, dear love," Himli breathed. "Touch me everywhere you can!" And she shivered as he pulled her atop him. Adlechis had never known such burning, such a crescendo of longing through every inch of his body.

"Himi!" He cried. "I must have you!" And he entered her,

remembering at the last minute to move slowly...for her sake. Her warmth enveloped him; her need matched his in every thrust. Together, they rose, up, up and up. There seemed no end to the upward climb, made piercingly desperate by their mutual desire.

Help me! Help me!" Adelchis heard Himli cry as their movement rose to an explosive pinnacle. They clung to each other, kissing and crying and shouting out their love. And, then, they flowed into each other as the apex of their desire burst open. Himli clung to Adelchis, trembling. She kissed his chest and, then, his navel, squeezing him happily.

Adelchis shifted his head and looked at her. She was propped on her hand, gazing at him adoringly.

"I love you, Prince Adelchis," Himli whispered and, then, squirmed over to kiss his lips gently. "Oh, darling..." Her eyes dropped from his. "I seem to have bitten your lip! Please forgive me!"

"Nay I don't feel it," Adelchis objected. Then, reviving a little, he noticed the soreness on the right side of his mouth. "Well, maybe." He gazed into her face. "I shall prize that bite all my life."

Himli smiled anxiously. "But I didn't wish to wound you, darling," she answered, trying her best not to smile at him. "You'll never want me again..."

"Ha!" Adelchis exclaimed. "That's not damn likely, my girl...not a chance in hell, as a matter of fact! Come here; here to my arms. I never want you more than an inch from me again." And he gathered her up, kissing and tasting again the woman he so adored.

Sometime later, Himli looked around the cave again. It's so incredibly beauiful in here, she thought, even as she laughed at herself.

"What's so funny?" Adelchis asked, tickling her side, just so he would hear her laugh one more time.

"I was just thinking how beautiful this cave is," Himli answered. "It's beautiful because of you, dear Adelchis." She rested her head on his chest. "I must tell you." Suddenly she was shy. "Everything is beautiful...because of you. I had forgotten... just how freeing being in love can be." She tried to snuggle even closer to Adelchis, but it was impossible. Nothing could make them closer, nothing but melting into each other.

"Aye. I feel free myself," Adelchis affirmed, drinking in her tousled hair, glowing skin, and blushing face. "Himli, I've destroyed your face. I never thought about my beard. Your dear cheeks are almost raw!" He was frantic, seeing the scrapes on her cheeks. Himli touched her face, surprised when he mentioned it.

"Oh, Adelchis, it's a small price to pay for such sweetness! I would my cheeks always be a testament to your love, dear." Her face clouded momentarily, but she shook her thoughts of the future away. "No matter, think no more of it." She regarded him keenly, tracing her finger around his jaw, tapping his lips gently. "Aren't you starving, my energetic lover?" She jumped up and began pulling on her clothes.

"I am really hungry, love," she repeated. "We must eat." And she held out her hands to pull him upright. Adelchis grabbed her hands and stood, bringing her to his chest in one gentle sweep.

"I would give up food, if you would replace my fire as we use it, Himli," he replied. "But, please, let me tell you again. I would say these words to you with each breath. Remember my words. Every time you breathe, know I love you!" He kissed her again and felt her heart jump. He held out his arms in mock despair. "I must dress....yes, and we must eat. I am exhausted, just like you."

By the time Adelchis dressed and washed his face, Himli had bread, cheese, ale, and nuts on the trenchers. They sat side by side, eating and constantly touching each other: a sharing of cheese here, a drink from the same flagon next, a piece of nut just perfect for the other one. Their happiness in each other radiated out, keeping them warm.

All of a sudden, Adelchis jumped up. "Oh, Lord!" He moaned. "I almost let the fire go out! Himli, why didn't you tell me?" He looked around frantically and, then, relaxed, seeing a stack of wood and old tree limbs in the far corner. He hurried to them, bringing back several pieces to throw into the pit. The fire blazed up, the coals red and glowing.

"This fire is perfect for roasting," Adelchis commented. "Did you bring any meat for Jaston?" He knew that the manor often paid for others' services with produce, meat, leather, or spun cloth.

"Aye, how stupid of me!" Himli exclaimed. "I buried a haunch in the snow right outside. Let me get it. We can make a hot meal for Jaston and Pippin. They will welcome it after so much time in the cold." She hurried out of the cave, returning in a moment with a sizable piece of lamb. Adelchis already had the split across the fire pit. As he made the meat secure, Himli took bread from her pack, put dried beans in a pouch to cook, and cleaned their trenchers, rubbing, then rinsing them with water. She propped the trenchers near the fire to dry and to warm. After the food cooked, she would place it in the warm trenchers, the trenchers would retain some heat. Juices from the meat sizzled on the rock lining of the fire pit, filling the air with tempting smells. Even though they had eaten, Himli and Adelchis agreed they looked forward to sharing the meal with the two animal-watchers. Noticing the cow's full udders, Himli milked her. As she strained the milk, she heard Pippin's tired voice asking Jaston a question.

"What is there to eat?" Jaston repeated. "I suppose there's bread and cheese, my boy," he replied. "Aye, and tonight, you must have some warm milk. I will ask Mrytle if she can spare some for us."

At that reply, Pippin's laughter rang in the cold air. "Ask Mrytle? She say AYE!" And he laughed again. All of a sudden he rushed into the cave, running directly to Himli and grabbing her legs. "Mom-a! Hello!"

"Hello to you, my brave animal hunter!" Himli shouted in return, swinging Pippin around and around. She set him on the floor and laughed as he turned, dizzy from all the whirling. Adelchis gave him a welcoming hug, then went to help Jaston take off his pack.

"This pack seems much heavier than when you left, Jaston," Adelchis observed.

"Indeed," Jaston answered. "I don't doubt it. It is filled with Pippin's treasures, things he could not bear to leave behind." He smiled as Pippin ran up.

"Me trey-sures!" Pippin exclaimed, looking sideways at Jaston. "Me and your trey-sures!"

"Suppose we see those treasures after you've eaten?" Himli asked. "There's warm food for you here and I found more tarts, in the bottom of my bag!" Her eyes were wide, her mouth smiling as she relayed this information to Pippin. Distracted, the boy rushed to the firepit and promptly sat down.

"Yum! Yum!" he replied. "Eat now!"

Himli watched open-mouthed as Jaston and Pippin ate. Although she and Adelchis talked to the animal watchers, Jaston and Pippin were too preoccupied with putting food in their mouths and chewing to offer a word. The cave was quiet, filled with delicious smells, Pippin's smacking, and desultory conversation. Refusing the tart that Himli offered, Pippin hugged Jaston's neck, gave Adelchis a sleepy kiss, and curled up in his mother's lap. He slept as soon as he laid his head against her chest. The adults watched the lad sleep, nodding at the happy smile which suffused his face. His eyes twitched, his legs moved and he murmured quietly in his dreaming: "Like turtle best!"

"He had a splendid time!" The herbalist announced, confirming with his words the pleased face Pippin showed to each of them. "He has more energy than I could ever imagine! I gave out long before he needed his second breath!" Jaston laughed, re-living some of their 'adventures' for Himli and Adelchis. "He's a natural with animals. I can tell you that. Even old Jeb plodded a little more quickly as we rode him toward the river. We left him there grazing as we returned, very close to where we found him." Jaston yawned openly and apologized.

"I don't mean to show my weariness in your faces," he admitted. "But I must to bed. The lad has worn out my legs." He laughed quietly, kissing the top of Himli's head as he passed her on the way to his ledge at the rear of the cave.

"Have a good sleep," he wished both Adelchis and Himli. The two murmured their own 'good nights'. As soon as Jaston ambled away, Adelchis' arms went around Himli's waist; he pulled her close to him.

"My dear love," he whispered. "This has been the happiest day of my life, being here with you and, now, sharing this meal with you. Your son is a bundle of energy. You deserve much credit...in the way you rear him, help him grow." Adelchis stroked Himli's hair, captivated by its subtle sheen and the way it fell from his fingers. She inclined her head slightly, savoring his gentle stroke and the love it reflected.

"Aye, this was a magical day," she concurred. "But most of the magic came from you Adelchis! I will never, ever forget my 'feast' or the glory of your body," she added. Sighing, she kissed his lips gently, nibbling a little at one corner.

"My dear, I could love you forever," Adelchis declared. "All I need is a little time for food and rest. Your love, the giving and the getting, is so uplifting! I never dreamed loving someone would produce such a warming glow." He snuggled his head under her chin and pulled her closer to his chest.

Himli laughed softly. She felt so blessed and so overwhelmed with thankfulness for her life--for Pippin's character and for Adelchis' tenderness. She wished never to lose this minute. She kissed Adlechis' temple, then his dear cheek. Before she realized it, their lips found each other. She felt the fire blossom in her stomach just as she felt Adelchis draw in his breath.

"Oh, my blessed Himli, we will surely consume each other!" She felt him shudder as he pulled away. "Wait a moment, love," he interrupted. "Aye, I want you. I want you as if we had never come together at all. And I will love you again...in just a moment...but." He took Himli's arms from around his waist and held them to his chest. "We must talk, my darling. We must try to arrange our lives." Adelchis stopped speaking and gazed into Himli's face. Her eyes sparkled; her lips were pink and glowing. He could see the love for him in her eyes.

"Aye, my dear, I agree. Of course, we must talk." Himli stroked his cheek, tracing the outline of his jaw. "I love you, Adelchis, my prince," she whispered. "I love you dearly." Adelchis held her face between his hands. He kissed each cheek, kissed her cute, little nose. Then, he folded her into his arms.

"And I love you, my Himli, more than you can possibly ever realize, more even than my own life," he added fervently. They sat as close as possible, basking in the sureness which comes from complete acceptance of a deep commitment to each other. "We must make plans." Adelchis pulled himself back from the dream he had just lived. "We must be together for all time. We just have to work out some practical means to do that."

Himli's head snapped up. She gazed into his eyes. Adelchis saw her face pale, her eyes drop away from his. She shook her head slowly.

"What is it, dear?" Foreboding made his voice tremble as he took both her hands is him. "You are to keep no secrets from me," he cautioned.

"Nay, I won't," Himli responded. "I promise. It's just…. Adelchis, we cannot be together. I mean, we cannot live together like other folk. I must stay here in my manor. I must devote myself to Pippin's future." Her eyes locked onto his, begging him to understand.

"Go on," Adelchis answered tightly, afraid of her next words.

"I cannot come with you, my dear man," Himli began. "I cannot risk it. Were I to leave here, Charlemagne would likely order Pippin to his court." She saw Adelchis frown and continued. "Charlemagne does not want the boy. But, if he thought you--or any other man--would teach and direct his firstborn, he would prevent it. I have no dissolution of my marriage. I am not a free woman, not free to marry you. Aye, the Church said my marriage was not sanctified. But, the Abbot said I would always be the Queen. I do not believe that either. Here is the fact: Charlemagne must announce the dissolution of my marriage. Only in his disavowal of me can I be safe. If he has done this, I know nothing of it. My marriage still binds me!" She noted Adelchis' frown.

"Aye," she accepted the direction of his thoughts. "Aye, I know the King released your sister from their marriage as well. But, it was a blessed marriage, blessed by the Church's ceremony, I mean. Surely your father and mother saw Desiderata's marriage as legal and binding. The Pope dissolved their marriage, but nothing has been done about mine. I suppose I am free, but only if the King desires it for himself." Himli paused for breath.

"I matter little, my love," she appealed to Adelchis. "I cannot risk losing Pippin. Imagine his life at the Frankish Court. Nay, nay, Adelchis! I cannot bear for my boy to be there!" Himli's tears coursed down her cheeks. She kissed Adlechis' face over and over, soothing and comforting him as she tried to cover her own anguish. Adelchis held her closely, thinking of her words.

"Aye, of course, you are right, Himli. Aye, I understand exactly your words...and the difficulty in your saying them. ... how stupid of me, how stupid of me--not to have thought of the King!" He stopped talking, realizing he could not take Himli away, could not ask her to leave her manor. Her life and Pippin's would be irreparably damaged by such an action. *King Charlemagne has a fiery temper. None of us will be safe if he thinks that Himli has embarrassed or wronged him in any way.* Adelchis stood abruptly.

"Excuse me, Himli. I must think...and I must think away from you. I do so love you!" He walked toward the front of the cave. Looking back over his shoulder at Himli, Adelchis suggested: "Go and lie down, Himli, there on the linens. Try to get some rest." At her step toward him, he waved her to stop. "Nay, nay, love. I must think. I'll be back with you soon. You have my word." He turned and walked toward the front of the cave... out into the night. Himli stood uncertainly.

"I certainly do not want to go to my bed," she declared. She wanted only to be with Adelchis and, now, he had motioned her away. She sat down by the fire pit, the tears beginning again. "How can I live without him?" The empty cave around her gave no answer. After his tenderness and passion—the magic of his hands, the joy of his lips, the depth of love in his eyes—how could she return to her old life? It was not possible.

"God?" she whispered softly. "God? How can you condemn me to such loneliness again?" Stumbling, Himli found her way to the sleeping linens and lay down. She was weary, but weary from loving and laughing and hopefulness. She could not imagine how she would deal with the aloneness now... after Adelchis.

Jaston heard the footsteps leave the cave. By the sound of them, he concluded Adelchis was the one leaving. The herbalist leaned back on his linens, catching slight sounds of Himli's weeping.

"This is no good," he muttered to himself. "Two people so concerned for each other, so united in their love for little Pippin must be together. This feeling between them must grow. If not, all three of them suffer." Jaston shook his head, turning his back to the faint glow from the firepit embers. "Those two have good heads on their shoulders, they'll find a way to make this work." So thinking, he was comforted and soon fell back to sleep. As the three in the cave slept, Adelchis paced outside of the cave, going over today's events in his mind.

The one thing I will not do, Adelchis thought to himself. *I cannot, I cannot give Himli up. I will find a way to make her mine. Never have I felt such longings for a woman!* He chuckled to himself. *I would move the river to see her smile,* he admitted to himself. *Her happiness, along with Pippin's, is the only thing I want. I will find a solution;   I will!*

Unlike his father, Adelchis was no dreamer. At King Charlemagne's court, he had made good use of his time. He quickly understood--the King was the only ruler of the Frankish empire. Oh, he allowed individual chieftains and, even, some nobles to rule their vast domains. But Charlemagne was ever in control. The King tolerated only those who followed his rules, who ruled in his name. Charlemagne may not call it so but his nobles lived in vassalage. Similiarly, Desiderius may not consider the Lombard kingdom part of the King's realm, but Charlemagne surely did. The King's acceptance of Desiderata as wife confirmed that. He wed the Lombard princess to garner the support of Lombard and its nobles. To him, it was a small price. The payment, though, was not sufficient. Charlemagne would take Lombardy; he would have it in his realm. Adelchis had no doubt.

Because Adelchis was the prince of Lombardy and expected to learn from the King, he attended many court meetings between King Charlemagne and his Peers. Each one of them had understood the King's desire for Lombardy. The Peers, often glancing at Adelchis with trepidation and apologetic looks, knew Charlemagne must befriend or overcome Desiderius. Other rulers would no longer support Charlemagne if he allowed an upstart like Desiderius to manipulate him. Charlemagne took steps to co-operate with Desiderius, to earn his support and that of the Lombard nobility. But if Desiderius did not willingly become subservient to the King and follow his commands, Charlemagne would absorb Lombardy into the empire and emasculate Desiderius. In fact, the process might already be well underway. Queen Desiderata was already back at home after all, no longer a part of Charlemagne's court or of his life.

Before he accompanied his sister to Charlemagne's court, Adelchis described this possibility to his father. But Desiderius convinced himself and some of his followers he need only defeat the King in battle. Then, Desiderius felt he could easily overcome Charlemagne's vast legions and rule the entire Carolingian empire himself. All he needed, he believed, was one decisive battle. Desiderius never dreamed the nobles were weak in their support of him. Indeed, his support was weak, compared to Charlemagne's.

Adelchis laughed as he remembered. *My father acknowledges only what he wishes to believe. I could never reason with him. He will NOT listen to the obvious. No matter my argument, he always returns to his plans. Before leaving Lombardy for Frankland,* Adelchis remembered, *I wondered if I were describing King Charlemagne's interest in our realm too seriously. But after a few weeks in the King's court, watching and listening, I knew my surmise was correct. Eventually, there will be no separate Lombard king; there would be only a figurehead, chosen by Charlemagne. Knowing that, I I decided to become a Peer.* Adelchis' breath caught as he realized all he had instinctively known.

Then, unexpectedly, Charlemagne annulled his marriage to Desiderata. She hurriedly left Charlemagne's court so I was left to pack her bride's gifts. I followed her in two days but fell ill and, so, returned to Lombardy late.

"But none of that matters," Adelchis spoke aloud. "None of my father's politics have changed. He is still set on his course."

He shall be destroyed. In his unreasonable certainty, he guarantees his own destruction.

"Naturally," Adelchis nodded his head. "Himli can never be with me, not in public, not acknowledged. We both risk our lives, not to mention Pippin's, if the King suspects any connection between us. Therefore, I must concoct a plan, a plan that will strengthen our feelings and keep our lives safe."

Chapter Seven

As Adelchis contemplated their future, Himli tossed and turned on her linens. She eventually fell to sleep, the sleep of the reassured and the loved. She awoke feeling more energetic than she had since that day long ago...the day she had come to her manor. Armed with happiness and good spirits, she began preparing breakfast for the men in the cave, calling them to come to eat while the food was hot.

"I need some herbs to take home with us," she said to Adelchis and Pippin. "Let's take a basket down by the river for our mid-day meal and gather herbs. It's early...but we might find some plants peeping out!" Adelchis and Pippin were excited about her plan, especially having their meal by the river. The three of them set out. Jaston gave them directions for finding early growing herbs but declined making the trek with them. He stayed at his cave to build drying racks for later use. "We will search for herbs, have our mid-day meal, and return to bid you farewell before we head for home, Jaston," Himli said as they waved goodbye. Hours later, they returned to the cave with thyme for Jaston, as well as early chamomile leaves and mint.

"Thank you for your hospitality, Jaston!" Himli exclaimed as she kissed the herbalist's cheek. "These days will be one of my most beloved memories. Thank you...for understanding."

Pippin hugged Jaston's knees and said he would be back 't'morrow' to see him. Adelchis pressed Jaston's hand.

"There is nothing big or warm enough to say, Jaston," Adelchis admitted. "You know the gift you have provided. You cannot know the depth of my, of our, gratitude." Adelchis had left a wool tunic, wool cap and new pair of foot-coverings beside the fire pit inside the cave. "I can never repay you." Jaston beamed at the three of them.

"Return whenever you can," he urged. "If I am traveling or gathering herbs, away from here, just make yourselves at home. Don't be strangers now. I will yearn for your laughter. Don't keep me waiting to hear and see you again." Thanking him repeatedly for his hospitality and care, Adelchis, Himli and Pippin finally put on their cloaks and left the herbalist's cave. He kissed them all and urged them to visit again. "I agree with Pippin," he added, "tomorrow would be ideal."

"Nay, we must give you time to do your work," Himli answered. "But we will be back, Jaston. This magical place will live in us always and we must return to refresh ourselves."

Adelchis was, again, warmly welcomed at Himli's manor. The days flew by, as happy days do. Adelchis knew his time there grew short. He must return to his spy network, to compare the rumors he had heard with the other men's reports. But he did not see how he could bear to leave Himli and Pippin again.

"My love for you grows and grows, Himli," he confessed to her on the day before he was to depart. "I would never have believed anyone could become so much a part of my life. You and Pippin are one to me — the most important unit I ever hope to have …or love," he added. He and Himli were riding with Pippin to the river. The lad was eager to show Adelchis all he had learned about fishing from Jakob.

"…s-o-o-o many fish, Adul-us!" Pippin shouted. "So many…but they are in the water!" And he laughed with glee. He had brought his cane pole and a bag of worms; both of them he held tightly. "Me take fish to Jakob," he repeated over and over. Himli brought her basket to pick wildflowers for drying. Adelchis and Pippin left her in the field, picking flowers, and walked toward a curve in the river.

"Here, Pippin," Adelchis took the lad's pole. "Let me put the worm on for you. Find a good spot." Adelchis baited Pippin's hook and, then, his own. He threw the hook into the water and handed the pole to the boy. But it was no good. Holding the pole over the water was too difficult for Pippin. His hunchback made the movement awkward. Adelchis looked along the bank. About forty steps away, the river dropped. A short bank hung over the water. "Let's move there, Pippin. You can sit on the bank and drop your hook more easily." Adelchis shouted Himli's name and pointed downstream to show their direction.

"Right here, son. Sit here. I'll prop the pole up for you. Just keep your hand ready, if the line pulls." Pippin nodded energetically and plopped down on the bank, looking out over the river. He held his hand directly over his pole, as Adelchis positioned it. "Watch it now," Adelchis cautioned him. "Let me know if you get a bite!"

"Me will," the boy responded, bouncing up and down with excitement. Adelchis dropped his own hook into the water and sat beside Pippin.

"Tell me about the puppies and their training," he said to the boy. And Pippin began to talk. Adelchis watched Pippin's pole. Something is nibbling, he thought, but I'll wait. *It might be a bite or small minnows nibbling at the bait.* Pippin was telling him about the brown puppy's hurt foot as his pole dipped quickly. Adelchis took the boy's hand and placed it around the pole. Pippin stopped talking, his eyes bulging as he felt the pole quiver.

"Fish! Fish! Adelchis, help!" he cried, just as the pole began moving toward the water. Pippin grabbed it quickly and held tightly. "Got a fish! Got a fish!" he cried. Himli looked up and, hearing Pippin's excited cry, began running toward them. Just as she ran up, Pippin and Adelchis pulled a large trout from the river.

"Look, Moma, look!" Pippin screamed. "Look at my fish!" He patted Adelchis on the head and danced around the flopping fish. "We eat it!" He exclaimed, not able to contain his excitement.

"What a big one, Pippin!" Himli joined in the excitement. "Another two fish this size would feed us all tonight! You are a fine fisherman, my boy." His eyes shining, Pippin patted his fish, getting in Adelchis' way as he tried to get the fish off the hook.

"Just a minute, Pippin," Adelchis said. "I can't see what I'm doing." Pippin laughed, stepping back just for a minute. Then, he was 'helping' Adelchis with the fish again. They put the fish on a thin branch, tied it to a sapling near the river and put the fish back in the water.

"That will keep it fresh 'til we're ready to go home," Adelchis explained. "We can get Cook to make your fish for the evening meal. Would you like that?"

"Aye," Pippin responded. Seconds later, he jumped up. "Come, Adul-chus, you got one!" Sure enough, Adelchis' pole was almost over the bank. Pippin grabbed it and fell back on the bank, the pole clasped in his hands. They landed this fish, too, agreeing these two large ones were more than enough for their meal. The fishermen were hungry so Himli offered bread and cheese, pieces of young, spring onions, and toasted hazelnuts for lunch. The sun beamed on their backs, making the breeze welcome. They were lazy, enjoying the spring day, being together, and the thrill of successful fishing. Pippin lay down to watch an army of ants marching away from the water. He was soon asleep, his hand protectively sheltering his fishing pole.

"What fishing he has had!" Adelchis said, smiling at Himli. He patted the ground beside him. She sidled over to that spot, reaching up to caress his cheek. "My darling," Adelchis acknowledged the caress, "be certain in these days to come. I love you. I will be thinking of you always...these many days we shall be apart." He knew his voice sounded as plaintive as he felt. He pulled Himli close and kissed her lovingly. "I do adore you, my girl," he whispered in her ear.

"And I you," she responded. Trying not to sound sad, Himli took his two hands and kissed them. "Adelchis, what shall we do? How can this separation be borne?" She asked. Adelchis swallowed. I must be strong, he thought. *I must show her we can and will sustain this relationship. There must be no doubt, no doubt Himli can hear in my voice.*

"I will not lie to you, my darling," he answered. "This will be difficult. But it can be borne...and it must. I want no one other than you, Himli. I can love no other as I love you. And I would have you under any conditions, any conditions. Do you understand me? The heart is not influenced by convenience, or by ease, my dear. It just loves whom it chooses. And my heart has chosen. I can do nothing but love you well." He held Himli as close as possible. "It will be horrible without you near," he added.

Himli sighed. "I do love you, Adelchis. I know my life is easier than yours. M y constraints do impose themselves on you. I would not blame you…if you found another." She felt Adelchis' body shift under hers. "But I pray every minute you will not!" She reached for him, finding his mouth already on the way to hers. "I love you so much," she was able to say before losing herself in his arms.

Adelchis rose early the next morning, well before the rest of the manor. He decided last night he would leave before anyone else was up. This way, he thought, I avoid the extra measure of sadness…and I will not have to see the sorrow tug at other people's hearts. *I know Himli will understand. Pippin? I'm not certain. But, surely, she can console him. If I hold her again, I don't know if I can leave her. So, 'tis better to be on my way.* He mounted his horse, turning it from the stable. Looking at the manor, he saw Himli standing at the front door, waving and blowing him kisses. He turned his mount toward her and, then, thought better of it. Adelchis gave one last wave and spurred his horse. It was the most difficult leave-taking he had ever made.

He gave his mount his head and made good time, riding alone. The days were warming, the leaves and grass competing with each other in growing. Had he not left Himli and Pippin behind, his journey would have been perfect. Adelchis was within a half-day's ride of the rendezvous location when he spotted a single rider, coming from the southwest. Surely I am in no danger from a lone traveler, he thought. *I will stay on the road and meet this stranger.* As the rider drew nearer,

Adelchis paused. One of King Charlemagne's small banners was fluttering under the rider's saddle. Now that Adelchis look, the man's seat in the saddle was familiar. Adelchis gave a cry of pleasure, recognizing Oliver as they drew closer together.

"Oliver!" Adelchis called, as he waved a greeting. "It's Adelchis here." He spurred his horse. "How good it is to see you! What are you doing out here, riding alone?" Adelchis cantered toward Oliver, beaming with joy.

"Adelchis?" Oliver asked, unable to believe he had run into Lombardy's prince. "What a pleasure this is! I never expected to see you here, so far from Pavia. Where are you headed?" Looking around expectantly, Oliver expected to see Adelchis' escort, but there were no other riders in sight. "Are you, too, riding alone?"

"Aye." Adelchis leaned from his saddle to hug Oliver. This man had earned a special place in his heart during the days he spent in the Frankish court. Oliver was the thinker, the one who deterred King Charlemagne from foolish, knee-jerk reactions. He was the true peace-keeper, attempting any negotiation to avoid fighting. Oh, he's no coward! Adelchis thought. *He's the only Frank who sees conflict as the last, truly the last, resort.*

"Had I expected to see you, Lord Oliver," Adelchis began, "I would have started my journey with a much lighter heart! How have you been?" He looked Oliver over from feet to head. "You look fit and well-fed."

"Aye," Oliver agreed. "I manage to survive, Adelchis. But what are you doing here? You are quite a way from home." He gazed at Adelchis keenly.

"You are the only man I can tell the truth," Adelchis replied. "I am on a spying mission for my father. You know the needs of kings, Oliver—always watching others and trying to read meaning into everything!" Oliver nodded his head slowly.

"...always reading meaning into every rumor, every action," he agreed, "...even when there may be no significance at all in the things they hear." He dismounted, reaching into his traveling bag for an apple from last autumn's harvest. "Luckily, my horse doesn't object to wrinkled fruit." Oliver grinned at Adelchis. "Otherwise, this apple would have been discarded long ago." He reached back into the bag and offered an apple for Adelchis' horse. Adelchis swung from his horse, took the apple, lay it flat on his palm and offered it to his horse. The two animals munched happily, their breaths steaming in the cool, morning air.

"What is your destination?" Adelchis asked Oliver, sharing a drink from his flagon. Oliver pointed as he swallowed.

"Actually, I am heading toward Pavia," he responded. "I deliver a missive from Charlemagne to your father." He looked at Adelchis, considering. "You may have helped trim my journey. I see no reason for not turning the message over to you...and continuing south, rather than west. My final destination is Septimania." He rubbed his horse's nose, scratching right above the nostrils.

"Of a certainty," Adelchis answered. "I shall be happy to take the missive, though I would welcome your company as I ride toward home. Is this a hurried trip or can you spend some time with me at the Lombard court?" Oliver laughed aloud.

"With Charlemagne, everything is hurried...as you know," he smiled. "Nay, I may not linger, Adelchis...no matter how high my spirit floats. It is wonderful to see you. Duty calls, though. Charlemagne seeks to reassure himself of his commanders' allegiance and I am his messenger. I fear the summer battles against the Saxons will be long and bloody."

"Have they offered a challenge?" Adelchis asked, surprised. "It is early in the year for the rebels to be moving, is it not?"

"Aye," Oliver agreed. "But they harry our outposts, parry and feint against our soldiers, undertake small raids against settlings. Commanders have already gathered informally to discuss battle plans, complete with vows of retribution." Oliver shrugged. "As always, battle is our destiny...at least, those of us aligned with Charlemagne. I do support his vision for trade, for safer and richer lives for our people, Adelchis. I just wish some of this could be obtained without constant fighting." Oliver hobbled his horse to graze and sat on a near-by stump. "Let's swap stories of the last few months, Adelchis; and, then, I must be on my way," he explained.

"It is a gift to see you, Oliver," Adelchis replied. "I have missed no one as much as you. Although I did enjoy the Frankish court, I found your company the most pleasant of all. You do look fit." Adelchis continued. "How are you and how are things at the court? Charlemagne, is he content...and Gisela? I trust they are both well."

"The King is excellent," Oliver answered, smiling. "Not to make judgment, Adelchis, but I think him well out of the marriage with your sister. You heard he and Hildegard of Swabia married?" At Adelchis' nod, Oliver explained. "Not knowing his own mind, the King was adrift for a while. He married Desiderata as a result of pressure from the Queen Mother."

"Aye, so I was told." Adelchis nodded his head, accepting Oliver's words. "I had little contact with Queen Bertrada. To me, it appeared she ruled all the court, her son especially," he said. "Make no apologies on my account, Oliver. My sister is not a wife I would recommend to any man." Adelchis smiled.

"There are few men as secure, arrogant, and stubborn as Desiderata. She genuinely believes she can do no wrong. Any negative event which she hastens, she believes to be totally removed from her responsibility. Never has she realized she instigates much negative herself."

"Charlemagne is blessed with Hildegard for his wife," Oliver stated. "He loved her long before he realized it and, therefore, his heart was incapable of drawing close to another. She is a kind woman, the kindest I have seen," Oliver explained, "and wishes the best opportunities for everyone. I do pray the selfishness of the Frankish court does not dull her dreams. She and the King will work well together for the benefit of the realm." Oliver paused, looking at Adelchis. "Did you hear about the new daughter?" Adelchis startled, looking into Oliver's face.

"Nay, I knew nothing," he exclaimed. "Charlemagne and the queen have a daughter? How splendid...for them and for the little prince," he added. He smiled, thinking of the blessing of a child but checked his enthusiasm when he saw Oliver's face.

"The little one is gone, Adelchis. She lived only a few months." He shook his head, his eyes full of sorrow. "It is one reason I sought this mission, to leave the grieving in the court. The Queen has been inconsolable."

"I cannot imagine such a hurt, Oliver," Adelchis responded, trying to imagine the pain and shock of losing a child. "How has the King managed? This is a challenge he cannot fix by sheer strength of will. I do mourn for him."

"He would thank you, my friend," Oliver answered. "He takes losses, ones like this and battle losses, hard. He does share others' pain, I think, more so than most men." The two men's thoughts drifted back to the Frankish court. Oliver grasped Adelchis' shoulder.

"The King missed you when you returned to Lombardy," Oliver continued. "We all missed you, if the truth be told."

"And I, you," Adelchis answered immediately. "I would gladly have stayed, Oliver, if I had had a choice. My dearest wish was to become a Peer. But you know my father and his expectations. I could do nothing but go home."

"Everyone knows," Oliver acknowledged, "but we miss you just the same. Let's not bring up hurtful subjects, though I did open the door, did I not?" He turned back the flap on his traveling pack to share food with Adelchis. "I hope the King and Queen will soon have another child. It will be a lucky babe, with Hildegard for a mother. And the King would be mud in a little girl's hands." Oliver laughed. Adelchis laughed as well, his eyes twinkling.

"Your praise of the Queen, Oliver, is the only recommendation I need," Adelchis replied. He cocked his head. "But, what about you, my friend? Surely, some enterprising young woman should have caught your eye!" He laughed as Oliver's face turned a bright pink. "Ahhhh, I see I have guessed a-right. You do have feelings for someone! Who is the lucky woman, Oliver?" Adelchis smiled, aware he had struck a nerve in the generally placid Oliver.

"I will not pressure you for your secret," he assured his friend. "You know I wish you the best woman in the world. But, beware, Oliver. You need a woman who will shield you from the criticism and contempt of others, a woman who holds values similar to your own." Adelchis opined. "Would you like me to list them?" He asked in merriment.

"Aye, I would," Oliver replied. "I would understand your comment completely, for I suspect much depth there." He looked into Adelchis' face, very seriously. Adelchis was taken aback. But, being sincere, he nodded.

"You need someone who is honest, straight-forward, and gentle, Oliver," Adelchis began. "Someone who reasons, analyzes, and compares options—not one who follows the old ways, repeats the old responses, or feels traditions are best! Oh, I don't necessarily describe a rebel." He grinned, as he held up his hand. "But you do need a thinker, Oliver...a woman who recognizes and values your forward-thinking ability, your questioning of traditions. I would not have you waste your gifts on just anyone. Your counsel is much too valuable."

Oliver grinned with pleasure. Adelchis may not realize it; but he warmed Oliver's heart with his words. *How many times had Charlemagne and Abbot Fulrad, too, scoffed at his advice; accused him of advocating the enemy's values; railed at his tendency to act slowly and judiciously? How wonderful to hear someone defend his deliberative thinking and carefully directed advice. Adelchis even thought a woman would value his efforts to keep the peace!*

"My thanks to you, Adelchis," Oliver replied. "Although I hesitate to bask in your glowing words, I do appreciate your thoughts. You have seen into my heart. I do try to think, deliberate, and choose the best response...not let anger and impatience propel my steps. But, you know how obtuse and slow the King believes I am."

"Mayhap," Adelchis answered. "But he does listen to your advice and ponder your words—even though he may not like them. He knows your value. Trust me in that. King Charlemagne's impatience does not make my words any less true. The world needs men such as you, Oliver, to keep it aligned. Were there only more of you, we would find ourselves in very changed circumstances."

"Thank you, Adelchis; you do honor me," Oliver replied, genuinely touched. "I appreciate your kind words." Then, he looked at Adelchis with twinkling eyes. "I did want to seek your advice." Adelchis' mouth dropped open in surprise. "Aye, truly. You must have much experience with women. I have almost none and, thereby, need your help. You guess rightly. I have great interest in a young woman at court; but I know not how to show my feelings or, even, if I should show them. Adelchis, can you help me?" Oliver asked, dropping his eyes to the ground in confusion. Adelchis kept his face perfectly still, surprised Oliver had found a heart interest but even more surprised he was asking for advice. *And from me,* Adelchis thought. *I...who have more than my share of difficulties with my own heart challenges!* Adechis cleared his throat and spoke.

"Firstly, let me wish you good luck, Oliver," he answered. He thought for a moment and looked into Oliver's eyes. "Of a certainty, I have told you all I can...in describing the type of woman whom you need. As for making your feelings known to her... are you ready? Are you certain you wish to move to the next step, ready to go beyond the watching and admiring stage, I mean?"

"Aye, I have watched and yearned." He stopped. "I have yearned for her, Adelchis. I can admit that to you, for many months now. It is time for me to determine if she returns my interest. I cannot say. I have no ability to read women," he smiled worriedly. At Adelchis' wrinkled brow, Oliver continued. "She is unfailingly pleasant when I greet her. She appears to like my horse." At those words, Adelchis raised his hands in bewilderment. Oliver tried again. "I mean, she is always asking about my horse. She comes to the stable to help me curry him and always brings him a carrot or an apple. I fear she plans to gift me with a puppy because she has asked, more than once, what kind of dog I fancy." Oliver's words tumbled over each other. He desperately wanted to convince Adelchis the young woman liked him. But his words sounded weak, even to his own ears.

"How have these questions arisen, Oliver?" Adelchis wanted to know. "Is she asking about your preference in dogs when you are in the stables, around the puppies, breaking your fast, at court events, when?" If she gives him a puppy, Adelchis thought, it may mean she considers him a good friend, someone interesting to talk to. *Many women think puppies are dear without realizing their long-term needs...or without caring if someone will fulfill those needs.*

"In one conversation and another," Oliver replied, not clarifying anything with his answer. "We often meet in the stables. We ride together in clear weather. I ask her to dance when the King commands all us Peers to 'entertain the ladies." Oliver rubbed his eyes wearily. "She just seems to appear. Just as I wonder where she can be, I look up and there she is." He smiled widely at Adelchis, not knowing anything else to tell him.

"Do you have a particular schedule for riding or for currying your horse, for example?" Adelchis asked.

"Of a certainty," Oliver replied. "Unless there is a meeting of the Peers or the King summons us for conversation, I curry my horse each morning after breaking my fast."

"And is this young woman always there to help you curry your horse, each morning?" Adelchis queried.

"Aye," Oliver affirmed. "She is there every morning. Even if I begin later than usual, she pops up...to help me, she says." He looked steadily at Adelchis.

"Then, Oliver, I believe she is already interested in you," Adelchis answered. "There are few women who come each morning to curry a horse which is not theirs. She may like your horse; but she, also, likes you." Adelchis stated quietly. Oliver rose from the stump, nodded his thanks, and walked about. He paced his steps deliberately. I wonder, Adelchis thought, is he trying not to jump or skip? Oliver's steps had a decidedly jerky movement, as if he were holding himself back. Adelchis laughed aloud.

"Do you want to dance?" Oliver's head jerked up at his words. Adelchis saw the slow blush move up Oliver's face and burst into laughter. "You do have a bad case, Oliver," he said, openly. "You must speak to the young lady." Oliver's face blanched white.

"What do I say?" he whispered. "I don't know what to say to her. What if we are mistaken? She will take me for a fool, Adelchis!"

"You must know if she is interested." Adelchis dismissed his fears. "You must. If she is not, it is better to know now, not keep hoping things will move forward for the two of you. If she is interested, you will know. Then, there is reason to move forward, to deepen the relationship. Don't you see? The time has come for a choice. It is not possible to stand still."

"I guess," Oliver replied. "I just feel so unworthy, Adelchis. What do I have to offer her?" He shook his head in despair.

"You have much to offer," Adelchis responded seriously. "You are a Peer in the greatest court in the land. You are thoughtful, kind, serious, and loyal. The King puts great value in your counsel. You can provide a comfortable home and a stable life for a wife. Come, Oliver. Don't be stupid. You have much to offer the right young woman." He gripped Oliver's shoulder, trying to reassure him. "By the way, who is she? You must tell me so I can suggest ways of interesting her." Oliver was frozen in position. He was so intent on Adelchis' words that, at first, he did not process the question. When he did, he answered without thinking.

"It's Jocelyn Hautgard," he said.

"Jocelyn?" Adelchis asked. "Is she not the sister of that little flirt, what is her name? Maria? Is Jocelyn Maria's sister; aren't they both good friends of Hildegard, Charlemagne's new queen?"

"Aye," Oliver replied. "Jocelyn is the oldest of the maids in waiting...and the smartest, Adelchis. She quotes poetry; she plays the harp; she even reads some Latin! She told me King Pepin encouraged her father to educate her, asking her to recite rhymes to him when the King chanced to visit Count Hautgard's manor. She helped the Count describe his 'delights' — the tarts, pies, and other sweets he supplies to the King's and the nobles' tables." Oliver's face smiled in praise of the young woman. But, then, his countenance fell.

"Someone so accomplished," he continued, "why would she be interested in me?" Adelchis laughed aloud, slapping Oliver on the back.

"Because, you idiot," Adelchis shouted, "you are just as 'accomplished' as she. You are lost, Oliver!" Adelchis chortled. "I do hope the young woman is as daffy over you as you are over her. But you must find out." His face sobered. "If she is this extraordinary, you must not risk losing her." He immediately regretted his gentle teasing. Oliver's face fell, turning white with fright. Adelchis saw the dismay cover his face.

"Oh, I could not bear it," he moaned.

"Then, speak with her," Adelchis advised. "Do it upon your return to court. You must not delay. You must not." Oliver wiped his forehead, looking over at Adelchis.

"I must, I must declare myself to her," he agreed. Then, he clasped Adelchis' shoulder. "Thank you, thank you, my friend.

I will take heart from your certainty and declare my affection to her." He sighed. "Thank you, Adelchis. If I am lucky, you will be among the first to help me celebrate." The two friends broke the mid-day fast together, sharing each other's traveling food and promising future meetings. Oliver knew Adelchis would not be welcome in the Frankish court for some time. His sister's leaving Charlemagne's court was still too new. But, eventually, with this new marriage, the situation might change. The entire court would delight in Adelchis' return.

Oliver and Adelchis bade each other goodbye, each turning in a different direction to complete his journey. Good friends, reunited for a brief space, both continued their journey with lighter hearts, looking forward to the promises of a new tomorrow.

Adelchis was genuinely happy for King Charlemagne in his new marriage. The king had always treated him honorably. When Adelchis had spoken with the King about becoming a peer, Charlemagne had peered at him keenly, reminding him he was his father's only male heir and listing his father's expectations.

'Yes, I know,' Adelchis remembered responding. 'But a father's plans do not necessarily come to fruition, not in the manner he expects.'

'That is true,' Charlemagne had replied. 'Fathers hope and plan and pray, but life has a way of interrupting those dreams. Let us see what the future holds, young Adelchis.' He had said. 'We all are in thrall to the future.'

As Adelchis and Oliver continued their journeys, both were unaware of the missive King Charlemagne had lately received from Pope Hadrian I. The Pope wrote.

King Charlemagne, King of the Franks, Defender of the Faith, Protector of Pepin's Donation, King of Military Valor, Purveyor of Religious Doctrine and Direction...

King Desiderius has asked me to declare King Charlemagne's nephew, Carloman's son, the lawful ruler of his father's realm. In fact, the request has come from your sister-in-law, the boy's mother. But I have been assured by several court nobles that Desiderius himself has instigated it. Gebnega regaled me with vows of Desiderius' and Carloman's friendship, even suggesting Carloman would wish the Lombard King to absorb his lands. This cannot be true, Charlemagne.
I am not at all interested in such a development. Is there any way to curtail the Lombard king's ambition? We must align forces to resist his stratagem.

Hadrian 1

If the Pope complied and the young boy became king of half of the Frankish realm, Desiderius, through his old allegiance with Carloman and his present sheltering of Carloman's two sons, would directly influence--if not rule--the other half of Frankish lands.

Charlemagne was maddened into action. Although he had tried to maintain harmonious ties with the Lombard Court, even after sending Desiderata home, the Lombard King would not cast aside his unholy ambitions. "Desiderius will not rule my realm!" Charlemagne shouted. "How dare he! I absorbed Carl's lands into my own; it is *my* realm. He will not use his connection to Carloman, his manipulation of my nephew to control the Frankish realm! I will have no more of it!" His face became so red it mottled, even as he strained his voice in anger. While Charlemagne no longer feared for the lives of his nephews, their mother's flight to Lombardy after his brother's death still rankled. "Gebnega's wish to distance herself from Carloman's family is one thing. But she has no right to take his children away from us as well." Charlemagne stated a long-held resentment.

"Desiderius has threatened to besiege Rome, if the boy is not named and anointed king. And, of course, Hadrian begs me to come to Rome to defend the city. Humph!" Charlemagne exclaimed. "I shall end this posturing now." As Adelchis visited Himli's manor, Charlemagne sent messengers throughout the realm, requesting additional military support and supplies for the summer battles. He wanted another two legions of soldiers to accompany his present army to Rome, knowing only an increased force would deter an immediate attack from Desiderius.

Had Oliver known of the impeding threat of battle, he would have hastened back to the Frankish court. Had Adelchis known of his father's move, he would have sped for Pavia, hoping to reason with the man. But both Oliver and Adelchis, protected by their unawareness, continued their separate journeys, oblivious of the confrontation in the making.

King Charlemagne decided to march for Rome, acquiring additional troops as he marched south. He set a record pace and arrived in Rome two days before Desiderius' army established its own camps outside the city. When Desiderius arrived, Charlemagne had already conferred with Pope Hadrian and had begun deploying his forces to protect the sacred buildings. Desiderius climbed the steps before the holy church with all the arrogance his personal vision gave him. The Pope bade him enter and speak. Desiderius' hearty greetings and scarcely veiled threats did not move Hadrian, not with King Charlemagne's army bivouacked on the western side of the city. Understanding the obtuse mind of the Lombard King, the Pope uttered his own threat. But he did not threaten Desiderius alone. With Desiderius' commanders and kingly guard listening on the steps of the church, Hadrian spoke.

"March on Rome, Desiderius," Pope Hadrian began, "and you march against all those who love the Mother Church. You have no authority inside the walls of this city. You have no authority within the Holy Church itself. The true son of the church is Charlemagne, King for the Franks. His father, King Pepin, promised us lands to support the Church; Charlemagne has honored Pepin's donation and has extended our lands. You, on the other hand, have given us nothing. Therefore, you have no reason to be in Rome. No temporal power may attack these walls." The Pope raised his arms, encompassing all the land before him.

"Lest you discount my words, through your own ignorance or your misguided ambition, take heed, Desiderius. March on Rome, harm a hair of anyone's head....and I shall excommunicate you." Complete silence spread across the court-yard. Even the pigeons ceased cooing.

"Not only you," the Pope continued. "I shall excommuni-cate anyone in your legions. You will all be forbidden to wor-ship God, unwelcome in any house of worship, denied partici-pation in the Eucharist, refused the celebration of the sacra-ments. Think well on your actions. You do endanger your immortal soul and those of all who follow you."

Soldiers in the front ranks of the army moved restlessly, startled by the Pope's pronouncement, but uncertain to whom they could speak. The military commanders at the head of their columns rushed to Desiderius' side, each one trying a dif-ferent argument, all frantic to give their opinion. Before a command could be given, the Pope's words spread among the rank and file of soldiers. Lines began to waver. Formations roiled, moving one way and, then, another. The infantry began a backward march away from the church. Commanders yelled for their men to stand firm. As they called, the army lines shuddered. Men began walking away. Commanders, their eyes searching for their own legions, turned from Desiderius and followed their troops out. Desiderius watched it all with-out expression. His dulled eyes stared into those of the Pope. Finally, after moments of tense silence, he gave an affirmative nod.

"As you suggest," Desiderius said, "I am with-drawing my army." He waved for his commanders to retreat. "The threat of excommunication has saved you this day, Hadrian. It will not work a second time. I vow to you." Then, the Lombard King turned from the Pope, saluted his departing army, and mounted his horse. The Lombard commanders did not hesitate, nor did they linger. They rolled their blankets, doused their fires, gathered their weapons and army hangers-on, and turned toward home.

Charlemagne celebrated with Pope Adrian, complimenting him on his creative threat. The men laughed, considered themselves lucky, and bid each other a fond 'adieu.' The Frankish army turned north as well, pushing Desiderius from the rear, thankful that a battle, inevitable still, was as yet still in the future.

As King Charlemagne turned almost directly northward toward Frankland, Roland—Charlemagne's most beloved Peer--turned northeast, still searching for men to swell the army's size. He called at the manors of those who supported Charlemagne. Many of these second and third sons will join us, Roland thought. *Their father's manors are not large enough to support them; most have no lands or wealth of their own. But serving with King Charlemagne will give them hope of land, of an improvement in their circumstances. Everyone will win in the end, especially the King.* He shook his head, well aware many of the young men would be lost to battle, never able to demand land payment. Available or not, land would make no difference to them. His thoughts turned to land and peace and the future, to the dreams of the King.

Returning from Himiltrude's manor, Adelchis—still unaware of his father's disastrous march on Rome--turned toward

Pavia. His spy mission, both east and west, had yielded important information. None of it would his father welcome, though. Of that, he was certain. King Charlemagne's forces were growing larger every day. The King's efforts to deflect or prevent the Saxon's incursions into Frankland were gaining him support from all the people. They had nothing but praise of the king. Adelchis stopped in villages and small settlings as he journeyed back toward Lombard. Here, as in the towns, everyone talked of the Saxon's forays, of the threat of constant invasions. King Charlemagne, they bragged happily, seemed to be everywhere at once.

"It's a shame," one old man said to Adelchis. "I hate to see the men soldiering all year. We need their hands here to plant and, then, to gather the harvest. But every man knows; peace comes at a price. All able-bodied men from here go to fight with King Charlemagne. He has a huge army. It spreads for miles. We saw him pass...oh, more than a fortnight ago. 'Tis early in the season for battle, but with these Saxons about....well, the King cannot be too careful, you see." Soldiers patrolled on the road, questioning Adelchis on his destination. He grew increasingly troubled. Soldiers, nobles, even peasants were moving—all hoping to meet the King and join his troops.

I must leave the road," Adelchis muttered, "and travel cross-country, avoid all the messengers I can. With such efforts to obtain more soldiers, Charlemagne may decide to call me to court, to get me out of Lombardy. Not that I would mind," Adelchis muttered to himself. *I daresay Father has allowed no Lombard nobles to answer the King's request for troops.* Seeing his rich clothing, soldiers on the road assumed Adelchis was traveling from the Frankish court, an assumption he did not try to correct. Soldier after soldier asked him if he knew the King's marching route, where a man might join his army. Adelchis, surprised at the increasing number of soldiers, was concerned. His Father would not take kindly to men wandering through Lombardy, searching for King Charlemagne's troops.

"Father will say this call for soldiers is short-sighted and belligerent," Adelchis murmured. He changed his fur-bordered mantle for a gray, nondescript one and decided to ride in the forest. He stopped beside a stream for his horse to drink and, then, rode toward the thick trees which banked the road on both sides. Although many of the trees were leafless, the thick forests of oak, birch, and maple were almost impossible to penetrate. The land was covered with trees for many leagues. All manner of wild beasts—men and animals alike—sheltered within those vast stretches. Adelchis rode slowly, letting his horse pick its way through the thick underbrush. His thoughts returned to the last man he had met on the road.

"The commanders say King Charlemagne's army will be fighting in six weeks." The strapping fellow told Adelchis. "It's eary for the battle season;" he declared, "but profitable for me. I'll transport foodstuffs to the camp--all the fruit, wheat, and vegetables I can buy. If the army marches long, everyone will need food. The longer the fighting season, the more money I'll make." He smiled. "As the days go by, the coin will fill my purse. I look to make my fortune." Taking Adelchis' silence for judgment, the man defended himself.

"I'll put coin by...for my wife and little ones. Then, in the last days of summer, I'll join the army. No one can question my allegiance then. Let the King march. I'll be just behind him!" Adelchis shook his head, wondering if the battle season would be anything like this man predicted. Some leagues farther, the road began slanting upward as Adelchis crested a hill. His mouth dropped as he gazed on the ocean of tents in the valley below. He looked for the highest knoll and, yes, saw

King Charlemagne's banners waving.

"My God!" Adelchis said aloud. "What is the King's army doing here? What is he about?" Fear rose in his throat. He was not a day's march from Pavia and home. "The King's army is camping in father's shadow!" Adelchis looked about carefully. I went to Himli's manor by the northern road, he thought. *Although I did not pass this way, I know there was no camp here two weeks ago. But here Charlemagne is, on the southern approach! I wonder how long he has been camped.*

Adelchis sat his horse, looking closely at the camp. His eyes roamed up and down the rows of tents, around the many campfires. The camp, while it did not seem newly pitched, did not have the look of a lenthy stay. The tents closest to him were stained with mud and water. But grass grew between the tents and ruts were not yet dug into the earth. Crusted mud lined the ruts made by wagon and horsehooves alike and bits of ice clung to the edges of the streams. But the grass was lush and brilliant green in the open spots within the trees. Adelchis reined his horse, the better to think. He felt well-hidden in the trees. As he turned his mount, two soldiers appeared across the road from him. Adelchis shrank back a little, anxious not to be seen.

"When do we move out?" A dark haired soldier turned to his companion. "I hoped to go home after this march to Rome. A man cannot march all year. There's necessary work to be done in my settling. But the nobles from Lyons say we're to begin a siege. I thought we were marching through the realm, hunting Saxons," he said. "Have you heard?" He turned to the horseman by his side.

"I know nothing. Mayhap, since we didn't fight in Rome, there's been a change in the King's plans. We all prepared for the worse there." He added. "But all was solved without battle.

Who knows what the King will do next? It's early for battle this season but late to send us home." He shrugged at his friend. "I just pray my village got the seeds in the soil. Most of the men are here, waiting for the King's orders. We won't get home for months now." His companion nodded.

"King Charlemagne seems as relieved as us at not fighting the King of Lombardy. But, wasn't he prepared for that? Rumors in the camp said the King grew tired of Desiderius' taunts. As for me, " he shook his head slowly, "I trust no king. They battle for their own reasons...and use the rest of us as their arms. Nay, this camp has a bad feel to it. Let's fight and be done with it, I say."

"Don't be so anxious," the other replied. "Are you in a hurry to die? I'd rather sit here and enjoy the sun than cut off another's head. Waiting, I agree, is wearisome but not nearly as bad as dying. Why a siege? Is that what you heard?" The other man nodded. "Why not fight?" The first man wondered. "We have strength, arms, fine catapults, infantry and cavalry. Why are we here, if we do not come to battle?"

"I over-heard the commanders last night. One of them, Ganelon, he said King Charlemagne lets his anger drive him." The first soldier responded. "Why else do we march like hell, like driven cattle, and then sit?" He gazed forlornly at the camp. "Surely we move out soon."

"Come," the other soldier motioned, "let's patrol the perimeter. I guess you're right, Tardt. Any duty is better than dying." The soldiers rode off, slowly increasing the pace of their horses, heading to the northern side of the large army camp. Adelchis stayed hidden in the trees. He was almost home. Pavia was just across the next small hill. And here camped the Frankish army. He looked back over his shoulder, re-affirming it was King Charlemagne's banner that flew.

"No doubt about it," he muttered. "King Charlemagne is going to attack Father or he comes to examine the fortifications these fools said they would strengthen. Would he make this marge to investigate such a claim?" Adelchis wanted to feel relief; but he did not.

"And what is this about Rome? Charlemagne was in Rome? He returns from a confrontation with my father in Rome? This is very peculiar. I do not understand." Adelchis reconnitored the area around him, determined to slip by the soldiers without being seen. His father and the King may not have battled yet, but this camp was a testament to increasing strain between them. "If Charlemagne was in Rome, perhaps Father will use this time time to consider the future more carefully." Adelchis shook his head sadly. "I believe father incapable of coherent thought about King Charlemagne. He just wants him dead, completely destroyed, if possible." His furrowed brow reflected his concern and his confusion. "Why would Charlemagne have gone to Rome?" He asked himself over and over.

Sometimes riding and sometimes leading his horse, Adelchis slowly made his way to the cave, hoping to rendezvous with his fellow spies. They did not disappoint him. Three of them — Gus, Hans, and Harry — were back and hunted to feed their fellow spies. They readily offered him venison and acorn bread which Adelchis gratefully accepted. He thought so much about Himiltrude that he cooked very little on his journey back home. As he ate, his friends recounted the information and rumors they gathered. They knew more of the army's movements than he guessed.

"The Frankish army pitched their tents here on the way

back from the holy city." Gus reported.

"Your father left to besiege Rome, Adelchis," Harry said, not looking into Adelchis' face. "He must have marched soon after we left. The Pope, uneasy by King Desiderius' continuous efforts to direct him and to control Rome, begged King Charlemagne to come to Rome and protect the Church. Of course, the King marched the day after he received Hadrian's missive." Adelchis listened in wide-eyed horror.

"What does my father think?" He asked, not expecting an answer. "He's not strong enough to hold Rome, even were the gods with him to overwhelm it in the first place. Surely, he can see the Pope's dependence, even his cultivation of King Charlemagne. The King loses his reason! Besieging Rome…it makes no sense!" His companions nodded, regretful they were the ones to describe King Desiderius' behavior to his only son.

"Charlemagne's army camped here four days ago. They're settled in, it seems," Hans reported."Your father predicted Charlemagne would not attack. So far, he's right. But we believe—Gus, Harry, and me—the attack will come soon. King Charlemagne will not hold back much longer. It will be a rout, Adelchis! The Lombardy army has less than one-third of the soldiers Charlemagne commands. We cannot hope to withstand his army; the numbers make it impossible." He sighed, giving Adelchis time to respond. Adelchis said nothing.

"I hope your father is well-prepared to explain, Adelchis…explain the strengthening of the fortifications. The King is likely to see such behavior as provocative, take it amiss, I mean," Harry added, almost as an aside.

"Our spying reports will be of no use now," Adelchis said, almost laughing at the absurdity of it all. "We shall each do as we must. I will return to my father's court. I surely do not ask that of you. In fact, I do not recommend it," he assured his friends. "My story is that I have not seen you, any of you." He looked into the eyes of each of his companions. "Sneak away in the dark. Make a new life for yourselves…somewhere beyond Lombardy. Pretend you've never heard of it. Mayhap, you should flee to the Anglo isle. Take your lives and live, I beg you." He grasped each man around the shoulders and wished them 'Godspeed.' "Guard one another and take care." Adelchis called out as the three spies mounted their horses. Adelchis climbed into his saddle, pointing his horse's nose back into the trees. He rode slowly for home, skirting the edges of the Frankish camp. He expected to die with his family. He doubted King Charlemagne would show mercy to them.

Ever after, Adelchis regretted not turning his own head away from his father's foolishness. How easily he might turn back toward the route he followed here. But he did not. He sneaked into Pavia through a meandering, over-grown hunting path he knew and presented himself to his father.

As it turned out, King Desiderius had no occasion to explain his march on Rome to his son. Adelchis arrived at a court filled with bombastic commanders, all giving their military arguments to his father. Now that battle was at hand, Desiderius seemed more muddled than able, more likely to be influenced by his companions than to follow his own plans for battle. Adelchis delivered the ill news of Charlemagne's camp to his father and the nobles. Desiderius laughed uproariously, boasting of the strength of the Lombard army.

"I did look a fool in Rome," Desiderius admitted. "But here, in my own land, the great King Charlemagne shall feel Lombard's wrath."

"You will not last a week." Adelchis gave his unsolicited advice. "Your army is one-third the size of his, not well-equipped, and led by less than courageous commanders. Prepare to die, Father, or to live in exile, if the King is merciful. Charlemagne may see banishment in a monastery as fitting tribute to your foolishness."

"Out! Get out of my sight!" Desiderius screamed at Adelchis. "You are a coward, unable to see the glory in fighting!"

"And, you Father, are unable to see the shame in straining beyond yourself, in being cowed into a hopeless situation. You do sacrifice us all." Adelchis said as he left the chamber.

Adelchis found a country monk to take his mother to a near-by abbey. Bidding her farewell, he joined his father's army in a defensible location among the ancient fortifications in the Susa Valley. Although the Lombard soldiers re-inforced the fortress, just as Desiderius suggested, Adelchis knew the forts would thwart Charlemagne's army only a short time.

His father, as usual, ignored his warnings. Desiderius, feeling confident and safe, hunkered down, waiting for Charlemagne to march into the lower Susa Valley and be entrapped. Instead, Charlemagne marched his army to Giaveno, as if leaving. Later, he turned back to Avigliana, coming in behind the Lombard army. Unwilling for his army to be massacred, Desiderius retreated to Pavia, hoping to be safe behind its walls. Charlemagne laid siege immediately, confident of its outcome. In the early days of the siege, Desiderius summoned Adelchis.

"Come," Desiderius said to Adelchis, as he pointed to a beautiful stallion. "Sneak out as you came in, my son. Ride this mount to Verona. Take refuge in a nunnery or a monastery. It makes no difference. The 'holy' Charlemagne will not dare harm you. It is his calling to be 'merciful,' as he deems it." Desiderius' face was calm, untroubled. He seemed to consider Charlemagne's army an irritant, rather than his likely destruction. "When it's safe, journey to Constaninople. Recount our defeat to the nobility there. They know you are my legitimate heir and will aid you in conquering the Frankish imposter! Go, go! There is no time to lose!"

"Won't you come, Father?" Adelchis asked. "My mother is safe, of a certainty. But you, you cannot stay here. Pavia is not strong enough to withstand a long siege. Charlemagne may sit outside the walls for months. You cannot know what may come!" He paused. "Perhaps King Charlemagne will be merciful..."

"Merciful?" screamed King Desiderius. "I spit on his mercy. Nay, nay; you must go! Your mother has, often, wished for a nunnery. She will be safe there. But you, you must flee! Go quickly. Do not hesitate and do not look back! Go!" Desiderius begged his son. "Trust me; you must go. This scout will get you past the Franks. Be still and do as I say. You must; I am your father and your king. Go!" He grabbed Adelchis' arm, pressing it—reluctant to let him go but knowing he could not remain. "Our friends in Constaninople are waiting, Adelchis," Desiderius insisted. "Eventually, they will lead a military expedition against Charlemagne and reclaim Lombard for you. If I send word, leave Verona and go to Constantinople. Begin recruiting a force to engage the King. Go now! Flee, my son!" Adelchis escaped the way he returned, creeping along old game trails through the forest.

Charlemagne's siege of Pavia lasted more than a year. The following June, in 774, Desiderius surrendered. By then, he was totally without resources. As the days and weeks went by, untold numbers of his men disappeared in the great forests. Charlemagne took Desiderius captive and banished him to the monastery at Corbie from which he never emerged. Adelchis, alerted to the imminent fall of Pavia, fled Verona to Constaninople and the Byzantine empire.

As Adelchis predicted, King Charlemagne appropriated Lombardy into the Frankish realm, though he governed it separately. Adelchis accepted the protection of the Byzantium nobles and the Church, secure in the knowledge that Charlemagne had the Lombard kingdom and did not wish his life. "

"At this moment, mayhap for years to come," Adelchis mused, "my life is all I have."

Chapter Eight

It was weeks before Himli and her manor heard about the siege of Pavia. She wondered and worried over Adelchis' silence. When she saw the courier riding toward her manor, she was positive this was a message from Adelchis at last. But such was not the case. The courier, come from Abbot Fulrad, made a twice-yearly ride, carrying greetings and concern from the Abbot and inquiring into Himli's and Pippin's health. On the parchment, the Abbot added a postscript, informing Himli of the siege of Pavia and the surrender of Desiderius. Himli could scarcely reply to the Abbot's missive, so worried was she about Adelchis. And, of a certainty, she could ask nothing about the Prince or his destiny.

"Dear God, dear God!" Himli cried. "Never did I imagine such a day as this. Charlemagne always tried to talk and compromise with Desiderius. Who would think they would battle? And that such a confrontation would ever affect me directly?" She wept in the quiet of her room at night, careful not to wake Pippin who would never understand the situation.

The heat of the late summer days ended; the beautiful color in the massive forests surprised. Its warmth and richness were a constrast to the cold fear in Himiltrude's heart. The winter months were colder still with far too many days of worry and despair. Finally, when the whole world seemed wreathed in snow, with no hope of sunshine, spring came to them. Its promise of renewal dulled Himli's fear into an ache which never left her heart. She kept hope alive in not having heard of Adelchis' death. Surely had he died, an internment would be announced.

One morning in late March, Pippin raced into the cook room.

"A missive, Moma, a missive!" He cried. "I not read it." In the evenings he begged Himli to help him read and grinned broadly when she asked him to 'read' a picture to her. Himli took the missive from his hand. He ran immediately out the door. Himli's heart dropped to her stomach. It was Adelchis' seal! And her name written on the front was in his hand!

"I'll be in the herb garden," she said to the cook. Himli grabbed her basket and rushed to the garden. The day before, she planted basil and oregano, rosemary and thyme, dreaming of the day she could smell their scents. She took refuge there now as she opened the parchment. Himli did not even read the words. She scanned the letter for the code she and Adelchis created and found his message:

'I am safe. Do not worry. I love you more than ever. When I can journey from Constaninople, I will send word. All my love.'

Himiltrude wrapped her arms around herself in relief.

"He's not dead," she kept repeating under her breath. "He's

not dead. Thank you, God. Adelchis is not dead." But as the days turned into yet more weeks, it sometimes seemed he was.

In any case, Himli reminded herself, Adelchis is not here with me and is unlikely to be for a very long time. But, when she thought of it--of his love for her and Pippin and her love for him--she could comfort herself. *Adelchis is just so easy to love!* She smiled, thinking of the wondrous days she, Adelchis, and Pippin spent with Jaston. She smiled broadly as Pippin skipped up the path to her.

"M-o-m-a!" He sometimes seemed to call her name, just for the pleasure of speaking it. "...Der you are!" He ran into her arms, burying his face under her chin. Reaching up, he patted her cheek. "You happy, Moma? I see you smile!" He smiled widely at her, as if encouraging her to grin even more.

"Aye, I'm happy, just to see my boy." Himli exclaimed. "But I was thinking of a special treat!" She raised her eyebrows and deliberately widened her eyes, looking into Pippin's face. He went perfectly still, holding his breath.

"What, Moma, what?" he demanded.

"I was thinking that it's time for us to visit Jaston again. Would you like that?" she asked. She could not have been better rewarded. Pippin's face brightened like a flower.

"He'll show me animals!" He screeched. "Jaston be happy to see me, to see us," he corrected as he ran in circles around Himli. He gave a small 'aye,' jumping up and down in excitement. "We go now, Moma?" He asked, already emptying his neck pouch to investigate the items he stored there. "I take trey-sur for Jaston."

"Nay, not now, dear boy," Himli laughed. "I think we should go after we sleep, after we break our fast. Tell you what we'll do." Pepin's obvious delight energized her. "We'll pack cheese, and tarts to break our fast on the way...and hike up to spend the night at Jaston's. Would you like that?"

"Wheeee!" Pippin shouted. "I miss Jaston. We go early!" Then, he stopped dead still, gazing at Himli. "Moma?" Seeing Himli nod, the lad reached for her hand. "Moma, Adel-chus come?"

"No, Pippin." Himli swallowed hard. "Adelchis will not be there this time." She saw his face fall, his left foot rubbing the dirt underfoot. "But Jaston, you and I will remember our good times with Adelchis. Remember how much you and Jaston ate after the animal visit?" And she laughed. She mustn't let Pippin be saddened by Adelchis' absence. "We all will miss Adelchis, but we will have a good time. You can be certain."

"Aye," Pippin agreed softly. "I miss him…I miss Adel-chus."

Himli and Pippin broke their fast in the cook room with Captain Mortimer. Himli told the captain that she and Pippin were going to check on Jaston, to determine when he planned to come to the manor to provide their annual spring tonic.

"Settlings all over this valley will expect Jaston to come," she said. "And he may come to us late. I have not been sleeping well, Captain," she admitted. "Mayhap, Pippin and I would both benefit from Jaston's spring tonic!" The Captain laughed; and then, his eyes became serious.

"Please, Mistress," he begged. "Pippin is energetic enough as it is. He can outrun and outplay all of us, except for the puppies. You take the tonic and ask Jaston to save Pippin's for next year." At the mention of 'puppies,' Pippin raced out of the cook room, heading for the stables and the latest litter. Captain Mortimer brushed the dirt off his trousers. He was digging holes for Himli to set out additional lavender bushes which she rooted in the stables.

"Let me go rescue the puppies, Mistress Himli," he said. "Pippin will have them worn to a nub in just a few minutes." Chuckling to himself, he walked toward the stables. Himli watched until he rounded the stable wall. Then, she rose to enter the manor and gather clothes for their overnight visit.

"Oh, Adelchis," she murmured. "If you only knew how much you're loved." She tucked one of his old shirts into the bag, all the better to remember him where they shared so much.

Himli and Pippin returned from their visit to the work of spring. Not needed in the fields, Himli concentrated her efforts on cleaning out stables and barns. Fortified with Jaston's 'tonic,' Himli seemed to blossom in tandem with the roses, sunflowers, and sweet peas in her garden. For a brief season, they could enjoy the rain which fed the crops, warm and nurturing—not the cold downpours of the autumn ahead.

Pippin watched a new clutch of eggs anxiously, befriending the mother hen as he offered more worms than she could eat.

"Moma, Moma," he called. Running to Himli, he pulled her arm. "Come see! Come see! We have a baby calf--a girl! Captain Mortimer told me so!" Himli hurried to see the new baby calf, delighted by her beautiful face. As she watched the calf nurse, Jakob reported there had been another birth in the early morning.

"Mistress," he greeted her. "We have a new male calf as well. He arrived just as the sun came up. He is strong and hungry but not as pretty as this little one!" Jakob smiled brightly. The more animals he could count, the more prosperous he considered the manor. Pippin laughed with delight as a mother hen led her baby chicks around the horse trough. There were nine yellow fluffs, following her and cheeping, each in it own way. The hen ruffled up her feathers. But hearing Pippin's voice, she calmed down right away. She watched him intently but stood still as he tried to pat her little chicks. Each side of the yard seemed to be full of new life: baby ducklings rushing to the pond; new-born lambs frolicking in the field; and one shiny, black colt hiding behind its mother's legs. Himli and Jakob congratulated each other on the new arrivals, calculating the extra oats they would need to harvest to keep all the animals through the upcoming winter.

"We always plant a little extra, Mistress," Jakob affirmed. "We'll just add to that, to provide for these babies. The berry nubs on the bushes are already heavy. I think the winter promises to be long. I'll sow extra seeds of anything else we plant," he promised.

"Good plan, Jakob," Himli agreed, turning to face him. "When those two mares died last winter, I did lose hope. And then, the wolves got the spring colt." She paused. "Those losses overwhelmed me and smothered my spirit. But, if we are cautious and careful with these new younglings, mayhap we will have them all next year this time."

"Aye, Mistress," Jakob agreed. "We must protect them more as they grow and wander. No excuse to lose stock after we get them through the first few months!" He paused, remembering something. "Hotford's son, he be nine years old, wants to groom the colts. Should we offer a job to him, do you think?"

"Of a certainty." Himli responded. "Let him learn, hone his skills with them. If he stays close round them, they will be safer." Jakob nodded in agreement, giving his basket to Pippin as they went to gather eggs from the coops.

As crops developed and animal babies grew, the cook and his assistants began preparations for preserving as much food as possible. The children spread fruit in the sun to dry, rubbed dried corn-kernels off the ears, and marked the walnut and pecan trees which produced the greatest number of nuts. The women of the manor sat late in the cookroom carding wool and, later, stitching new tunics. Everyone told Jakob the location of downed trees so the logs might be added to the woodpiles growing large beside the stable.

Himli and Jakob looked up as they heard the hooves of a rider. Himli shaded her eyes, trying to determine if more than one horse approached. The man slowed, directing his horse toward the stables. As he drew near, Himli's intake of breath caught Jakob's attention.

"But, no wonder!" he whispered under his breath. "Even I can see! The man would take any woman's breath away...so handsome does he look! Huh! I wonder what he does to merit such favor from God...or what will be asked of him!" Jakob sent Pippin to the chicken coops, walking toward the man. He nodded to the rider.

"Good morrow to you. May I ask your business on our road, Sir?"

The rider dismounted, smiled widely at Jakob and replied.

"Good morrow to you! And what a beautiful day this is! I would that we see this kind of day from now til Yuletide!" He laughed. "Or, at the least, impress it in our memory for later reflection." He turned a bit and noticed Himli walking toward them. "Mother of God, what a stunning woman!" He spoke under his breath. Jakob was surprised. The men he knew seldom made such an open comment about a woman. At least, Captain Mortimer and his men would never say such a thing...and neither would the manor's workers.

How dare he speak so of my Lady! Jakob growled to himself. And he opened his mouth to reprimand the rider. He looked over at Himli, with newly aware eyes, and closed his mouth. This man speaks true, Jakob realized. *She is beautiful, just glowing with health and surety.*

"One moment," Jacob announced, as the man turned toward Himiltrude. "I still wait, Sir, for you to state your business." The rider, startled by Jakob's words, turned his eyes back to the farmer.

"Aye, of a certainty," he answered. "I am Count Wibod, from King Charlemagne's court. I am traveling, seeking small-boned but wiry ponies to breed with the Arabian stallions which the King so loves!" He laughed. "We want a lithe, spirited horse with much endurance," he explained. His eyes moved back to Himli who paused to speak to Marsta. "Who is that exquisite creature?" He asked, turning back to Jakob.

Jakob scowled at the man. "You are in the court, Sir?" He asked caustically. "I cannot believe you do not recognize Charlemagne's first Queen, Queen Himlitrude—the King's first wife." Jakob was well-rewarded for his response. Count Wibod stared openly at Jakob.

"Queen Himiltrude...truly?" He asked. "I have been at court but this half-year, Sir. I did not know the lady...more's the pity." He rubbed his chin. The frown between his eyes deepened. "He banished this one? ...what a fool!" Seeing Jakob's reddened face, the Count realized his discourtesy. "I pray you; pretend you did not hear. I am too free with my opinions. I have mis-spoken!" The Count paused, his hand moving to rub his neck. "I cannot understand the mind of a king."

"We have no horses of interest to you here, Sir," Jakob replied. "We have no skill in the breeding. We have three plow-horses and three for riding. Nay, there are no horse breeders near-by. I have heard of one in the valley beyond this one, but have never seen his animals." Jakob looked at the Count. The more he saw, the less he approved. "There is nothing for you here." He spoke firmly.

Behind his back, Jakob moved his hand, motioning Himli back. He saw Marsta hesitate, then take Himli's hand and draw her to the house. At that, Count Wilrod nodded and bade Jakob farewell. Jakob turned back toward the stables. As his hand pulled the door, the Count rode up beside him.

"Excuse this question, good man," the Count began. "Do you know…. Is there anyone… I mean to say… does the lady seek another marriage?" Jakob's mouth dropped open. His eyes bored into the man's face. His face flushed with anger.

"Surely," Jakob enunciated clearly, "you do jest! The King would never countenance another. The lady is alone, if she wish it or not, Sir." Jakob glared at the Count, daring him to say another word.

"I see," the Count responded, shaking his head with regret. "Good morrow to you." And he rode away.

Jakob worried much about this count and his open interest in Himiltrude. And, then, he found an even greater worry. If he finds my lady so beautiful, Jakob thought, how many more men, discovering her, will try to make her their own? Jakob walked slowly to the stables, seeing Pippin searching the new spring grass for eggs.

"How many eggs did you find, lad?" he asked. Pippin moved back a tuft of grass and held up three fingers. Then, he gave a screech.

"Four! Four!" he cried as he proudly displayed another one to Jakob. The little boy actually patted the hen's back as he slid the egg out from under her. "How many chicks will Princess have, Sir Jakob?" the child asked. As spring arrived, Jakob had finally gotten used to the 'Sir.' Months ago, Himli told Pippin he should answer Jakob with an 'aye, sir.' The child begun putting 'Sir' in front of everyone's name, even the young girl Gerta. Everyone laughs happily when he does it, Jakob thought, so I guess this is the "Sir Manor" of Frankland. He could not bear to hurt the lad's feelings so he ignored the title.

"How many chicks?" Jakob asked. "Oh, you can never be sure, Pippin. We'll let Princess have a clutch of chicks soon, and Queenie and Sweetie as well. We shall be over-run with chicks." Jakob felt ridiculous. Imagine! ... naming the hens, he thought. But, truth was, Pippin had a name for every creature he saw.

"Ladies like babies." The lad declared. "Princess, Queenie, Sweetie—all need babies, babies to love."He smiled up at Jakob. "I not a baby any more," he added solemnly. "But ladies love me!" He laughed happily. Then, he sobered and looked into Jakob's face. "You love Pippin, too! And so does Capt'n Mortimer, Jaston...and Adelchis! Ladies and menses love me!"

"Of a certainty, that's true!" Jabob agreed. "All of us love you, dear boy!" All of a sudden, Jakob rolled that realization around in his mind. Of a certainty, he thought, Adelchis loves Pippin. He remembered seeing Adelchis' face softening when he picked the boy up, smiling widely as Pippin gave him a kiss, beckoning Pippin to sit on his lap. He does love the lad, Jakob thought, as he loves his mother. Jakob eased himself to the ground, leaning his back against the stable wall. Aye, he thought to himself. *Adelchis loves Himli and she loves him. I have no doubt of it.* Pippin came to sit close beside Jakob, turning his eggs around in their basket.

"Are you resting, Sir Jakob?" the child asked.

"Aye," Jakob replied, "resting before we go to break our fast. What say you to sharing your eggs with me?" At Pippin's enthusiastic agreement, Jakob stood, put his hand on the boy's shoulder and walked toward the cook room.

"Eggs good, Sir Jakob!" Pippin shouted. "Yummy! Yummy! Let's hurry!"

Talk at the cook table was about the news brought by the courier last week. Marsta fed the man well, flirting with him between refilling his flagon. As a result, he lingered over his meals, sharing any court talk or rumor he could remember. The King's successful conquest of Lombardy, without the loss of a single soldier, proved amazing to the courier.

"The King, he's a God-fearing man," the courier continued. "He did not even behead the Lombard king, though he did deserve it! Nay, King Charlemagne just banished him to a monastery. Many nobles called for his death. The King said he was being merciful, that God the Father demanded it!" He glanced around the table. "He is a godly king." The courier told them all.

"And what of King Desiderius' family?" Jakob asked. "If the King did not kill the usurper, surely he spared the family as well." Jakob held his breath, waiting for the man's reply.

"It is said the Lombard Queen fled well before the siege, Sire," the courier responded, "took refuge in a nunnery. The princesses, they're both married, you 'member? King Charlemagne has no quarrel with them. Neither of them was in Lombardy anyway."

"What about the Prince, Prince Adelchis, I mean?" Jakob pressed further. "He seemed a fine man...when I met him there at the King's court some years ago." Jakob embellished his sentence.

The courier's brow wrinkled. "Aye," he admitted, "he did escape. Some say Desiderius' bargained for his freedom, that the King sent him to a monastery, too. But others say he escaped and fled. Who knows? I suspect that if King Charlemagne wants him, he'll turn up. The King, he does make his dreams come true." The courier finished with a self-satisfied smile.

"Mayhap, mayhap," Jakob answered, doing his best to be noncommittal. He glanced at Himli. She was staring steadily at her porridge bowl. No one but Jakob saw the trembling in her hand. Pippin stirred on his bench, looking with fear at the courier. Himli squeezed his shoulder and slowly shook her head. He settled immediately, sidling closer to his mother. She whispered in his ear. Jakob saw the frown ease from his face; the boy nodded. Well, then, Jakob thought. *For now, all is well. Some word has come from Adelchis. Thank God!* Himli looked across the table and saw Jakob observe her reassurance to Pippin. She smiled and nodded.

"Pippin is anxious for everyone to know that we have two new colts." Himli announced as she beamed at those seated around the table. "...one born last night and one very early this morn. I am sure he will introduce you to them as soon as you like." She squeezed her son who wiggled in his excitement.

"Soon as you cum to see 'em," Pippin promised. Himli's comment served to move the conversation away from the King's conquest and back to the concerns of the manor. All finished their morning meal and left for their separate duties.

Late that same afternoon, Himli and Jakob mounted their horses. They, along with Pippin, rode to search for an additional plot of land. Jakob wanted to plant more wheat. Oats yielded the best harvest. But he found the animals ate more consistently when given both oats and wheat in the cold, winter months. Last week, he stumbled upon an open area within the forest which might yield well. He wanted Himlitrude to see the field and tell him if it were too far from the manor to cultivate. Pippin scrambled up in front of Jacob, preferring to ride double than to sit on the slow, plow horse which was his usual mount. Jacob planned to take his field hands to this plot of land and have them break a trail through the trees.

"It does seem good soil, Jakob," Himli observed as she knelt to dig into the earth. "This will be a goodly amount of work, though. The grass cover is thick; its roots go deep."

"Aye," agreed Jakob, "but I do hope that means the soil is richer, Mistress, richer to support such grass. Mayhap, the wheat stalk will yield more than normal," he added.

"If we have the seeds, Jakob," Himli answered, "let's try it. Just hope the grass does not take over, grow over our plantings, I mean." she clarified.

"We will try to keep the plants weed-free, my Lady," Jakob answered. "That young boy, the one who curries the horses, he does love to pull weeds!" Jakob laughed. "Though this is harder work, mayhap his energy can be used here!"

"If he does such work, Jakob," Himli responded, "give him an extra bag of wheat for his mother's house. He will earn it, pulling this grass!" Himli pointed to Pippin who was at the edge of the field, examining the blackberry bushes which were blooming in profusion.

"Pippin's looking for the sweet things," she observed. "Wheat and blackberries together, now that's a hopeful grow- ing!" She smiled at Jakob.

"All substance has some sweetness, my Lady," Jakob re- sponded, barely realizing his words. "It is good, if this be a goal the lad seeks." Himli looked at Jakob in surprise.

"Jakob!" she exclaimed. "You remind me of the learned men in the King's court. They often spoke in just this manner." She sighed. "That was the amazing thing about King Charlemagne, Jakob. He could speak of battles, and soldiers, and bushels of wheat. But he could, also, quote words which were like a bird's melody, smooth and pleasing to the ear." She shook her head. "Charlemagne could best anyone with his words. King Pippin, on the other hand, seldom said anything, though he did love to hear the arguments. He was a dear, loving man." Her voice sof- tened.

"Was he a good man, Mistress?" Jakob asked, flattered that Himli was disclosing her past to him. "I came to Frankland just as the illness took the King's life, though he did take a battle wound, too. I never knew much about his ruling."

"He was a good man, Jakob," Himli confirmed. "He was very protective of the young, of the vulnerable. Ha! He asked me if I were really so foolish as to want to marry his son! Then, I hardly knew his meaning; but, now, I understand too much, mayhap."

Jakob sighed. He hardly knew the response he should make. I must sympathize but not discourage her spirit, he thought to himself.

"My lady, looking back is always clearer than the living of a thing. The living, though," he continued, "is the important one. In the living is the hope, the courage, and the love." He paused as Himli's eyes met his. "Only in strengthening that hope and courage may we love as we should." Jakob paused, searching to explain his meaning. "Not a trite love, my Lady, a love for doing, for understanding, for growing--not just a love of people." Himli smiled at Jakob softly. She reached out to touch his hand.

"Why, Jakob, you are a philosopher. The King would greatly value your words. And, though I cannot appreciate them as he would, I do thank you, for your good thoughts, for your good heart. I thank you daily for your care of Pippin, even though I do not say it to you near enough. You are a constant source of strength and, aye, of love for him."

"You are my responsibility," Jakob replied, "you and the lad. It is my blessing...that I do like you." He saw Himli's brief smile. "...that I do love you. And you are blessed: there are so many others who do the same. The entire manor is your garden, my Lady. Our colors and good scents, if we can claim them, come from you!" Jakob surprised even himself. He never found such words before...and to speak them so easily to this lady! He laughed self-consciously. Himli nodded.

"This talk of love, all the different kinds, is startling, Jakob," she answered, equally unsure of where this would go. "I have never spoken thus, not with anyone. I have wanted to say these things, I suppose, but I was never sure..."

"...if the other person would understand?" Jakob asked. At Himli's slight nod, he replied. "It is good, don't you think, to say the words, my Lady? So often we do not confirm all we feel. That's a mistake. How can feelings be improved if no one speaks of them? Ha!" He caught himself. "Mayhap, I do speak too much!" He sat quietly, trying to recapture their conversation.

"Nay," Himli objected. "This has been a true gift! I will

count this talk of ours as one of the most important of my life! We must be honest with each other, Jacob...if only because so many lives rest in our hands." She smiled to herself and nodded. "I must admit something to you, because we speak of love. This must remain a secret, Jakob, to protect us all." Himli shifted, clarifying her thoughts in the process.

"I know," Jakob interrupted, trying to put her at ease. "I know you and Adelchis are...are lovers. I figured it out for myself. It *is* a good thing, Mistress, a good thing...for you and your little lad. And, I suspect, more than a good thing for the Prince." Jakob patted her hand.

"Let's go see about Pippin. I fear he may try those green blackberries!" He laughed as Himli hugged his neck and gathered her reins. Jakob did not see Himli's eyes fill with tears as she thought about his words. Neither could he know the comfort they gave her. But he felt her thankfulness every time she looked into his face.

Pippin was not eating green blackberries. He was attempting, gently, to separate a skunk kit from its mother. Jakob assured him this would not be positive in the coming months.

"You have no way to protect him from other people, Pippin," Jakob said. "Some of the boys at the manor and, of a certainty, those in town, would hurt or, even, kill this skunk." Pippin's face turned pale; he looked at Jakob in horror. "It's just the way of things, lad," Jakob told him. "Some people don't think. They hunt and kill. They just destroy. We don't want to encourage that." Pippin shook his head, still trying to process Jakob's words. With a heavy heart, Pippin stroked the baby skunk one last time as the mother led it away. The lad watched forlornly, waiting for Jakob to put him in the cart. They turned the horses toward home.

The days went by, as days will. Despite her worry and loneliness for Adelchis, Himli realized the constant work of the warm spring days and the summer growing season would soon be behind them.

"I cannot believe autumn is here." She exclaimed to Captain Mortimer. "Before we're ready, winter snows will be falling." She and the Captain hauled hay from the fields to store in the stables. "This hay seems to have trapped sun inside it!" Himli exclaimed.

All of a sudden, Pippin rushed in and did just as she dreamed of doing. The lad took a running leap and jumped into the mound of hay. Giggling and with hay clinging to him, he popped up and ran again.

"Pippin found the perfect use for this hay." The Captain laughed. "Never mind that we need it for warmth and bed." He paused and looked intently at the lad. "Come, Pippin," the Captain called. "Jump on every mound of straw. Press it down as much as you can. The more you press, the more this place will hold. We have, at least, two more wagon-loads to store. Jump, my boy, jump!" Pippin startled at the request. But seeing the Captain was serious, he gave a whoop and fell into yet another mound of hay.

"I get Paul!" He cried, running to the stable ladder to call Paul, Jakob's son, to help him 'jump on the straw.' The two boys had a great morning. Their efforts were well-rewarded when Captain Mortimer announced all the hay was in the barn. Pippin and Paul puffed with pride when praised for their enthusiastic efforts.

After the mid-day meal, Captain Mortimer left to check on

the progress of the bean picking. One look at the bean vines told the Captain the harvesting of the beans proceeded too slowly.

"We need more hands to pick," he muttered to himself. "But where will I get them? Everyone in the valley is searching for people to help with the harvest. So many soldiers have not returned. They are caught with the King's army." Captain Mortimer mounted his horse, heading toward the manor. There, way in the distance, almost directly east, he saw a cloud of dust billowing behind three riders. Who might that be, he wondered. No one in Frankland traveled these days; everyone was in the fields picking, cutting, or gathering crops. As the Captain rode toward the manor, the three riders increased their speed. All met at the stables.

The tallest rider leaped from his horse and clasped the Captain's shoulders. At first Captain Mortimer could not see the man's face, so covered with dust was it. His cloak, as he raised his arm, rained fine particles of dirt and dust on the ground.

"Good morrow to you, Captain!" The man greeted him. "Say that you know me, so speedily did I ride to get here!" Captain Mortimer grinned in delight.

"Adelchis!" He laughed. "Is it? Welcome! Welcome! How are you, my friend? Does my lady expect you?" The Captain was confused; he had no word of Adelchis' arrival. Then, he remembered the news of Lombardy. "Are you well?" We ve had word of the siege of Pavia," he dropped his eyes, not knowing all the Prince may have suffered. "It's good to see you safe!" Captain Mortimer grabbed the Prince, dust-covered cloak and all, and hugged him enthusiastically.

"Aye, Captain, I am well, now—better than ever," Adelchis responded as stable workers came out to greet him and his escort. The men with him were the ones whom everyone knew from Adelchis' days in the cave. Everyone welcomed them warmly. "I know it's a shock to see us. But I could not stay away another season. It was not possible." Adelchis's grin spread across his face. But, suddenly, his face grew still.

"May I speak with you alone, Captain?" he asked. Mortimer nodded at the other men who walked slowly toward the stable, drawing the others with them. Understanding the men's intent, Adelchis put his hand on the Captain's shoulder and turned him toward the near-by orchard. "I have come to visit, Captain, but I need your help to make that possible." Captain Mortimer turned a puzzled face to Adelchis..

"My help...?" He asked Adelchis. "Whatever I can provide, I gladly give you, Adelchis, but I don't understand."

"If I am found here or if the King learns that I was here, everyone's lives may be in danger," Adelchis said. He watched the Captain's startled face. Then, pointing to a near-by stump, he gestured to the Captain to have a seat.

"I don't understand, Sire," Captain Mortimer repeated.

"I am in limbo, Captain," Adelchis clarified. "After I fled the siege at Pavia, Charlemagne stripped my father of his kingdom and cloistered him in a monastery. Charlemagne declared my father a traitor and forbade him to leave the monastery at Corbie. The King never mentioned me by name but must know that I fled to Constaninople. I fear the King will discover me in Frankland. Judging me through my father's actions, he will execute me or, mayhap, confine me to a monastery." Adelchis' eyes were full of pain.

"We must expect that anyone who shelters me, who even speaks to me, may be considered an enemy to the King. I will not compromise your security in this way, none of you. But I had to see your Lady and her son again! They are dearer to me than anything else in the world." Adelchis stopped speaking. He did not know how to continue.

"No need to worry, Sire," Captain Mortimer replied. "I have seen your care for my Lady and for Pippin. All of us here recognize the great bond between you." He laughed at Adelchis' surprised expression. "You did not think to keep such feelings a secret, surely?" Adelchis sat on the ground, holding his head between his hands.

"I am a fool," he admitted, looking into the Captain's face. "I made great efforts to be discrete, to cover my feelings! Oh, God! What have I done?" He exclaimed. His face turned pale, his eyes darted one way, then another. His forehead wrinkled.

"Nay, nay!" Captain Mortimer cried. "Do not despair! You gave nothing away! I saw the little skip in my Lady's step, the smile that often danced around her eyes—just as I feel with Mollie, Sire." He paused. "But all here are not aware of your feelings. Aye, they know you love Pippin. But I do assure you, that is all."

"How can you be certain, Captain?" Adelchis asked quietly, his eyes still troubled, his mouth trembling slightly.

"Because," the Captain replied, "most people see what they want to see, Sire. And though they would, likely, be undisturbed by such knowledge, neither do they suspect it. You were very careful. I know that. I used some of your same tricks when I tried to interest Mollie in me!" He laughed aloud as Adelchis' head popped up. "Wait. Wait. You need to see the lad and Himli, too. Let's not postpone this meeting. Come, come. I will announce you." He gave his hand to pull Adelchis from his seat on the ground and clapped him on the back. "It is good to have you back, Sire," he added, "very good, for us all!"

Captain Mortimer knew Pippin was in the oats field with Jakob. He walked Adelchis to the manor, taking him around back to the herb garden. As the day cooled, Himli was always there, gathering leaves for drying and picking late-appearing seeds. She even dug up some of the roots, to grind and use for healing...or for dyes.

"I leave you to your greetings, Sire," the Captain said as he heard Himli's steady humming. "Try not to startle her," he whispered as he squeezed Adelchis' shoulder in support.

Adelchis stood just to look at her. *She is so beautiful.* His heart whispered, as he watched her pick the larger herb leaves and place them in her basket, being careful not to bruise them. Thinking of Adelchis' last days at the manor, Himli hummed softly. Adelchis began humming with her, exactly matching the pitch of his voice to hers. It was some minutes before she realized there was another humming. At that moment, he moved toward her and caught her eye, just as she turned. With no words at all, they flew into each others' arms. He held her face to kiss every part of it as softly and quickly as he could. Her arms, warmed by the sun, circled his neck; his lips, salty from her tears, kissed her more and more deeply; her smell, redolent of herbs and sunshine, broke through his defenses.

"Himli, Himli, my love," Adelchis murmured. "My darling, how I adore you!"

"Are you really here, Adelchis? Or is this a dream? Are you here, my love?" She asked quietly, her voice full of love.

"Oh, Himli! I could not stay away—not another minute!" Adelchis exclaimed. "It seemed impossible at first--impossible to come, I mean. But I knew I must find a way. Finally, I just rode as quickly as possible to you. Himli, you are an angel, my love. I did not remember how wonderful you are. Nay, nay, that's not what I mean. That's not it. I forgot your magic, how the world feels for me, just being near you. I love you so much, Himli, sooo much!" Adelchis whispered. Himli squeezed him that much harder, murmuring sweet words back to him. She raised her head.

"But I can never find the words to show my love, Adelchis," she admitted. "I think even the poets at court could not express my feelings for you. You must see it in my eyes, feel it in my lips, and read it in my arms around your neck." She snuggled her head below his chin, sighing with complete contentment. "If only we could stand here in my herb garden forever." She laughed and looked into his face. "Did you travel long today?" At his slight nod, she released her arms and took his hand. "Come; let's get you something to eat. You must be hungry."

"Nay, not for food," Adelchis replied. "But I am hungry to gaze into your face, to hold you close, to bury my face in your hair. Might we take some food along the river? I want just to look at you and hold you…before the manor celebrates my return." Himli smiled and nodded. "I love them all, my dear," he confirmed. "But I must have you to myself for a little while and, then, see my boy, Pippin. Is he well, Himli?"

"He is," Himli replied, smiling. "He is happy, loved by all in the manor and secure. I thank God every day we are here. The manor and our lives here protect him…til he can strengthen himself, become who he is, and not care about the rest of the world. He is my joy, Adelchis; but you are the earth on which we both rest that joy." Adelchis took her in his arms again, kissing her, stroking her hair, and murmuring endearments.

"Come," Himli made herself draw back. "We should start

for the river. Mayhap, we shall run into Pippin and Jakob on the way."

Adelchis listened to Himli's voice as he scanned the riverbank for a protected, shady spot. Seeing no other person about, he pulled Himli down into the grasses and kissed her passionately. Her arms stole around his neck, her hand rubbed his neck. He felt her press more closely against him and, then, her hands were sliding under his tunic. Adlechis slid his body down so his lips were against Himli's breasts. He slowly pulled her tunic low, kissing the space between them, feeling her nipples harden. She was breathing more quickly now. He pulled his tunic over his head as Himli did the same and they were in each other's arms once again. It was agony to pull away from her for even one minute, their bodies molded together perfectly.

"Thank goodness the day is warm!" Adelchis laughingly teased. "The sun will kiss us both as we worship each other." He gazed at Himli's body, taking pleasure in the single freckle at the base of her throat, the small scar on her left breast, and the up and down of her breathing. Himi reached for him, pulling him yet closer as she pressed his body against hers. He felt her stir, heard her whisper 'hurry, my love,' and basked in the heat of her passion. He stroked her inner thighs as she moaned. He knew she yearned for him but he knew, also, her pleasure would escalate if he waited. He kissed her neck, first one breast and, then, the other and moved his tongue down, down, down, to her navel. Then, he entered and thought no more. There was only feeling, giving, sharing as they moved together. As their passion peaked, they held each other tightly, tears leaking from eyes which could now admit the long loneliness of the past months. They could not stay out of each other's arms, even as their bodies cooled and their need lessened.

Finally, Himli pulled her tunic back on and held Adelchis' tunic for him to slide into.

"There is nothing to say, my love," she looked into his face. "I love you, I love you." Adlechis and Himli spread a linen, took their bread, meat, and onions from the carrying sack, and began their mid-day meal. Just as they were sharing an apple, they heard a happy shout. Pippin, spying them from the river path, came running with delight, rushing into Adelchis' arms.

"ADEL-CHUS!" The child screamed. "Where you been? I miss you!" And he hugged the man's neck with enthusiasm. "Moma! Adel-chus is here! Adel- chus is here!" He laughed as he settled into Adelchis' lap. Jakob came up smiling at them all, bidding Adelchis welcome.

"Come, come, Jakob," Himli invited. "We brought you a mid-day feast. Sit down."

"Nay, nay, my Lady," Jakob replied. "I did promise Gerta to taste one of her new tarts this meal. I must get to the manor. Welcome home, Sir," he said to Adelchis. "It is good to have you back. I'll see you at the evening meal." Turning toward the manor, he added: "It is a good day for a meal by the river, I do say. I'll see you later." And he walked away.

Pippin took the meat and bread Adelchis offered him, motioning for a small piece of onion. "Thank you, Adel-chus," he said, "…tastes good!" He leaned against Adelchis' chest, slowly eating his food. "He's come, Moma," he repeated. "Adelchus come at last!"

Chapter Nine

Later that evening, Adelchis and Himli sat in the herb garden, drinking *chai* (which they both learned to like) and recounting for each other all that had happened since they had been apart. Himli repeatedly kissed Adelchis on the cheek, squeezed his arm or brushed his hair from his forehead—anything to touch him. He leaned gently into her, drawing love from her nearness. Adelchis sighed, content that Himli and Pippin thrived. Their good spirits lifted his own..

"My dear," he took her hands in his, "I have dreamed of this moment since I rode away from your manor those many months ago. It is such a relief to me that the two of you are safe and happy." Himli gave him a soft kiss.

"You worry too much, my dear." Himli replied. "Captain Mortimer and his men are devoted to our safety. You must give this up; you worry, make yourself ill for nothing." His arms stole around her waist, pulling her ever more closely to his chest..

"Aye, I know," Adelchis agreed. "It's not worry for your safety, I guess. I worry I am not here with you...should you need help or protection. The male wants to protect his cave." He blushed, embarrassed Himli heard this from him.

"I love you, all the more for that, Adelchis," she responded. "But there is no need for worry. The King fights to protect all of us. And, here, deep inside the Frankish realm, we are not threatened by overnight invasions, by barbarians from afar. What will be, will come, Adelchis. It's foolish to think you can control every possibility."

"Why, look at us!" She continued, changing the subject. "Who would ever think you and I would find each other? How likely was that? I ask you." She pushed her body closer to Adelchis, delighting in his nearness.

Adelchis laughed, squeezing her hands. "Not very likely, I assure you." He answered. "But, what a gift—a blessed gift-- you are, my dear." His eyes scanned the mountain range low on the horizon. "But, I want your opinion about a possibility," he continued as he turned to face Himli. She immediately saw the seriousness in his face. Her breath caught.

"What is it?" she asked. "Is something wrong?" In that moment, all kind of dire thoughts zipped through her mind. "Are you ill? Has your life been threatened? My dear, what is the matter?"

"Nay, nay, Himli!" Adelchis quickly responded. "Don't worry, love. I am fine. In fact, I am better than I have been these past months. I received a missive from my father." He saw Himli's face pale. "He is fine, my dear. There are no worries about him. Free from the thrust of his obsession, he seems content. Nay, he reminded me I have a small manor in Septimania. For some reason I could never understand, father insisted the manor was mine, even before I was ten years old." Adelchis shrugged and continued speaking.

"For years, he required I visit there, meet the people who care for it, and understand its bounty." He smiled. "The sweetest grapes in the realm are in that region. Its wine is much sought-after." Himli nodded, seeing the pride in his eyes.

"Adelchis, that's wonderful. You, then, are not caught in

Constaninople. You can live…" Her voice trailed away. "Nay, nay," she realized. "That is still in the Frankish kingdom. You cannot go there." She lowered her eyes, unconsciously massaging Adelchis' hand.

"That's just the question, Himli," Adelchis answered. "I think I can.." At her startled look, he continued, wrapping his hand around hers more tightly. "You see," he was unable to keep the excitement out of his voice. "I cannot live there…I mean I cannot stay there indefinitely. But I do think I can go for extended visits. Everyone there knows of my circumstances, of course — being banished by the King, having lost my family and my home. But," here he hugged Himli to his chest, then released her to look into her eyes. "…but, they do not know where I am, only that I fled from Pavia." At Himli's quick glance into his face, Adelchis consciously tried to calm his enthusiasm. "Charlemagne has never said a word about me! He did not banish me, as he did Count Marston and his family…neither did he speak of imprisonment or beheading!" Adelchis gazed into Himli's face. He did not want to attribute positive characteristics to Charlemagne. He knew how Charlemagne's rejection of her, his sending both Himli and Pippin away, hurt her.

"It may be deliberate…his saying nothing, Adelchis," Himli slowly agreed. "He ever tried to be merciful, thinking God expected it of a king. Mayhap, he just wanted to forget you. As you said, he knew you wished to be a Peer. When you said that to Oliver, it proved you had no interest in the rule of Lombard…or of anything else. Aye," Himli slowly nodded her head. "Aye, he may overlook you — intentionally or not. We will never know. I cannot explain the way Charlemagne thinks."

"I never could explain my own circumstances," she admitted. "Charlemagne has, for years, send foodstuffs, linens, even jewelry here. But he never does anything personal. As far as I know, he does not mention my existence to anyone. But he never suggestsI leave Frankland either." She paused, trying to see Adelchis with the King's eyes.

"It is possible, Adlechis. You might go to your manor and never be challenged," Himlitrude decided. Her eyes were far away, considering the likelihood of Adelchis' hopes. She smiled into his face. "It's a risk, for a certainty."

"Aye, it is," Adelchis agreed. "But it is an acceptable risk, don't you think, my dear?" Adelchis let his breath out. He had considered this possibility in his own mind so many times he was incapable of being reasonable in his evaluation. "Mayhap I shall ask Captain Mortimer's opinion," he suggested, "…not that I will be led by his view. But he will be more realistic and, mayhap, more blunt than you in his appraisal, my love." Himli smiled and hugged him.

"Of a certainty," she replied. "I want whatever is best for you, dear man. And I can see this idea delights your heart. I would see you happy, Adelchis, happy beyond measure."

"I am happy," Adelchis asserted, "happy because of you. But this happiness makes me want more of you, every day which passes. I want days and weeks of sitting by your side, just using up the days together." He pulled Himli into his arms, kissing her gently but, then, pouring his love for her into his kiss. She ended the kiss breathlessly and kissed him again immediately. "Wait! Wait!" Adelchis laughed. "We have not mentioned the best part of my plan. I thought it through very seriously, Himli. I am secure in my decision." He stood up, gestured for Himli to remain seated, and began talking.

"I know my next words must be well-considered, Himli. I want you to think about them for the next few days. I will give you time alone, away from me, to think." At Himli's startled movement, Adelchis pressed her shoulders, urging her not to stand. "Now, you must think deeply, my dear. Do not be misled in your love for me. Think of your futures—yours and Pippin's." He ran his hand through his hair, tousling it as he did. Himli smiled; he looked so frustrated with his hair standing out every which-a-way. Adelchis did not notice.

"This is my thought," he continued. "I believe it will be safe for all of us--you, Pippin, and me—at my manor." He forestalled her reaction. "Nay, nay, hear me out. I have had weeks to consider alternatives." He assured her. "Neither of us is able to stay there indefinitely. You have this manor to run. My friend in Constaninople expect me to be there...at least some of the time. My friends there do beg me never to stray. But they demand nothing and keep no record of my comings and goings. However, should King Charlemagne ever ask about me, they must be able to say I spend time in Constantinople. I think it makes little difference where I am otherwise; but I must be physically present some of the time."

"Frankly, Himli," Adelchis continued. "I doubt the King ever thinks of me. He is unlikely to search for me. If he believes I am not in Frankland, not in his realm, I should be safe." He waited for Himli to respond. She did not. She sat very still, looking over his shoulder at the far away mountain.

"Adelchis, even though I understand your need for your own manor, I would not have you risk your life," she finally replied. "But this idea, it may not be such a risk. Let me think." Himli stared off into the distant, unconsciously counting on her fingers. Long minutes later, she turned, again, to Adelchis. "From all I know of the King, you are correct-- he does not concern himself with you. But neither does he forget. Believe me. In these past months, if he did not seek you out or verify your presence in the Byzantine empire, he considers you beneath his interest. His knowing you have no interest in ruling eliminates you as a threat. So, I think you may spend time at your manor with little fear." She smiled at Adelchis, thankful he did, indeed, have his own home again.

"But, don't you see?" Adelchis asked, trying to stay calm. "You and Pippin can come to my manor! You can spend as much time as you wish there...even stay when I have to return to Constantinople." At Himli's surprised look, Adelchis continued. "Nay, listen. Sit still one more minute. Listen, listen to my thoughts." He took Himli's two hands in his own, kissing first one finger and, then, the next.

"Himli, as you just pointed out, Charlemagne has no concern for me. He has no fear of me either. The same lack can be said of you! He may wonder about Pippin, wonder how you are doing...but he has sent no word since you came here. Right? He sends no greetings, no Yuletide blessings, no invitations for Pippin to the court... nothing to acknowledge him?" He paused and caressed Himli's check.

"Oh, my dear, I don't mean to hurt you. I never wish to give you pain. I am just trying to be realistic....about the King's concerns. This lack of interest from him does protect us! Aye, truly. I think you two you may be wherever you choose, as long as you reside in your manor some of the time." Adelchis squeezed her hands. "My love, my love, don't you see? Because of the King's neglect, his lack of concern — for you or for me — we can be together. Don't you think it possible?" He asked, with such yearning and hope Himli stood to wrap her arms around him.

"Aye, dear Adelchis," she whispered. "It might be. As long as we draw no attention to ourselves, we quite possibly can do as we please." She looked into Adelchis' eyes. "Is that what you mean?" He nodded, unwilling to cover the hope in his face. "Let me reflect on Charlemagne's previous actions and recall his thoughts on those he banished," Himli answered. "There were a few after King Pepin died. He did talk much to me after Pippin's birth. His vision and his ambitions never changed...or they did not, according to all I heard. Mayhap, he lives by those values still." She shook her head as she slowly smiled. "My dear Adelchis, what an incredible idea. May it be true...that we can do this!" She looked into his face, basking in the love and care it reflected. "If we can be together, just a little more than in the past months, my world will be complete...totally complete, my dear Adelchis."

As Himli took time to consider his plan, Adelchis spoke with Captain Mortimer. He, the Captain, Jakob and Pippin were fishing on the river bank. Each man took turns helping Pippin with his bait and pole, all of them trying to assure the lad caught a fish. Pippin spent much of his time running back and forth, examining the fish that each man caught, and taking as much pride in each one as if he caught it himself. Jakob took Pippin to look for his favorite turtle while Adelchis sought Captain Mortimer's opinion.

"It makes good, logical sense, Adelchis," Captain Mortimer replied after hearing Adelchis' plans for returning to his own manor. "Septimania is a lengthy journey south and west of the King's usual circuit. There could not be a better location for losing oneself within the kingdom." The Captain nodded slightly. He looked at Adelchis. "You know, with all the couriers we receive--some coming specifically for us, some passing through--no one ever asked about my Lady---to return information to the King. Some of them do not even know who lives at this manor. They deliver their messages, ask for directions, go to the cook room for food, and are on their way. I daresay very few people ever wonder about her fate. Strange, is it not? Perhaps, they don't even remember her."He frowned at Adelchis.

"This ease of forgetting, I do not understand it," Adelchis admitted. "Himiltrude is the kind of woman we all seek: courageous, spirited, yet able to accept her fate. How...?" He raised his hands in inquiry. "How can one forget a wife and a son? Truly, can he *never* think of them?" He paused.

"I cannot imagine such a thing." Captain Mortimer rubbed the back of his head. "Please pay no attention to my words. God knows, I am no one to judge a King. I am thankful, though, that I am not in his place." The Captain returned to the subject. "But, as for your question, I do believe you will be safe....and my Lady and Pippin with you. You should all spend some time where you are thought to be. Aye. But, spending weeks—even months—together in Septimania, it does seem reasonable. Aye, I am sure of it, Adelchis. That will be possible."

The Captain was rewarded for his words by Adelchis' brilliant smile and a hearty slap on his back. He saw the Prince hurriedly wipe a tear from the corner of his eye, just before he stooped, selecting worms for Pippin's fishing hook. "It should be mentioned, Adelchis, another thought. Being in a less-isolated manor will help Pippin as well. He needs to interact with different people, practice the manners of a noble, learn to make his way with strangers. Your manor would be beneficial for that opportunity as well."

"Thank you, Captain," Adelchis answered. "Thank you for your thoughts." He paused and said: "I must rescue Jakob from Pippin!" Laughing, he began to call the boy's name.

The fishing party returned to the manor, bringing more than enough fish for the evening meal. Adelchis acted as young as Pippin as they cleaned the fish. Both the Captain and Jakob reassured him of the soundness of his plan, renewing his hope of taking Himli and Pippin to his manor. Adelchis did not mention the journey to Pippin, not knowing when he would begin or, even, if Himli could be convinced to journey with him. Himli thought of nothing else in the coming days--to be with Adelchis with no separation in sight, to plan their days with no goodbyes looming before them.

"What heaven that would be!" Himli whispered to herself. She carefully reviewed her memories of Charlemagne's thoughts on those he conquered. He had often described a bat-tle and its consequences to her. It was his, and King Pepin's way before him, to evaluate their successes and quantify their failures before the next battle. Himli remembered Charle-magne's insistence on mercy, the mercy a sovereign should re-flect. As far as Himli could remember, the King's punishments were always tempered with mercy. He had almost never sen-tenced a Frankish man to death. He preferred banishment, im-prisonment, or bondage to the finality of taking an enemy"s head.

Himli did not fear King Charlemagne's final evaluation of Adelchis. She doubted that the King had changed his mind about Adelchis from his first opinion. He liked Adelchis. He told her so...before she realized that Adelchis was her replace-ment's brother. At first, Adelchis was only another noble, come to hunt. She remembered Charlemagne's praise of the Prince's hunting skill, his quick kills, and his admiration for the animals they tracked. The King even offered him a faster mount during those hunting expeditions. Valuing Adelchis' interest in becoming a Peer and knowing his ambition did not include ruling, Charlemagne felt no threat from him then and, of a certainty, did not fear him now. Himli decided. He just pretends that the Prince no longer exists. Stating her views to Adelchis, Himli breathed a sigh of relief when Adelchis told her that the Captain and Jakob shared her opinion. Her eyes opened widely as Adelchis grinned. The way was clear for the two of them to make a life together!

Himli fell to her knees. "My Father God," she prayed. "Thank you, thank you for your blessings. Thank you for Adelchis, my love, and for Pippin, my son. Please I pray Thee, protect us all."

Chapter Ten

Jaston traveled with Adelchis, Himli and Pippin toward Septimania. He was eager to check on particular settlings before the dreaded snows of winter began and, knowing the area, was an excellent guide. Captain Mortimer and Jakob, both, reluctantly deferred to Jaston's experience traveling through Frankland. They agreed to remain at Himli's manor to oversee the work and secure its safety. And, if a frantic summons should arrive from any direction, one of the two men would respond to it immediately, even coming to retrieve Himli and Pippin if that proved to be needed. Adelchis would have kept to the manor for days longer, to guarantee that Himli and Pippin had a happy leave-taking. But Captain Mortimer insisted that the small group begin their journey.

"Had I realized you would be going to Septimania," he allowed, "I would have had you packed and on your way two weeks ago. After darkness falls, the cold seeps into your bones. And soon, snow will be our daily companion. You must begin your journey/ Tomorrow is almost too late," he fussed at them, grinning at the same time as his eyes flashed and he frowned.

"We are going. We are going," Adelchis responded. "There is just so much to decide. Will we need three or six mantles? Is one saddle sufficient for each of us? Should we take extra mounts in case one of our horses is crippled along the way?

What should we do about…?"

"Say no more," Captain Mortimer commanded. "On the morrow, at dawn, you shall begin this journey. Dress warmly. I will give directions to Mollie about your provisions. You will be a number of days on the trail… seven at least," he added. "I must be certain to remind her to pack 'traveling sticks,' dried fruit, and cheese. You may not wish to cook every night, Adelchis," he turned to the Prince. "But, do build a fire to take the chill out of the air. Your provisions will be plentiful…"

"I know, I know, Mortimer." Adelchis replied, reaching out to squeeze the Captain's shoulders. "Don't worry. Jaston and I both are old men at traveling. You seem tot hink we are all babes in arms. I do bet that Pippin is more accomplished than you think! Ha! Don't be such an old woman, Captain. We shall journey safely and in good time."

"Damn right!" Mortimer exclaimed. "I am sending Nordt to accompany you. He'll deposit you at your Septimania manor and accomplany Jaston on his continuing route." The Captain shook his head. "Nay, nay. I have decided this is the best way." He waved them toward the manor.

"Go, eat," he directed. "You must say your farewells this night and be off without a murmur on the morrow. Go, eat! And, then, sleep," he commanded.

As it happened, they left the manor early the following morning. Despite their efforts to be quiet, to mount their horses and leave quickly, the manor's residents lined up to bid them farewell. Nothing would do but that they dismount to give and receive hugs, kisses, pats on the back and the best wishes of everyone for a safe trip. It was an excited lad who sadly bid his friends goodbye but, the next moment, jumped in impatience at their delay in 'hitting the trail,' as Pippin described it. He rode with Jaston on his horse but squirmed this way and that so often that Jacob said he rode with each of them.

Finally, the small group waved their last farewells and began the first day of their journey. Captain Mortimer continuously checked the clouds for signs of snow. He held his hand high above his head, judging the speed and strength of the wind. Quickly, he rode to Jaston's horse and reached to pull Pippin's hat further down over his ears.

"My dear boy," the Captain said, "keep your hat low on your forehead and tuck your scarf into your collar. The cold wind around your neck will make even your toes seem frozen." Pippin ducked his head and smiled at the Captain. Holding with one hand on Jakob's jacket, he reached for the Captain, giving him one last hug.

"I love you, Capn Morti," the boy whispered. "Bc back soon as I can." The Captain grabbed Pippin and kissed him soundly.

"You stay safe, you hear me?" He gruffly replied. Pippin smiled as he patted the Captain's cheek.

"Aye, stay safe," he agreed. Nordt led the procession, followed by Himli, Adelchis, and, then, Jaston with Pippin in the rear. They had gone only twenty feet or so before Adelchis dropped back behind Jaston.

"I'd feel better bringing up the rear, Jaston," Adelchis explained. "I can have my eyes on all of you but, especially, Pippin. If he gets weary, I'll be glad to relieve you for a while." Jaston nodded, thankful that there were three of them. Three men could surely protect one woman and a small child from any harm.

Pippin turned to check on Adelchis, then turned back to check in front of his horse. He seldom had the opportunity to visit other manors and, as yet, had not spent a night away from his home. Trying to imagine the trip to come, he was excited and nervous, both at the same time. Himli, feeling inexperi-enced now in dealing with noble visitors, grew quiet, over-whelmed by the changes which would soon define her day-to-day existence. Adelchis, overwhelmed by his good fortune-- to have both the family he so loved and a manor of his own— alternated between bouts of spirited laughter and quiet revelry.

"I never believed it would happen," he repeated over and over. "I did not think t one man could be so blessed."

The journey, though grueling, was uneventful, except for the challenges of the weather. The snow clouds which threatened the first two days of their riding broke early on the morning of their third day. The wind quickly picked up speed, lifting bursts of snow from the ground up into the faces of man and beast alike. The snow, wet and heavy, settled on their shoul-ders, its cold seeming to sneak into their clothing, skins, and then bones. Finally, just after mid-day, Jaston covered Pippin entirely with his mantle, urging the boy to keep his head and arms underneath. Jaston assured Adelchis and Nordt that he knew exactly where they were and kept them plodding over slight hills and mild inclines until late afternoon.

"We'll camp in a cave near-by," he told Nordt as he rode to the head of the column. "It has a stream close so if we have to stop for a couple of days, it will be little hardship."

"I would as lief press on," Nordt answered. "If we wait, a more serious storm could delay us for days."

"Aye," Jaston nodded. "This is but a hindrance," he admit-ted, "though I know the cold seeps into the Lady and the lad. Mayhap, tomorrow will bring sun...an easier condition for our journey."

On the morrow, the sun did, indeed, rise early and beam on them steadily all day. After a small flurry in the morning, the snow ended. The world was white, pristine, and full of promise. Adelchis, Himli, and Pippin looked toward the west with great hope and enthusiasm, each sure an exciting world beckoned to all three of them. And so it did.

About The Author

Acacia Oak, a dedicated researcher, has dreamed of fictionalizing Charlemagne's story since she taught 'History of the Book' in 1969. In a world which cries for heroes, Charlemagne's vision for his people claims our attention. He redefined our concept of king. His vision of a progressive, humane nation which educates its children—boys and girls alike; which values the differences of its neighbors; which anchors its society around the tenets of brotherhood are ideals we need for our own century. How amazing they are reflected in the world view of an eighth-century barbarian king!

"We all need heroes," she says, "even with their ever-present feet of clay."

Acacia Oak is a southerner by birth, a world citizen by outlook, and a hopeful writer by inclination. She lives in California with her family and their three 'girls,' rescue dogs who keep life mellow as well as interesting.

www.ingramcontent.com/pod-product-compliance
Lightning Source LLC
Chambersburg PA
CBHW050036180626
46810CB00002B/739